CW01558846

"More twists and tu   h"

MICHAEL HAINGE

THE ANCIENT SOCIETY OF
HYPNOTISTS

PREPARE TO BE MESMERISED

For Katy, my therapist, who helped me fall apart.

For Alison, my wife, who helped me put myself back together.

And for Mary, my sister, for a lifetime of love and support.

Book One

Identity

"I am not what happened to me, I am what I choose to become."
— ***Carl Gustav Jung***

Chapter One

Monday

0618

I'm heading towards consciousness. Like a large hand pulling me out of the deep, warm waters of a tropical ocean, I am starting to break the surface that marks the boundary between sleep and consciousness. Light. Sounds. And a faintly unpleasant taste on my tongue, inform me of my arrival in the land of wakefulness.

Fragments of the previous night's events flicker in my memory. Tempting as it is to wallow in the occasional triumphs of my performance, my head is calling for coffee, and loudly so.

I follow the familiar routines of waking as if from a script: stumble out of bed, look for my tracksuit bottoms and then my slippers. All the while my need to pee becomes more and more urgent.

So I head down the hallway to the toilet without any tracksuit bottoms. I sit down to pee (it may be some time, despite the urgency which summoned me to this place). As my pee drains away, so too does the cloudiness in my head in some peculiar synchronicity between bladder and brain.

The stiffness in my limbs begins to subside as I walk back to the bedroom in search of the tracksuit bottoms. By this time I'd have expected to hear the cat. Damn. Four years on from his very timely death, I still miss his demands for, well, something. Food. Water. A stroke or just company. My own circumstances are not so dissimilar to those of the dearly departed Iago.

I still do see him from time to time. Not just a 'corner of the eye' appearance, but a fully rendered, what? Ghost? Hallucination? Strangely, the appearance of Iago has never bothered me. Surprised me from time to time, but never something frightening or unsettling. Often the opposite, in fact.

I remember snatches of a dream – my dreams have always been most vivid and occasionally disturbing – I am surrounded by faceless people and feel their threat and malice keenly as they circle me, weapons in hand. Oddly, I don't feel in the least bit fearful. And just like that, the vapour of the dream disappears and eludes my conscious grasp.

In the kitchen. Lift the kettle and happily find there is enough water in it for my coffee. On it goes. As I assemble the essential ingredients to the morning's beginnings – coffee, inulin and vitamins – I try and remember what the day has in store.

0713

I'm in the gym. However long I've been doing this, the mindless pounding of expended calorie upon expended calorie, breath upon breath, never cease to bore me. The cross trainer describes its ceaseless, elliptical path through space and time, whilst actually going precisely nowhere. Endless, for all eternity.

Music usually helps. It weaves an uncomfortable symmetry between the beautifully crafted compositions I like to listen to and the ungainly and laboured movements I feel compelled to exert. Nevertheless, it can, on occasion, be a transcending experience. But not today - my mind is too full of the previous day's exploits to find the stillness that I crave.

0759

Back to the house for a shower and the usual ablutions.

0821

Dressed, I return to the kitchen for my second coffee and some breakfast. Almost always the same: two slices of toast, one with Marmite and the other with peanut butter. Upstairs with my breakfast ensemble, and into the office to see what's afoot. It's the usual fare. Offers of sex, money, and shopping vouchers all neatly lined up in my Junk folder.

But today, there's something more, shall we say, unusual in store.

Interlude

Before I resume with this day's chronology, there are some things I need to explain. Prior to the 22nd of December, six years ago, I was married and living in London. On the 22nd of December we sold the family home and I moved into a house I'd bought with the help of a sizeable mortgage.

On the 31st of December we were divorced. Happy new year.

I was left alone, with the cat. Over the following months me and the cat would occasionally cross swords but, more often than not, we would exchange knowing looks and glances as we each went about our business inside the house and in the back yard. The narrative of the looks and glances, if there were such a thing, would go something like this:

Me – "So, Cat, it's just us. I know you'd rather be back where we were and with more family around – who I think you prefer to me anyway, by the way – and with a garden and grass to lay on in the summer and the area beyond the house where you loved to patrol. Still cat-of-the-walk, despite your age and growing infirmity."

Cat – "Yup."

Work was ok. Since I'd given up full time employment, I'd taken some interim roles and consultancy gigs. Neither of which made my heart or soul sing. I felt out of step with myself, as if I was missing the point somehow. So, I needed a change.

And change is what I got.

0824

An email announced its arrival in my inbox. The sender was not immediately familiar to me – one Pascale Blanchet. Presumably a woman and with her first name I imagined the surname was pronounced in the French way, not the Cate Blanchet version. It read as follows:

Dear Simon

I enjoyed your performance last night and was moved to write to you to ask a favour.

It may entail some travelling on your part as well as a degree of discomfort, though nothing which a man of your stature could not endure.

If you are interested, can I suggest we meet in The Eagle and Child in St Giles, Oxford, today at 2.30pm? A simple Oui or Non by return will suffice.

Yours in anticipation,

Pascale

In anticipation of what, I wondered? I couldn't recall anyone particularly attractive to me at last night's performance, but that is not so surprising given the limited view of the audience any actor has when on stage. Even an amateur actor. The email address was @gmail.com so no clues there. And a quick Google for one Pascale Blanchet provided me with "About 1,510,000 results (0.48 seconds)". Even adding Oxford to the search didn't help. But why would it? Just because she was in Oxford last night…

I decided that my sleuthing was unlikely to reveal anything more about the intriguing Pascale Blanchet than she had intended for me to discover. In other words,

9

precisely nothing. The only clue might be in the location of our *rendezvous*. The Eagle and Child is best known as the haunt of JRR Tolkien and CS Lewis. Often together, indeed.

The question remained, should I meet her? A quick glance at my diary confirmed my lack of any appointments for the rest of the day. I looked down and saw the cat once again, as if reading my mind he replied:

"Oui" he said.

1310

And so it was that I found myself on the 1315hrs S9 Bus from Wantage to Oxford city centre. You'd imagine the S stood for speed or speedy? No.

1405

55 minutes later I disembarked in Park Street and made my way over the Castle Mill Stream and cut across towards George Street. I passed the Old Fire Station, the scene of last night's performance of Beckett's End Game. Was the French connection (so to speak) the reason for Pascale Blanchet coming to see the play, I wondered?

Left turn on to Magdalen Street and past the Randolph Hotel on my left before the widening road announces my arrival in St Giles. Perhaps Pascale Blanchet is staying at the Randolph? I'd like to think so. It paints a more salubrious picture of the object of my forthcoming meeting.

I paused outside the jauntily named noodle bar, *Ramen Kulture – Anytime's a good time!*

Indeed.

I went inside the Eagle and Child and approached the bar. My immediate orientation to an Oxford pub led to me to order a pint of Morrells Best Bitter. I was reminded that the brewery had, in fact, closed down in 1998. Not in so many words, but by the blank look of the barman who had the misfortune to receive my request.

"We've got Stella?" he replied.

A quick scan of the beer pumps brought my reward.

"A pint of Hook Norton please."

Taking my drink to a small table with an excellent view of the door, I settled in. The beer was good. Very good, in fact. And there was a reassuring smell of ancient tobacco and spilt beer that few old pubs have managed to preserve. The olfactory equivalent of the patina old objects acquire with the passage of time.

There was a copy of the Oxford Mail on the table next to mine, so I picked it up. I'd barely had time to read the headline about a burglary at the Ashmolean museum and the theft of some Saxon artefact, before I was interrupted.

"Simon, so glad you could come."

I looked up towards the unmistakably French voice that greeted me. With her back to the light of the open door, I could make out little of her features but instead saw the woman in outline accompanied by a halo of reflected sunlight.

"Pascale Blanchet, I presume," I said as I stood up and extended my hand in greeting. A redundant gesture, as it turned out. Pascale kissed each cheek and left a

11

delicious lingering scent which I recognised but couldn't immediately place.

"Can I get you a drink?"

"Thank you, no. Would you mind coming with me?" Without waiting for my reply, Pascale turned towards the other side of the bar and opened a door through which she disappeared from view. I hesitated only slightly before picking up what remained of my pint and followed her.

1426

As my eyes adjusted to the gloom of this inner room I was struck by the absence of any windows. One door from the bar, through which we had just come, and another door on the opposite side of the room, leading to who knows where. A simple fireplace, a table and three chairs and a single pendant lamp completed the scene.

"Please, sit down."

I sat down. I could now make out her features. Best described as refined. Age, hard to tell but somewhere between 40 and 50. Well dressed and with a presence that I found both attractive and slightly intimidating. Radiating confidence and self-assurance with the slightest hint of threat. I was, to say the least, intrigued.

"Thank you for coming, Simon. I'm sure you have many questions to ask me but if you can wait until I've set the scene, so to speak, that would be most agreeable."

I nodded my assent.

"Excellent. What I am about to tell you must remain confidential. Is that ok?"

I nodded again. Truth be told, I was captivated by her. Anything to keep her talking in her smooth, resonant voice. And her scent, which insinuated itself into my senses once more. As if sensing my transportation, Pascale continued.

"It's important that you take in everything I'm saying. If you don't, then the risks to you are multiplied and that's something we should both do our best to avoid."

"Please go on – you have my full attention." She is clearly off her rocker, I thought. Or trying to scam me – what on Earth am I doing here...

"For some time now, the organisation I represent have been looking for someone like you – "

"Oh really? And what am I 'like' then?" My suspicions were raised, as were my hackles, for such a gauche effort in flattery!

"No, I mean we have been looking for someone who is literally, like you. Looks like you. Appears as you appear," she added, to emphasise the point.

"We needed to find someone with your facial features, age and physicality. As unlikely as this sounds, that's really all we needed to know before I approached you."

Somewhat embarrassed, all I could manage in response was "I see". Not that I did. Not yet anyway.

"We found a match for your face through extensive web-based research. We then found that you were performing at the Old Fire Station last night, so I came to see you. You were very good by the way. And acting skills, a strong imagination, are a significant advantage for what we are going to ask you to do."

My head was spinning, and I wasn't sure whether I should be outraged, flattered or both. I decided to remain silent and as inscrutable as my non-poker-playing visage would allow. Pascale paused, as if reading my face.

"I know this probably sounds a bit... creepy. But please bear with me. Four years ago, one of our associates went missing when he was engaged in some very sensitive work. We have been looking for him relentlessly since then. When we first came across your image, we thought it *was* him. Your resemblance is remarkable. We need you to complete the work he started – it won't take long – and we will be *very* grateful.

"Meaning?"

"Meaning you can have pretty much whatever you want in return."

"Meaning?"

"I don't know – you tell me."

Before getting carried away with the untold riches I had in store, I swallowed a large mouthful of reality. Here's a woman I don't know offering me anything I want, to do some work that is yet to be defined. Having found me because my face looks the same as someone who has apparently gone missing.

Wake up.

"It was interesting meeting you, but I can't help you and I think I should leave." With that I headed to the door of this strange, inner room and I made my way back into the bar and finally onto the street. I looked up at the noodle bar as I passed by.

Anytime's a good time!

But not today.

1514

Sat on the top deck of the bus, I was lost in my thoughts. The glorious, chaotic greenery that is mid-summer streamed past. Even the occasional rap of a branch against the bus did little to disturb me. Back in the market square, I was the last to leave the bus before it filled up with waiting passengers and began its circuit again. I started the short walk back to my house.

1543

Somehow, I knew what was coming next. A mental image had been forming in my mind. A little out of focus, perhaps, but it was there. As I turned the corner towards my front door, there she was.

1544

Sitting confidently on my doorstep, seemingly entirely at ease in the afternoon sun, her face inclined towards the sky with eyes closed. Yeah right.

"Hello Simon," a broad smile flashed on her face. But not so much her eyes. A chink in her immaculate presentation at last.

"Why are you here?"

"Can I come in? Please..."

I reached for the door key in my pocket and hesitated.

"And if I say No?"

"Then I will leave."

"You'd better be quick, the S9 is filling up."

"I'm sorry?" A genuine look of confusion, vulnerability even, passed across Pascale's face. I've always found it easy to resist entitlement, arrogance and anger. Vulnerability or sadness, however, have always pulled on my heart strings.

Speaking as much to myself as Pascale,

"Oh for fuck's sake. Come in."

1525

As I opened the front door, the relative cool of the house washed over me, returning my mood to something approaching its normal affability. Pascale followed me, a little gingerly I thought, into the house.

"Let's sit in the garden," I said as I opened the back door and led Pascale up the stairs to the small courtyard. Despite being in the middle of town, the courtyard was not really overlooked and only a faint sound of the day's hustle and bustle underscored the peaceful atmosphere.

"Please," I said as I gestured to a galvanized metal garden bench. She sat down.

"How about you start this right at the beginning? The whole story please. I want to know who you are, what the organisation you work for is and does, and what you want me to do. Please don't give me anything but the full, un-sugared truth. If I think you're bullshitting me then this meeting will be over. Immediately. Do you understand?"

I'm not quite sure where this surprising, authoritative streak came from, but I embraced it. A serious, intense gaze accompanied my dialogue. It appeared that I had Pascale's full attention. She broke gaze from me, casting her eyes down for a moment. Shifting on the bench, ever so slightly, she let out a breath, looked at me as she appeared to make up her mind, and said

"Yes. I understand."

"Good. Go ahead then."

"I'm going to explain some things to you. Some of them you may find hard to believe and others you may dismiss or laugh at when I tell you them. I want you to know that I am entirely serious in everything I am about to say to you. Ok?"

"Fine with me."

Pascale appeared to draw a deep breath while looking around her. And then she began.

"The roots of our organisation go back to the 1700s. It was Franz Mesmer, in fact, who first used the term *Lebensmagnetismus* to describe the invisible natural force possessed by all living things, animal and vegetable. The term is German and translates as Animal Magnetism."

She paused.

I studied Pascale's face for signs of a joke, a slight tension in her mouth perhaps. There was none.

"Go on."

"Animal Magnetism," She repeated.

Oh dear, I thought. Pascale was now scanning my face for signs of, what? Disbelief, contempt, ridicule? I probably showed all three but made strenuous efforts to return to a neutral, even, interested, disposition.

"Go on, go on."

"Well, Animal Magnetism was Mesmer's theory that there is a universal magnetic fluid flowing between all living things, and that this fluid is essential for good health."

"Obi-Wan Kenobi eat your heart out," I muttered.

Ignoring my mutterings, Pascale continued.

"Anyway, his ideas were developed by Armand-Marc-Jacques Chastanet, Marquis de Puységur. Puységur adapted Mesmer's ideas and practice and became one of the first practitioners of hypnosis. After him came many notable figures. James Braid, for example, was a Scottish surgeon who carried out scores of operations using hypnosis to anaesthetise his patients."

"Seriously?", I asked, somewhat incredulous.

"Yes, seriously." Pascale replied with a profound sense of both conviction and intensity. My interest was piqued.

"Many notable scientists and doctors have shown the effectiveness of hypnosis. Sigmund Freud practised hypnosis, sometimes regressing his patients to assist him in his psychoanalysis. He was a follower for ten years until he left us...".

"Left who, exactly?" I felt, at last, that we were getting to the heart of why Pascale was here.

Pascale took a breath and paused, ever so slightly.

"I am member of the Ancienne Société des Hypnotiseurs. The Ancient – "

"Yes, I get it. The Ancient Society of Hypnotists. Sounds like a blast. I still don't know what this has to do with me and why you want me to keep this knowledge to myself. All this history will be on Wikipedia anyway, in all probability."

18

"Some but not all. Certainly nothing about ASH."

Oh god. The way she said ASH was so delicious. Borderline erotic, even. I always had a soft spot for a French accent. I brought my attention back to the present moment.

"ASH was founded by the Marquis de Puységur. He created a public organisation - Société Harmonique des Amis Réunis, or the Harmonic Society of Reunited Friends. With the coming of the French Revolution, revolutionary powers started moving against the Marquis. In response he created the Ancienne Société des Hypnotiseurs. This was a secret society whose purpose was to keep the methods and secrets of hypnosis out of the hands of people and state actors who would use this knowledge for harmful ends."

"Oh, come on – you can't be talking about stage hypnotists, surely?"

"Of course not!" Pascale retorted, showing for the first time that her patience and charm were not limitless.

"You have no idea how powerful the techniques are that ASH developed under his leadership. The Marquis spent two years in prison, for his pains, and was only released when Napoleon was overthrown. But to this day, to this very day, the secret knowledge entrusted to ASH has been honoured and preserved."

Silence flooded the courtyard garden. Pascale looked away from me as I looked down to the uneven, block paved floor. The sounds of a lorry reversing to replenish a nearby Waitrose filled the air, until I broke our uncomfortable silence.

"I'm sorry Pascale. This is a lot to take in and I'm having to do so entirely on trust. I find that difficult in any circumstances, yet alone with a mysterious, beautiful stranger I've only just met."

As I'd hoped, the insertion of 'beautiful' into my apology had disarmed Pascale. A cheap trick, yes, but I thought a smile played across her lips and perhaps even just the merest hint of colour rose and quickly subsided in her cheeks. Or perhaps it was a grimace and a flash of anger? Either way, it broke her silence.

"Well, ok. If you want me to continue, I will. But I think we should move indoors for the sake of complete privacy." I nodded my assent and we went down the steps to the house, pausing only for me to gesture towards the drawing room forward and to her right.

"Perhaps I can make you something to drink before we begin again?"

"That would be nice. A cup of tea. No milk. No sugar. And not from a tea bag, s'il vous plaît."

As I walked down the corridor to seek out some loose tea in the kitchen, I looked over my shoulder and I saw Pascale begin to scan the drawing room. No doubt she would be looking for clues as to my personality, interest and who knows what else? The inside of other people's houses is a fascination for most of us. As I rooted through my food cupboards, a memory of a 1980s TV show, Through the Keyhole, came back to mind.

I was tempted to return to the drawing room quickly to disturb Pascale's investigations. But, on reflection, I let her have the full time it takes to boil a kettle, make the tea and then return.

"No biscuits, I'm afraid. Je suis désolé," I said as I passed her the mug (not cup) of tea. She took the tea with a shrug and sat down in a comfortable old armchair made of a deep brown leather. She had her back to the window but facing the door. This had the effect of me not being able to fully make out her face, being backlit (again). I wondered if that was deliberate as I took my seat on a sofa adjacent to where she was sitting.

"Good tea, thank you. Shall I continue?" I nodded.

During the time of the Société Harmonique des Amis Réunis, the Marquis and his friends took the work of Anton Mesmer and developed new techniques and approaches that had startling effects. They knew that if their discoveries were more widely known, the establishment in France would move mountains to discredit them, whilst using their discoveries for who knows what ends? Instead, the Marquis continued to give all credit to Mesmer and publicly showed little deviation from Mesmer's techniques. It was only in 1884 when Charles Richet, the Nobel Prize winner, discovered some of the Marquis' writings, that the extent to which others had claimed the credit for his work was truly revealed."

"Pascale, what were the developments in hypnosis that produced such startling effects and why do you need to keep them secret?"

"Oh Simon. I can't tell you, obviously. But please trust me that the effect on your fellow humans is serious. And in the wrong hands, it can be used to achieve many awful ends."

I sensed something in the way Pascale had spoken that didn't add up for me.

"*Can* be used or *has* been used?"

The air in the room seemed to get sucked out, up the chimney or somewhere. Pascale was tense as she considered how to reply. After a considerable pause she replied:

"Has been used."

The air returned to the room, like a sigh.

1613

Silence.

"Assuming I am prepared to help you, you're going to have to tell me *something*. How about you start by describing my mission or what have you?"

"Simon, I can do better than that but you're going to have to trust me completely."

"How come?"

"I want to show you, using hypnosis. Perhaps that will impress upon you the seriousness of this matter and the powerful nature of what we are dealing with."

I was seriously uncomfortable about this. Images of stage hypnotists sprang to mind, with me prancing about as if I were a chicken or a horse. Only in this case it might be something considerably worse.

"Pascale. It would be untrue to say I am not intrigued. But I'm also more than a little anxious about this. You're not going to make me believe I'm a chicken or something are you?"

"Yes. That's exactly what I have in mind for you. How did you know that?" She said with an extraordinary straight face.

For a moment I believed her and I must have shown it in my expression. She burst out laughing – real, genuine laughter – and she melted my sceptical heart in an instance. How could I resist.

"Ok. So what do we do now?"

"Just sit down in that chair," she signalled to a recliner chair by the door.

"Make sure you're really comfortable as you'll be sat there for at least an hour, probably nearer two."

I did as she asked, in silence, feeling rather like a small boy who's been told to sit down in a doctor's surgery. Was this me creating these feelings, or it was it her? Sensing my unease, she continued.

"It's ok Simon. Everything that's going to happen to you will be enjoyable, deeply relaxing and even beautiful, ok?" I nodded.

"So, let's begin."

She began talking to me in a deeper tone of voice, slightly husky even, and with a more pronounced French accent it seemed to me. At first this was amusing – she's using her hypnotist's schtick, I thought – but very quickly I tuned into her voice. Or rather, it felt as if her voice tuned into me. She took me through some basis relaxation techniques, as I recall, and then conjured up some beautiful imagery for me to engage with. It felt more and more real and I felt more and more absorbed by the beautiful images and places we were creating around me.

The next part I have no memory of, other than a strange sense of detaching from my body, a kind of peeling away. Afterwards, I asked Pascale why I couldn't remember this bit. And she told me it was because she *told* me to forget it. This was the phase that brought me to the most startling experience of my life. To that point at any rate.

What I do remember is emerging through some kind of doorway. The doorway led directly into my drawing room. It was so bizarre. I entered the room to see Pascale exactly where she was when I closed my eyes. She looked up.

"Hello Simon."

She gave me such a beautiful, understanding smile that was full of kindness and connection. I wanted to cry and to laugh, full of unadulterated human joy. I was immediately at my ease. This was fortunate as the next thing I noticed *was* me. Me, sitting in the reclining chair. A wave of what I can only describe as vertigo washed through me, followed by nausea. Pascale had clearly seen this before.

"Don't worry Simon. It will pass quickly."

And so it did. I'd heard of people having out of body experiences before, but this was extraordinary. Vivid, full colour and every detail of the room, and me, was there.

"This is unusual," I said. Pascale nodded in agreement.

"Welcome to the world that ASH is protecting. I need to explain a few things to you before we get started."

Chapter Two

Monday

1625

Approximately 159 miles away in a corner of a dingy, seaside café, sat a woman of indeterminate age. Her clothes were unremarkable, as was her hair, her facial features and just about everything else. As she stared out across the main promenade, she appeared for all the world to be lost in thought. And indeed, she was. In a way.

Isobel Fernandes (her real name) moved to Aberystwyth some 14 years ago after a rather unfortunate incident in Edinburgh. She was younger then, she often reflected as if she still might find redemption, or at least forgiveness, from those who controlled her destiny. There was little chance of that although, as events unfolded, it wasn't that there was *no* chance.

Particularly as a younger woman, Isobel had a certain weakness for hard drink and young men (often together), and she found herself during the course of one evening consuming rather too much of both. The details were somewhat vague in her memory now, a neat trick given her extraordinary mental abilities, which suited the growing sense of embarrassment she felt with each passing year.

The second rule of ASH is discretion, and the Edinburgh incident was anything but discreet. Complaints made to the police by many of the young men involved (though not *all* as Isobel pointed out with some pride when interviewed under caution later) threatened to produce a scandal the size of which hadn't been seen since the Marylebone Incident in 1879. Suffice to say, that particular scandal also involved a degree of 'persuasion' of many of the male participants.

The first rule of ASH is that members never use their remarkable abilities in pursuit of personal satisfaction or gains, and the Marylebone Incident was a transgression that saw the ultimate penalties being given to the transgressors. In the case of ASH this was not death but something many regarded as worse. It was permanent expulsion from the organisation and removal of any memories or abilities that they had acquired when they *were* members. As if this was not sufficient, a hypnotic lock was put on each transgressor that made it impossible for anyone (including themselves) to induce a hypnotic state of any kind in the future. Use of the hypnotic lock was infrequent and seen as especially harsh. Except, of course, when dealing with ASH's enemies which meant practically anyone who discovered the secret ways of Puységur and sought to use them for what ASH regarded as improper purposes.

And so here she was. Exiled to a small, seaside town on the coast of West Wales. A strange choice for the power

26

brokers of ASH in many ways as, being home to a university, the town had many pubs and plenty of young men. Perhaps that was part of Isobel's punishment, living, as she did, under a strict edict of alcohol-free sexual abstinence. Hard to imagine any other kind...

However, for members of ASH, even those in some disgrace, physical exile was simply just that – a limitation on where they can physically reside. Very few had ever been subjected to limitations on the Hypnotic Plane. And that, while staring out to sea, was where Isobel was.

1034

Earlier that day, Isobel had felt a strong sense of things being off. Just not quite all lined up the way they should be. Anyone who has ever experimented with psycho-active drugs will be able to appreciate that sense of detachment, of being out of phase with the world. In Isobel's case, she had learned to pay close attention to any feelings of things not being just so. Since the morning, the equivalent of a dull headache had been accompanying her every activity. Experience had taught her not to ignore this. She tried to zone in on this disturbance at home in her terraced house in Chalybeate Street, next to the wholefood shop. She couldn't quite find it. Somehow it kept escaping her grasp.

As the day wore on, she relocated several times. First she tried sitting in the castle grounds, then the South Beach and eventually she made her way into the Old College library. She loved it in here. The 70 year construction began in 1795 and the building was only turned over to the University of Wales in 1872. Here in the 21st century, it was a beautiful, if somewhat faded example of Victorian gothic architecture.

Sitting silently in the library, she closed her eyes and, using the techniques handed down from Puységur, entered a state of deep hypnosis. Beyond this, she pushed further on until she was able to manifest herself *extra corporelle,* or outside of her body. As usual, a sense of the ethereal accompanied her transition to the hypnotic plane. Over the decades, she had spent so much time in this plane that the world that most of humanity regarded as reality, felt rather humdrum and drab.

As she was contemplating her surroundings, her sense of unease grew an at alarming rate. She had felt this before, of course, though many years ago. She braced herself for what was about to come as she felt a tremendous thud on the back of her head that sent her tumbling forwards. As her feet kicked up to where her head should have been, she could see her attacker behind her, rapidly closing the distance between them. Stabilising her position, feet pointed forwards and her body almost horizontal, she focussed all her concentration through her hands and launched a massive bolt of energy directly at her assailant. It was a direct hit. She quickly got to her feet and, all senses primed, waited for her attacker to get up. He didn't. She knew from experience that somewhere, wherever they had manifested from, a real-world body would have drawn its last breath. The hypnotic plane version simply evaporated before her eyes, a slightly quizzical look passed across the face of what she estimated to be a 25 year old male.

"Fuck you," said Isobel in a tone that spoke more of a minor inconvenience than a threat to her life.

Whoever he was, or had been, he was a strange choice as her would-be assassin. She'd been at this game for far too long to be taken out by some child, she thought to herself. Whatever the reason, she'd been careless. Living a relatively quiet life by the seaside had made her lazy. Basic precautions were still important, as this attack demonstrated. She scanned the immediate area but could detect no other presence. Once she was certain no imminent follow-up attack was likely, she re-joined her real world self and, being careful to check for anyone following her, made her way to her favourite, dingy, seaside cafe.

1625

They were used to this rather quiet, non-descript woman coming to the café and sitting there, as if in a dream, for hours at a time. They used to think it might be bad for trade but after a while, Ioan and Annie Price grew accustomed to her presence, and even quite looked forward to her visits. They couldn't say what, exactly, but there was something rather... magnetic about Dawn (as they knew her). Quiet, yes. Talkative, no. But something...

Today as she sat in the Penguin café, Isobel was meeting on the hypnotic plane with the Ancient Society of Hypnotists Council of Elders.

Having just described the circumstances of the attack, the Council of Elders sat in silence, each of the five members wearing their deep concern in their already lined faces. Two men and three women comprised the Council. Antoine (the président of the Council), Rebecca (his deputy), Patrick (the longest serving member), Claire (rumoured to be having an affair with Antoine) and Fay (famous for being single minded if somewhat suggestible).

29

Isobel looked around the Council Chamber. It resembled an operating theatre from the 18th century – dark wood and steep tiers of seats around a relatively small central space. The lights were dim in the periphery and bright in the centre where the Council members sat, forcing Isobel to squint from her seat in what was, for all intents and purposes, a small enclosure like a witness box in court.

"And you're sure, Isobel, that this assailant was targeting you?" asked Antoine, an older man with unnaturally dark hair and a strong jaw line.

Wouldn't you be pretty certain if you'd been lumped on the back of the head? She thought.

"Yes, absolutely. I'd had a sense of something not being right all day, I – "

"And you didn't report this immediately?" interrupted a woman of about Isobel's age.

"Now, Rebecca" Antoine raised a hand, palm down, as he spoke in an unmistakable gesture designed to bring calm to proceedings.

"Isobel, I'm sorry you had to endure this attack and I want to assure you that the Council are behind you 100 percent. We will put in place protective measures immediately and consider whether you should be moved. In the physical world, that is. We can't discount the risk of you being attacked in your home in…,"

He leaned towards one of his Council colleagues with a questioning look. Isobel heard the colleague whisper "Aberystwyth". A look of faint displeasure crossed Antoine's face and rapidly disappeared.

"Your home in Aberystwyth." All reassuring smiles now, composure fully regained.

"May I speak?"

An incredibly rich and resonant voice reached into the ears and mind of all those assembled. A much older man, dressed in a black turtleneck with black jeans, leaned forward into the light. His features were, to be kind, craggy. Topped off with incredibly thick, afro hair. He was fit too. The outline of a well worked body was visible in the gloom.

"Patrick, of course," said Antoine with great reverence, even toady-ness, as he bent forwards and gestured in what to Isobel looked almost like an act of supplication.

"I have been thinking carefully about what you have told us, Isobel. I commend you for your skill in despatching your assailant. I am concerned you felt a sense of unease this morning, and when such a distinguished practitioner of the Ancient Art – "

Rebecca snorted, involuntarily, and drew the slow gaze of Patrick while the other Council members looked away. Uncomfortable, embarrassed, scared, even.

"Forgive me Patrick I..."

Patrick looked at Rebecca with such an intensity and absolute focus, that Isobel almost felt sorry for her. Almost, but not actually. Rebecca had damaged Isobel's reputation or rather had made the most of the self-inflicted damage that Isobel had brought upon herself in Edinburgh. As Rebecca sat in a state of obvious and excruciating discomfort, Isobel knew what Patrick was doing, as did the other council members. He was reaching deep inside her and reading her real motives, emotions and sentiment. It was a skill only the greatest practitioners of the Ancient Art possessed. In the present company only Patrick and Isobel were capable of such feats, and of all the ASH members worldwide, only Patrick new of Isobel's prowess.

Patrick's continued gaze led Rebecca to leave the table and exit the room. No words were necessary. She would not return to the council again.

Turning to Isobel, Patrick's face was instantly transformed to kindness itself, a beguiling smile and even a hint of laughter in his eyes.

"It's been a long time Isobel. Not since Edinburgh, I think?"

"It has Patrick," Isobel replied. She scanned Patrick's face for any signs of approbation or censure. She saw none. And perhaps, just perhaps, she saw a few laugh lines briefly draw themselves around his eyes and quickly disappear.

"When you started feeling uneasy today, tell me how that felt?"

"It was very unusual. I haven't felt like this since," Isobel stopped mid-sentence.

Recalling, painfully, the last conflict between ASH and their enemies, she had lost many friends and had been called upon to use her considerable skills in many unspeakable ways to secure victory. Silence filled the room.

She looked up at Patrick, tears rolling down her cheeks. Patrick gazed deeply inside her – she felt his presence in her consciousness – and he spoke to her directly, without utterance in the room.

"Isobel, I felt the same thing, but we cannot speak of this in the company of others. You must explain your uneasiness away. I will come and visit you soon."

Isobel finished her sentence.

"-not since just before my father died."

The council members, who had been anticipating a different explanation very much on the lines of Isobel's real explanation, drew a sigh of relief and visibly relaxed. Patrick, now speaking to everyone in the room said,

"I understand. We will speak of this again. And in the meantime, we will send ASH security members to Aberystwyth to protect you in the real and hypnotic realms."

"Thank you Patrick," replied Isobel.

*

"Miss? Miss?," a hand was gently touching her shoulder, trying to gain her attention.

"Is everything alright?"

Isobel found herself back in the Penguin Café with the owners, Ioan and Annie Price looking at her with concern in their eyes. She looked around and saw that she was the only one left in the café and that it was long past 5pm, the official time the Penguin closed its doors.

"Yes, I'm fine thank you," Isobel felt her wet cheeks and realised she had been crying here, as well as in the hypnotic plane. Under the concerned gaze of Ioan and Annie, she gathered up her things and ventured out onto the street. She looked over her shoulder to see them both still looking at her, with equal measures of kindness and sympathy, for their regular, slightly unusual, customer.

33

Isobel made her way from the Penguin towards the pier. Past the garish amusement arcade, improbably shining its lights on to the facade of what used to the theological college.

She walked along the prom and cut inland towards the castle. Walking through the castle grounds she found herself under the magnificent sculpture of a naked woman, part of the town's war memorial.

The bronze was created to represent humanity rising from the horrors of war, and she often came here to seek both solace and resolve.

As she stood under the sculpture and looked out across the Irish Sea, Isobel knew that things were going to change and change quickly.

Chapter Three

Monday

1625

I looked around the room in absolute wonder and awe. Everything looked as though, I don't know, as though it was *breathing*. Everything – inanimate objects, the walls the sky visible through the windows.

"Try imagining someone or some place that is familiar to you,"

"Ok. I'll think about a place."

I thought about a flat I lived in once, in central London.

"Nothing's happening."

"Really imagine it. The environment, the sounds, the smells the texture of the place."

I closed my eyes briefly and recalled some of the good times I'd had in the flat, the furniture, the smell of the old, waxed parquet floor – and then it happened. Like a zoom lens being turned really quickly to maximum, I felt propelled towards the flat. My eyes were well and truly open when I found myself standing in the flat or at least in what passed for the flat in this plane. I panicked wondering how the hell I would get back and felt a hand on my shoulder.

"It's ok Simon, I'm here."

Pascale had somehow come with me on this lightening quick trip across the home counties to the Smoke.

"What just happened," I barely whispered.

"You've just experienced one of the features of the hypnotic plane. I want you to try again, only this time imagine a public place, with people around you."

Warming to the idea (and perhaps even beginning to enjoy the possibilities of what this offered) I did as Pascale asked.

In an instant, we found ourselves inside the Tate Britain, on London's South Bank. People milled around, albeit in that ethereal shimmer that was present in everything I could see. Pascale was standing next to me. I asked the obvious question.

"Can they see us?"

"No. But some, those who are more susceptible to hypnosis can sense something, perhaps a presence, but they cannot see us."

"And can they feel our touch, can we touch them?"

"Not in the way you mean. If we enter the space of their physical form they will have some kind of sensation. In English I think you talk about someone having walked over your grave, or something like that? Of course there are those who do rather more than just enter the space of the physical form." Pascale gave me a knowing look that was completely wasted on me.

"Like what?"

"Some seek out sex."

"You mean they assault, sorry, rape people from this plane?"

"Yes, unfortunately. In mythology they are known as a succubus or an incubus, depending on whether they are male or female."

"That's appalling," I said.

"It is." Pascale replied.

For a moment Pascale looked perturbed – no doubt considering the dreadful conduct she had just described – but in a moment she said,

"We have to go."

Pascale grabbed my wrist and everything around me was a blur as we travelled in an instant back to my drawing room.

"What was that all about," I asked

"I just thought we should return here, "she replied, forcing a smile.

Just before we'd left the Tate, I'd followed Pascale's gaze and saw three, black-clad figures moving quickly towards us. At the point of our departure, they were very close.

"It was the people in black wasn't it? That's why you took me out of there so quickly."

She hesitated and replied "Yes. How did you spot them?"

"They were the only ones not, you know, shimmering, in the way that everything and everyone else does."

"Well spotted Simon. It's important for you to know that. If we're going to work together."

"What did they want, Pascale?"

"We need to leave this plane and return to the normal world. Then I'll explain."

Pascale asked me to close my eyes. She placed a hand on my forehead. I felt a tremendous warmth on my head and a sense of falling.

"Ahh!" I shouted out loud and sat forwards in the chair, back in my drawing room, back in the real world. Looking around everything seemed slightly flat, muted. Like an old fashioned TV with the colour turned down.

*

"ASH has had enemies since before it was even formed. You'll recall that Puységur was imprisoned by the revolutionary powers and only released when Napoleon was sent into exile. And this without our enemies even knowing the full extent of what we could do.

In those days the only other people on the hypnotic plane were so called primitive people like shaman and healers. They'd been traversing what we call the hypnotic plane for thousands of years before we stumbled across it in our clumsy way," said Pascale with a look of regret in her eyes.

"Do you mean to say others were here before you discovered it? "I asked in utter astonishment.

"Of course. And don't say we 'discovered' it. It's like saying Columbus discovered America or Cook discovered Australia – he wasn't even the first European to find it by the way. It's more likely that Europeans forgot how to access the hypnotic plane in our rush to become scientific and rational."

Pascale practically spat out these words, fierce anger burning within her propelling them outwards like projectiles. She paused, seemed to take a breath, and continued.

"And once we had rediscovered what our ancestors knew well, we knew we had to protect it against the *colonisateurs*, who would be sure to follow once they knew of its existence. Just like the worst excesses of your country and mine, right around the world. Only this time they would have the power not just to colonise the hypnotic plane but to use those powers to take control of most of the world. Unthinkable."

My head was swimming. Rather lamely I said,

"So it's really quite important, what you do then?"

And instantly regretted it.

"What the fuck? *Quite* important? It's absolutely CRITICAL!"

Pascale's face had reddened as her volume had increased. Bizarrely, my entire field of vision was affected, as though waves were travelling through the air around me, distorting my sight. I also noticed that her palms had reddened as well, almost glowing from within. It's fair to say I was terrified, and I didn't care that I was showing it.

"Oh Simon!," Pascale exclaimed, with an emotional content I found hard to decode.

"I'm so sorry. I nearly lost my temper with you and that's inexcusable."

Holy shit, that was *nearly* losing her temper? I stopped myself thinking about what a full-blown paddy would look like. Pascale looked at me. I mean really looked at me and I simultaneously felt a strong connection with her and a degree of violation.

"What are you doing?" I asked.

"What do you mean?" Pascale looked sheepish, just for an instant.

"I think you know exactly what I mean."

Another silence fell between us. This time, I was the first to speak.

"So who were those people in the Tate? The ones who were coming towards us when you yanked me back here."

Pascale looked thoughtful, as she often did, apparently transported by those thoughts to somewhere else. Come to think of it, she might be somewhere else, I reflected.

"I'm not sure."

"Then why the drama?"

"There are very few others on the hypnotic plane, and when we do, very occasionally meet, there is an agreed, well, protocol if you like."

"Go on."

"As I mentioned, the Plane is somewhere that many civilisations have travelled for thousands of years. ASH was never intending to be some kind of colonial power in the Plane, we didn't want to impose our view of world order or dominate something so precious. A land, if you like, of which we had no knowledge nor any right to be there. "

"To begin with, we never saw anybody else. And why would we? Just like colonial explorers stumbling up a beach on a newly 'discovered' island, those on the Plane could easily avoid our gaze. We thought we were the first! So arrogant and so naïve. "

"Then, over time, they began to show themselves in various locations in the Plane. Briefly, at first, and then for longer periods. If we moved towards them, they would disappear, so we learned to keep still, keep our distance, and let them come to us if they wanted to. "

"Very slowly, that's what they did. And as they came closer, we felt what you felt just now: a sense of being interrogated, no?"

I nodded. Somehow, Pascale's explanation and the whole experience of the last day was beginning to make sense. It was almost as if I recognised what she was saying. Not quite déjà vu but something close to it.

"This interrogation was subtle and at first we didn't appreciate what was happening. But, as time went on, the others on the Plane began to trust us, and our intentions, more and more. Eventually we reached an understanding."

"What does that mean, exactly? An understanding? "

"We came to learn that over thousands of years the Plane had been accepted as a sacred place. A place where all are welcome so long as they travel in peace and with no malice or corrupt intent. In other words, using the Plane for personal gain, power, violence, or domination was completely forbidden. There was no single group to enforce these ancient customs and rites, rather it was a responsibility shared by all those on the Plane and it was accepted that transgressors should be dealt with without mercy."

"Meaning?"

"Meaning travellers on the Plane could destroy any transgressor immediately."

The Hypnotic Plane was starting to seem like a highly dangerous place to be in my mind.

"And how, exactly, can anyone on the Plane make that kind of judgement? It sounds like some kind of vigilante rule."

"By using the technique you experienced just now, by remote sensing. In the physical world it's almost impossible to determine someone's motives or whether they are lying. Polygraphs are a complete joke by the way – but on the Plane, once you have mastered the technique it is as easy as reading words on a page."

"So, forgive me, but who were those travellers dressed in black, and why haven't they been... dealt with?"

"Of course, I'm sorry. I said I didn't know, and I don't. Not for sure. But in recent months we have been encountering more and more travellers in black. Their outer clothes seem to act as some kind of shield and it is very difficult for us – me and my compatriots – to use our remote sensing skills to determine their motives, which is why- "

"Which is why you only pulled me back as they were bearing down on us." I interrupted.

"Exactement."

Although the danger of being on the Plane was apparent, I had liked it. I'd really liked it. Enough to want to go back again and explore some more, especially now Pascale had started to give me some of the history. I was more than intrigued, I felt a real pull towards experiencing it some more.

"Pascale, what is it that you actually want me to do?"

"Simon, I think we've covered enough for today. I want to let you rest and think about things for now. I'll come back tomorrow and I will tell you everything we want you to do for us."

I sighed, audibly. I was not sure whether it was a sigh of relief or frustration or fatigue. Probably all three.

"Yes, I think you're right. I need to sleep on this and see how I feel in the morning. "

And with that, I showed Pascale to the hallway and saw her out of the front door. As I watched her walk away, she turned around.

"Be careful, Simon."

"I will be," I replied. Not really knowing what that would entail. I turned round and pushed the door to. And then secured both bolts, top and bottom, as I never usually did.

*

2330 hrs

43

In bed that night, I knew I wouldn't sleep well. There were too many thoughts spinning around my head. Instead, I wondered whether I could project myself onto the Hypnotic Plane, without any help from Pascale. It was a very stupid thing to do.

Initially, I got nowhere. I could use relaxation techniques to completely let go of any specific sense of my body. Just a generalised feeling of my physical form remained. But all too soon, my head would resume its seemingly endless cycle of thoughts.

Just as I thought I was tipping into sleep, that point at which we are conscious of both impending sleep and developing images and dreams, I felt the same detaching feeling I had experienced earlier in the day when Pascale had taken me onto the Plane. I was still in my bedroom, but instead of being in bed, I was sitting on the edge of the bed facing the bedroom door. I turned round and there was my physical self, looking peaceful and fast asleep.

I felt exhilarated! The same shimmering effect was everywhere I looked. I went downstairs. It was such an odd sensation – everything as I would expect it to be only less substantial somehow, a mirage of itself everywhere I looked. I decided to venture outside, despite the fact that I was only dressed in pyjama bottoms and a tee shirt, as I had been when I went to bed.

I walked down to the junction with Grove Street and turned left towards the marketplace. Approaching me were a couple of drunks. I had no watch but looking up at the Clock House on my left, the eponymous clock showed 11.45pm. Perhaps they had spilled out of the Swan or King Alfred's Head – Fred's Head as it was known locally. I could hear them arguing as they got closer. Some finer point about of debate surrounding when exactly they had been on holiday somewhere was in full swing as they passed me. They looked in my direction but seemingly saw nothing. Feeling emboldened, I thought I would continue to the marketplace and see if there was anyone else around. As I turned the corner past Mill Street, a small crowd were gathered around King Alfred's statue. I walked straight towards them.

The crowd comprised of mainly young men and a couple of young women were busy passing around joints, casting furtive looks towards the roads entering the square, presumably scanning for parents, police or perhaps just a taxi to get them home. I stood no more than two metres away. No recognition, nothing. On a whim I started dancing around the group and around the statue. I was enjoying this! It was thrilling to be invisible to those around me and I got a sense of how intoxicating, and potentially corrupting, this kind of power could be.

I continued my adventure by walking up Newbury Street. My intention was to head for the recreation ground in Manor Road, but as I was passing the row of pizza shops on my left, two people emerged from Post Office Lane. They stopped dead in their tracks and looked directly at me. For the first time since venturing out I had a sense of how absurd I must look, dressed only in my nightwear. The larger of the two was a woman dressed in black jeans, white trainers and a dark hoodie. The smaller, a man, was in blue jeans, brown shoes and a blue bomber jacket. They looked at least as surprised as I must have done. Whether this as due to our mutual visibility to each other, or my choice of clothes, was not clear to me. In either case, I decided to run.

Benefitting from local knowledge, which I assumed these two didn't possess, should give me some advantage, I reasoned. If only I knew how Pascale had transported us to the Tate earlier that afternoon, I'd be home free.

I accelerated towards Church Street. Passing the Thai restaurant as I did so. I considered briefly turning towards the Beacon Hall car park but this is too open with no chance to lose my pursuers, who were now gaining quickly on me judging by the sound of their footsteps behind me. I pressed on towards the church. Looking briefly over my shoulder, the shorter man was struggling to keep up, but the taller woman was lengthening her stride with little seeming effort. I needed to get out of her immediate vision, and quickly. I ran round the corner, past the Swan's beer garden and then darted into the elevated graveyard next to the church. I spotted a tall gravestone and ducked down behind it. As I looked back between gravestones I saw the woman round the corner. She paused, scanning the view in front of her, before she ran past the Swan, turned right and went back towards the market square. Eventually, the shorter man turned up, wheezing and gasping. He bent over in the road with one hand propping him up against the wall of the Swan. Then, as if he'd had a word with himself, he drew himself up to his full height and began walking after the woman. Before he turned the corner, presumably in case she was watching, he started running again.

I was terrified. Now the adrenaline was beginning to subside my imagination started suggesting all kinds of equally gruesome reasons why these people in black were chasing me. Were they the same ones as we saw at the Tate? I'd only caught a glimpse of them, if it was them, earlier but that was enough for Pascale to whisk me away in an instant. I wish I'd asked her more questions now. And I wished she was here. And that I hadn't ventured out on my own, idiot!

I looked around, gingerly raising my head above the top of the gravestone. I could see no-one. Had they gone away, would they come back? More importantly, what the hell am I going to do now? I sat back down on my haunches and let my finger idly trace the letters engraved in the gravestone I sat behind. I pondered my own mortality and wondered if I would ever end up in a place like this...

Enough. I needed to get back home and out of the Hypnotic Plane. I listened for any sounds. Footsteps or conversation. I heard none. I stood up and looked around me. I saw no-one. Right then, I thought, time to go. I tried to imagine my bedroom so I could transport myself there directly, just as I had done earlier in the day when I imagined my old flat. Nothing. I tried again. Still nothing. Maybe the adrenaline was stopping me, or maybe the two who were chasing me were inhibiting this somehow?

So instead, I headed towards the marketplace and skirted in front of the café and the Fred's Head towards Alfred Street. As I approached Mill Street, I looked around. Still no one. I crossed the road and walked towards Sainsbury's, avoiding the upper end of Grove Street. The town was very quiet, but not untypically so for the time of night. I turned past Sainsbury's towards Grove Street. Still all clear. I was beginning to relax.

I walked on the pavement, crouching, more or less, behind the parked cars as I passed the tyre place. The Clock House clock showed 12.23. I darted across the road and turned up Stirlings Road. I only need to make it round the corner to the back gate and I'll be home, I thought. As I did so I saw a cat crossing in from of me. She turned to face me and hissed. How odd, I thought, before replying

"Screw you."

I carefully reached for the latch on the back gate, opened it, and made my way inside. I was expecting the security light to come on and felt a little foolish waiting for it to do so. In the dark I easily made my way to the back door before climbing the stairs and getting back into bed, more or less over the physical form of me which remained there, asleep.

To my relief, I felt my body almost snap back into place with my other self. It was like a magnetic catch, clicking into place. In a moment I felt a tremendous sense of vertigo, before opening my eyes and sitting up. It was then I noticed her. She was sat in the armchair in my bedroom, between the two windows, her arms placed on each arm of the chair, back erect.

"Ah. Hello." I said.

"Bon matin Simon," Pascale replied.

Chapter Four

Tuesday

0925

The day after the incident in the Old College library, Isobel was sat at her kitchen table, her hands cradling a cup of tea. Her gaze was fixed at a point some 50 centimetres beyond the edge of her teacup, a pose in which she had remained more or less motionless for the last 33 minutes. She had barely touched her tea and that which remained was now, at best, merely tepid.

The kitchen had barely seen a lick of paint in the last 14 years. The Elders had arranged for the house to be decorated before she was sent here, but the job was not done well and the whole place was starting to look rather sorry for itself. "A bit like me," reflected Isobel out loud.

When she had first arrived in the town, in winter, her initial impressions were not great. Apart from the beauty of the prom, Old College, and of course the sea, the town was dreary and somewhat down at heel. An absence of green space in the town meant that the winter grey of the sea merged with the sky, slate rooves, tarmacadamed roads, and faces of the town folk that went about their business. Only the cheerful, sometimes garish, painted houses scattered on the sea front and in the town made an effort to lift the mood. In the summer though, and on occasional sun-filled winter days, they shone as brightly as the sky.

Once, on her first winter in the town, Isobel turned the corner from Pier Street onto the Prom and the view took her breath away. The sun caught the white tops of the waves, whipped up by a strong wind, as they dance on a pale blue sea. As ridiculous as it felt to her at the time, it reminded Isobel of southern California. Every time she makes the turn from Pier Street since, she hopes she'll be greeted by that same vision. And sometimes she is. Over the last fourteen years, that's just one way that this modest little town got under her skin. The prospect of leaving the place, that once would have filled her heart with joy, now only brought a sense of overwhelming sadness.

1001

The doorbell rang. Isobel was immediately entirely present in the room and, even as she made her way to the front door, was preparing herself for an attack or whatever other hostile presence was standing on her doorstep. Walking down the narrow hallway that almost always smelled of damp, she paused. Her senses, sharpened and honed over many years, picked up the presence of another traveller on the hypnotic plane.

"Shit," she whispered out loud. Then, turning her full attention to her front door, she struggled to determine whatever and whoever was there. Even before the doorbell rang again, a faint look of pleasure crossed her face, followed by puzzlement which was replaced with pure joy.

"Patrick!," Isobel practically screamed his name as she threw open the door and embraced the man with whom she had shared so much. Patrick returned her embrace whilst skilfully moving her back into the house and closing the door with a gentle pirouette of his left foot.

"I can't believe you've come," Isobel said as she held him at arms' length to look at him, to gaze upon his face.

"You're looking tired Patrick. Come into the kitchen and let me make you a coffee."

Isobel turned and led Patrick down the hallway towards the kitchen at the back of the house, where he sat down at the kitchen table. She continued talking without looking at Patrick. Her voice steady but her hands fumbling and mishandling the coffee, cafetiere and mugs she was trying to arrange.

"It was always your hands, Isobel."

Isobel stopped what she was doing and stood still. Her back still turned to Patrick. The slightest drop of her shoulders the only sign that she had heard what he had said and that his words had found their mark.

Isobel turned to face Patrick. Tears were streaming down her face and the look of joy at seeing her old friend was now replaced by a look of sadness washed with fear.

"I know." He said.

With a deep sigh, Isobel abandoned the coffee and sat down opposite Patrick at the table.

They sat in silence for some time, the way old friends can, until Isobel said,

"To ask the obvious question, Patrick, why did you come?"

"My answer is no less unexpected, I think. You know why."

Until Patrick uttered those three words, and despite what she knew intuitively to be true, Isobel had hoped that there was another reason.

"So, they're back.

Patrick gave an almost imperceptible nod.

"Patrick, I don't know if I can do this again."

"You're not the only one who questions their preparedness, and even stomach, for what we both know lies ahead," he replied.

"If only Hugo was here to help us…"

"Ah, Hugo," said Patrick with all the cares of the world crammed into those two words.

*

Hugo Durand was, quite simply, a legend. The son of one of ASH's most accomplished travellers, Marine Durand, no-one ever knew who his father was. Marine was certainly not giving up that information and the younger, irreverent devotees to the cause even suggested she produced him on her own. A suggestion that Marine rather warmed to when the gossip inevitably reached her ears.

She brought up her son with peculiar devotion and affection and fiercely protected their privacy as a family. She introduced him to the Ancient Art at a tender age – just six years old. There were some in the Society that were scandalised at the time. The Council of Elders certainly took an interest but, whether through ample evidence of Marine's outstanding motherhood or the intensity with which Marine defended her family's choices, they decided to leave her well alone.

Within six months Hugo was accessing the hypnotic plane with ease, and within a year he was travelling unaccompanied. As a child, he was quick to gain the trust of native peoples all over the Plane and it is said that during these early adventures, he acquired the extraordinary skills and abilities that served him, his mother and ASH so well.

Between the ages of six and eighteen he continued to develop his skills. He also assisted the research arm of ASH in evaluating new techniques and cataloguing new abilities that he was able to demonstrate. One such ability was legendary.

On a warm summer's day, in Hugo's twelfth year, had been playing outside with his friends, most of whom were not part of the Society. It has always been important to Ash that its members were fully integrated with the 'real' world. This was both for reasons of understanding what was happening in the world and also as a means of concealing themselves from their enemies and any other interested parties.

On this particular day, Hugo's best friend, Claudine, was expected to arrive back from her summer holidays with her parents. Neither Claudine nor her parents were a part of ASH. That made no difference to the 11 year old Hugo. He loved Claudine with all his tender heart. The same could not be said of her parents. They were overprotective and perhaps because of this, they were suspicious of Hugo. He felt that they didn't really approve of the friendship, the close bond that he shared with their daughter. He was right. And from their perspective, his mother left much to be desired – a strongly independent woman who kept herself to herself, apart from the occasional visitor. It was these visitors who aroused even more suspicion, and even fear. Nothing they could put their fingers on, but they didn't like them, nonetheless.

Hugo knew what time Claudine should arrive home and he decided to wait outside her family home to surprise her. They had been exchanging message for the entire two weeks they were apart and both were as excited as they could be to see each other.

The family were driving back from a holiday in Scotland, the Western Isles in fact. A place steeped in folklore and legend and somewhere Hugo had been to on his travels many times, though never in the real world.

Just south of Manchester, a lorry driver was tying on a load of timber. He'd been up very early that morning following a poor night's sleep due to his neighbours partying until the early hours. He knew one of the ratchet sets, with which he secured his loads, was in need of replacement, but in his haste to leave home he'd left it on a table in the hall. By the time he realised his mistake he was already in the depot and his supervisor was admonishing him for being late. Ah well, the old one will have to do, just for today. Just for today.

The driver joined the M6 at junction 19, about three miles ahead of Claudine and her family. The lorry was travelling at 55 mph compared to Claudine's family car travelling at 76 mph. In just 8 minutes, 34.2 seconds, they would be alongside the lorry. Another 3 seconds they would be past it. Would have been past it.

As they approached the rear of the lorry, Claudine's mother indicated to enter the middle lane to go past. At the same time, the broken ratchet finally gave way. This made the load of timber shift. The driver felt a change in direction of the lorry as a result and, being tired, over corrected. It was this sharp turn to the left that sent half his load tumbling off to the right, onto the roof of Claudine's mother's car.

Hugo was still waiting for Claudine an hour after she was due to come home. At the time, he had no idea what had happened on the M6. It was only when Marine came to find her son that he sensed something was wrong.

"What is it maman? What's happened?"

Marine looked on her son's face and thought about how the next few seconds would hurt him, deeply. Deeply enough for the pain to last a lifetime, she thought. She was not a believer in the existence of so called Closure. A ridiculous American invention, like so many things that plagued the world. No, she knew that grief and hurt were always with us, we just learn to accommodate them, like an unwelcome guest, in the home we call our heart.

She told Hugo what had happened with great tenderness but directly. With deep love but with clarity. Hugo could understand the events that his mother described but he simply could not understand that he would never see Claudine again. It was beyond his eleven year old mind's comprehension. In fact he *refused* to accept that Claudine was gone.

After his mother had told him the dreadful news he asked if he could go to his room, to be alone with his thoughts for a while. Marine understood and even said she thought it would be a good idea.

"It is a good idea," thought Hugo "but perhaps not one of which you would approve, dear maman."

It only took Hugo a few seconds to access the Hypnotic Plane. He often found that, if he was charged with emotion, accessing the Plane became easier and quicker. In time, he leaned to summon up intense emotion just to facilitate this rapid transition. No-one could do this quicker than Hugo and it became one of the many skills for which he would be known.

He travelled at immense speed across the m

Midlands towards Manchester. He didn't know where he would find Claudine but he thought she would probably be in a hospital somewhere, despite the fact that she was dead. Finding hospitals was not too difficult either. Hugo just hunted for an ambulance with its lights on and sirens sounding. He had worked out that it would either be on the way to a casualty or on the way to a hospital. It was a rough and ready technique, but one that worked. Eventually. It was not until late that night that he found Claudine, or rather Claudine's body. She was covered in a sheet, just like in the movies, awaiting a postmortem. The room was empty apart from Claudine and her parents. There were security doors at the end of the long, lifeless room, and beyond these a security desk staffed by a lone woman, looking bored, which of course she was.

He could tell Claudine was dead, even from the Hypnotic Plane. Perhaps that made it easier to tell. There was a kind of emptiness about her, like she had left her body, which of course she had. Hugo didn't really know what he was going to do next, he just knew that he wanted Claudine back in the real world. Like so many of his abilities, he had never been taught *how* to do them, he just reached for what he wanted, intuitively, instinctively.

He stood over Claudine's body. She had died from her neck being broken, snapped, as the tremendous weight of the wood fell onto the roof of her family's car. Apart from that, her body was undamaged. To begin with, Hugo placed his hands on the body of his best friend. He was not surprised at the coolness that met his hands, but he was shocked at the absence of anything he could sense as life. Normally, even from the Plane, a person's vitality was sensible.

Hugo closed his eyes. He began to try and imagine Claudine as she was. It was not difficult. Both because of the love he felt for her, and the fact that the imagination of an 11 year old has still not been conquered by the adult world of science and rationality. It is alive, an open channel to greater creativity and possibilities. He soon found himself immersed in the images of his dear friend. His imagination conjured up incredible levels of details. He began to imagine Claudine coming back to life. He imagined the blood flowing around her body, nerves firing, her lungs filling with air. He knew something was wrong with her neck so imagined her neck being complete, whole, just as it used to be. He couldn't sense any change in her, so he tried again. And again. And again.

"It's not working!", he said out loud. The grief came over him like a torrential downpour, every part of him drenched in it, to his very core. He had failed, failed his best friend. It was all too much for Hugo. From the bottom of his soul he cried out Claudine's name. If there had been anyone there to hear it, it was the very definition of heart-wrenching. It was a cry that carried all the intensity of human grief and love and loss.

Hugo collapsed onto the body of his best friend and soulmate. His body, even on the Plane, conducted the emotional energy he felt, in twists and spasms, as he wailed in response to the unbearable pain he was feeling. He could see Claudine in his mind's eye, with startling vivacity. An imaginative power he had never experienced before, and completely without conscious intent.

He felt the slightest twitch. Then a breath, yes a breath! He pulled away from Claudine's body and looked at her face. Colour was returning to her skin. With great tenderness, he touched her cheek with the back of his hand, scared in case his touch would banish her again from this mortal life. Gently stroking her face now, she opened her eyes. For a brief moment, through the hypnotic plane, she saw him, she saw her Hugo.

"I knew you'd come for me," she whispered before she closed her eyes again and fell into unconsciousness.

Hugo, almost blind with tears of joy, knew he needed help. Help from the real world to make sure that whatever had just happened, Claudine was kept alive. He turned over an adjacent metal table, scattering the hideous tools of the mortuary technician all over the floor. Then he pulled the sheet covering Claudine into her hands, to make it look as though she had tried to get up off the table. Soon enough the security guard came racing into the room. As if on cue, Claudine let out a quiet moan. That was enough for the guard who called in the extraordinary scene from her radio, attached to her belt.

Despite taking some convincing, the junior doctor who answered the call was quick to action once she saw that Claudine was alive. Or rather that she was *not* dead.

"This is going to take some explaining by someone," she said out loud. A sentiment shared by an 11 year old boy, some 184 miles away, who had just returned to his own body in the real world.

*

1036

The two friends sat in silence for some minutes more, only this time it was Patrick who spoke first.

"You know, we never stopped looking for him. Never." Patrick's eyes began to fill, and Isobel reached across the table to take his hands, now pressed together in a reflection of his inner anxiety.

"I know." Just two words conveyed so much more than an acknowledgement of the statement Patrick had just made. They conveyed a full understanding of the current facts as well as the pain and despair they had all felt when Hugo was gone. Patrick looked up, as tears ran down his face. Isobel reached out into Patrick's soul, in a state of openness and vulnerability that so few had ever observed in him. Their connection transcended words. Instead they sat still, staring into each other's eyes, hands clasped, motionless.

The doorbell rang and the moment transformed from deep connection to being instantly on high alert.

"Were you expecting someone?" asked Patrick.

"No." Replied Isobel. "Could you have been followed here?"

"Anything is possible, of course, but I think not. Answer the door and I will take the back door and circle round to the front. There's no point both of us tackling an aggressor in your narrow hallway."

Without speaking, Isobel steadied herself and made her way to the front door. The bell rang again, only this time with more urgency. At the same time, Patrick left through the back door, let himself into the health food shop's rear door and entered the shop. Without glancing at the startled shopkeeper, he moved quickly through the store, passed all the neatly stacked wooden shelves, towards the entrance on the street. Before he could reach the door, he heard a scream. He quickened his pace immediately, moving with extraordinary purpose and grace, slipping through the front door and turning to his left. He saw someone move inside the from door with their arms extended towards, presumably, Isobel. There was three metres between him and Isobel's doorway and he knew he had to cover that ground in an instant, before the door could be closed and god knows what else might happen. In that strange way that time both stands still and moves incredibly fast in times of great stress, Patrick remembered just how much he cared for Isobel and how much he wanted to keep her safe.

Focussing all his efforts on closing the ground between him and Isobel's assailant, he threw himself through the doorway before the attacker had time to close it. In doing so he tripped on the threshold, flying forwards, hands outstretched. He also crashed his head against the door frame, sending his vision spinning until at last he passed into unconsciousness.

1642

Unbeknown to Patrick, it took some time for him to regain consciousness. It was late in the afternoon before he finally began to come round.

"That was quite a dent you made in my door frame Patrick." He recognised Isobel's voice immediately, despite struggling to open his eyes fully. He became aware of a dull thumping in his head, as well as a sharp pain on his right temple where he had, presumably, crashed his head into the woodwork.

"What the hell happened? Are you alright?". Patrick's vision slowly started returning to normal. He looked around the room. He was upstairs, lying on an old fashioned brass bedstead in a room with a low ceiling and small window looking out over the back yard, as far as he could tell. A four panelled door was ajar.

"I'm fine. It's you you should be worried about. You've been unconscious for hours."

"I heard you scream, I'm sure I did. And I saw someone attacking you, arms outstretched as they made their way into your hallway. I knew I had to get into the house, to help you- ".

"Ah yes. I'm sorry about that. It wasn't a scream of fear, but of delight and completely involuntary. And those outstretched arms were going in for a hug, not a kill." Isobel looked sheepish. Patrick looked bemused then cross, then furious.

"Jesus fucking Christ, Isobel. What was I supposed to think?!"

An awkward silence filled the bedroom. Isobel looked down at her hands and Patrick looked down at the duvet. Then she let out a snort. Patrick looked up. He saw that Isobel was trying desperately to stop her face from cracking into a broad grin. She was trying so very hard not to laugh.

"You are an incorrigible bitch!" Patrick exclaimed, before he was overcome by laughter of his own. The pair of them were laughing so hard when Patrick heard the sound of crockery being moved around, items gently banging against each other from downstairs, the kitchen presumably. He tried to sit up.

"What's that – ". The effort of sitting up brought a flash of excruciating pain across the front of his head and he collapsed back against the feather pillows behind him.

"Shh, it's ok, "said Isobel, wiping tears of laughter from her face. The sound of footsteps coming up the stairs caused Patrick further alarm, despite Isobel's reassurances. She placed a gentle hand across his chest to prevent him from sitting up again.

A figure, silhouetted against the opened door, entered the room.

"Hello Patrick. Having fun?"

As he struggled to focus, Patrick connected the familiar voice to the emerging image appearing before him. As soon as he recognised this other person, he was filled with both delight, excitement and trepidation.

"Pascale Blanchet – for once you have caught me by surprise."

"Oh, I'm full of surprises, Patrick. You have no idea…".

Chapter Five

Tuesday

0025

We sat in complete silence. And whilst I spent most of my time looking at the end of the bed, eyes slightly cast down so as to not meet Pascale's gaze, when I did look up, she appeared to be regarding me with a sense of amusement, anger, thoughtfulness and frustration. Each in their turn.

I was beginning to feel tired. As the adrenaline left my body it was rapidly replaced by fatigue.

"You look tired Simon. And I don't think I'm ready to have the conversation we need to have."

I must admit I felt a certain sense of relief. I really wasn't ready to receive a bollocking from Pascale or anyone else if it comes to that. I said nothing but looked at Pascale. She returned my gaze with something rather surprising. I couldn't help thinking she was checking me out. She broke her gaze as if she had made a decision. She was the first to speak.

"Move over," was all she said. I quickly made space for her at the side of the bed which she was approaching. She quickly undressed, pulled back the duvet, lay down, and turned her back towards me. Within seconds, or so it seemed, I could hear the sound of her breathing. She was clearly asleep and even beginning to snore, very gently.

So much for checking me out! Unless her looks were in fact some kind of threat assessment, the result of which was clearly that she regarded me as not being particularly dangerous. I was not entirely sure how I felt about Pascale's perception of me, but perhaps it was for the best.

*

0609

I woke up around the usual time. I was lying on my side facing away from Pascale. I'd been aware of her presence for most of the time I had been in and out of sleep. Now, with the morning light bouncing around the room, I felt somewhat self-conscious as I considered getting out of bed, seeing Pascale, and facing whatever censure she had in store for me.

I simultaneously sat up and swung my legs over the side of the bed. Facing the wall, I drew in a deep breath and turned round to see if Pascale was awake yet.

Clearly she was, as her side of the bed was completely empty! I instinctively reached out my hand to feel the mattress where she had been lying. It was stone cold. I set off in search of Pascale, along the landing towards the bathroom, then down the stairs to the kitchen. Nothing. She must have left long before I awoke.

Walking back through the dining room, I saw Iago sitting in the hallway. My dead cat staring at me intently. I shut my eyes and attempted to erase him from my mind's eye. When I opened them, he was gone again.

0614

I went back to bed but found I couldn't sleep. Memories of the previous day's adventures kept intruding on my mind. In less than 24 hours my rather hum-drum world had been invaded, turned upside down and I'd been introduced to things that made my head hurt. Literally.

I'd been having headaches for as long as I could remember. Or at least for the last four years and certainly since I was divorced. Popular wisdom would suggest that headaches (both literal and metaphorical) should stop after a divorce but in experience this was not so. And it felt like the events of the last 24 hours had only served to make the headaches worse.

Something odd was going on, and not just the obvious strangeness of the last day. Every time I now thought about Pascale, ASH or our brief travels on the hypnotic plane, I received a flash of intense pain across my left brain. I emptied my mind (as much as I could) and the pain subsided. As soon as I returned to matters of hypnosis, the pain returned. I found the packet of Sumatriptans on the bookcase in the dining room. I pushed one out of the blister pack and swallowed it with a gulp of water. My GP had prescribed these anti-migraine pills some time ago, and I was running low. Time to re-order, I thought.

I returned to the kitchen and began assembling my usual breakfast: toast with marmite and with peanut butter, and a strong coffee. I took my modest repast outside into the courtyard garden. The sun was up but would not shine onto this space for another four hours, at least. Nevertheless, the early mornings always held great joy for me. The effect of the caffeine, the fresh air and the sounds of a small market town coming alive are both reassuring and full of promise. Accompanied by brawling sparrows in the tree at the end of the yard, I am always filled with hope that, despite increasing urbanisation and our best efforts to undermine nature, it always finds a way to not only coexist but even to exploit our clumsy approach to our environment. I closed my eyes and began to count my breaths, in and out. Mindful meditation came easily to me, and I found I could practice it almost anywhere. Today was no exception and before long my mind was emptying, and a blissful calm was filling my soul. Breath in, breath out. Breath in, breath out. Those thoughts that did arise floated through my consciousness like clouds, I had no desire to engage with them. Sometimes this reminded me of the Chuggers that filled our high streets for a while. Charity Muggers would always take advantage of people's good nature.

"Hello sir, how are you today?"

"Could I just ask you a question, it won't take two minutes of your valuable time?"

And so on.

If you engage with them in conversation, even for a moment, you would be sucked in by your own good manners and kindness, while they spend the next 15 minutes trying to get you to sign up to regular contributions to some charity or another.

And so it was with thoughts. Better to let them drift by and not engage with them at all.

I felt the vibration of my phone in my hip pocket. Ignore it, I thought. Sure enough it stopped. Then it started again. This pattern went on for three more cycles, disturbing my calm and starting to annoy me.

I took the phone out of my pocket and squinted at the screen: private number. I answered the call this time, if only to make it stop.

"Simon speaking"

0657

"Simon, it's Pascale. I need you to leave right now."

"Pardon?"

"I need you to leave right now. Don't pack a bag, don't pick up a toothbrush, just leave. Now. There'll be a dark blue Ford Focus pulling up outside your back gate in about a minute. Get in it and then I'll call you and explain."

Pascale rang off. And for the second time in seven hours, I was feeling very scared. Reflecting on Pascale's voice, I could detect fear as well as concern. What on earth is going on? Should I even trust Pascale and why do I need to leave with such urgency? My thoughts were interrupted by a knock at the back gate. I hadn't even heard a car pull up, was this the blue Focus or someone else?

I looked through a crack in the gate. Fuck! It was the short, unfit man from the night before. Unmistakable, despite the dark glasses and a baseball cap. He banged again on the gate, only this time much harder. It's not a strong gate and one hearty kick would see it fly open.

I turned tail and bounded towards the steps back to the relative safety of the house. If I could get out of the front door I could be away in no time. Quietly closing the back door behind me and sliding the bolt to slow down any pursuers, I moved towards the front door. Without checking the spyhole, thoughtfully installed by the previous owners, I threw open the door. Even as I did so I remember seeing the tall, athletic woman I'd evaded the night before. And then, everything went dark.

*

The first thing I noticed was the smell. I couldn't quite place it, despite the intensity with which my nostrils were assailed. Something like jasmine combined with damp mould. It made little sense to my poor brain. The left-sided headache had returned, strongly.

The second thing that struck me, as I emerged into consciousness, was the fact that I was tied to a chair. The chair had a high back, and I was secured to it by my wrists, as well as by my waist and, most alarmingly, also by my neck. From what I could tell from the touch of my hands, the chair was made of wood. The third realisation was that I was blindfolded. Thankfully not hooded, as you see in various movies and reality TV programmes. My claustrophobia would have been triggered if I'd come round to that sensation. No, rather surprisingly, the blindfold was soft and even soothing to my closed eyes.

I could hear... nothing. Absolutely nothing. The air felt still, and I sensed I was alone. As became clear later, I was wrong. I was not alone.

In a bid to clear my headache, I started to count my breaths, in and out, in that cycle of one to ten, over and over. It took surprisingly little time for me to start dissociating from my current predicament, to quieten my thoughts, and to enter a state that was at least an approximation of calm. As my counting progressed, my mind started filling with unusual images, of being surrounded by bright, white light, and an assortment of voices instructing me in some way or other. It was very unnerving and felt like a dim memory of something that had happened a long time ago.

Perhaps sensing or even perceiving my mental processes, a voice brought me back sharply to the present moment.

"Simon. Shall I call you Simon?"

It was a woman's voice, strong and resonant. I said nothing, resolving to keep schtum for the duration.

"Do you have any idea where you are?"

Such a ridiculous question.

"Do you know why you're here?"

"Why don't you tell me?" my resolution falling away after only two more questions.

"It's not quite that simple, Simon. Simple Simon. Simple Simon. Maybe not so simple, after all."

What the hell did she mean by that? Presumably she was referring to my recent adventures with Pascale, a fact that my questioner confirmed almost immediately.

"We know about your meetings with Ms Blanchet."

Just the mention of Pascale was enough to bring a flash of pain to my head. I flinched, involuntarily.

"Interesting," said the woman's voice.

"What can you remember, Simon?" She asked.

About what, I thought. What could this disembodied voice possibly want from me?

"Ah, forgive me. That's rather a broad question. How about this one for size? What's the earliest thing you can remember?"

I started to try and plumb the depths of my memory (which has never been good as far as I can recall) when a sharp, excruciating pain ran across my temples, causing me to gasp out loud. I tried again.

"Fuck!" I half shouted, half screamed."

"What are you doing to me?" As the pain subsided, I sensed someone close to me. My head was pushed to one side and I felt sharp sting in the side of my neck and then all went dark again.

*

When I came round this time, it was to full-on hallucinations. From what I can recall, some were hilarious, some bizarre and some downright terrifying. All the while, this same woman's voice was asking me question upon question, most of them I didn't even understand. And I kept on laughing, which seemed to make her more and more angry. I really couldn't stop myself – throughout all of the hallucinations, Iago, my long dead cat, was with me. Sitting on my lap, touching noses with me, and most weirdly of all, standing on his back paws whilst facing me and holding my head by the temples.

This made my headache feel considerably better and induced a kind of tingly, tickling sensation. Hence my laughter. As the rate of questions subsided, I was about to talk to my cat-hallucination. In a brief moment, seemingly anticipating my speaking, he moved his paw to cover my mouth. I knew exactly what he wanted. He wanted me to say nothing.

*

The next time I was awake and in something approaching a normal state of mind, I found myself lying in a double bed in a large, white painted room. I sat up and looked out of the window beyond the foot of the bed. When I say window, the whole of the wall was glass. It framed perfectly a beautiful garden consisting of a recently cut lawn and a few specimen trees. The garden went on for as long as I could see, into the middle distance.

Looking around the room, everything was white and minimal. There appeared to be a door out of the room, but there was no evidence of a handle or even a lock on this side. A single, open doorway led into what looked like an ensuite bathroom. I contemplated taking a shower and wondered what clothes I could wear. It was at this point that I realised I was completely naked.

Taking advantage of my apparent lack of immediate supervision, I ventured towards the ensuite. There, on a chair (white, of course) were my clothes from when I was taken. I find it hard to say 'kidnapped', although I suppose that's what it was. They looked washed and pressed, almost presentable. Me and ironing had long since parted company (about the same time as my divorce) and the sight of neatly ironed clothes was strangely nostalgic.

I turned my attention to the shower. There, sat neatly, as only cats can do, in the middle of the minimalist shower tray, was Iago.

I stood still and simply regarded him. He did the same. He seemed more vivid that he had ever been, unless you count the hallucinations which were beginning to come back into my memory.

I closed my eyes to test if I could make him disappear. He didn't. Instead, he spoke to me. I mean he spoke to me *inside* my head without making any noise.

"We don't have long, and I've got a lot to tell you." He said.

I wondered whether I was still hallucinating.

"You're not hallucinating. Just listen. I will explain everything."

My life was getting stranger and stranger.

Chapter Six

1642

Isobel and Pascale perched either side of the bed in which Patrick lay. The dim room casting a sombre veil across the reunion of three old friends.

"How's your head?" asked Isobel.

"It's fine. Can we please get out of here, out of this room? It's starting to feel like a Victorian death bed scene - something I am particularly keen to avoid."

Isobel began to protest but was silenced by a discreet shake of the head from her old friend Pascale. In resignation, she helped Patrick out of the bed until Patrick made it very clear he was going to move entirely under his own steam. Despite his fabulous physique, he was looking more like his actual age, after his injury that morning.

The friends sat down in the kitchen, round the kitchen table once more. In silence, Isobel filled the kettle and switched it on.

"You're looking tired, Pascale." Patrick observed.

"I'm *feeling* tired Patrick."

Isobel placed a fresh pot of tea and three cups and saucers onto the table, then took her seat. There had been a degree of tension between Patrick and Pascale following Hugo's disappearance. Each quietly blaming the other, at least in part, for the fact he was gone.

Pascale was considering her next words carefully. During the long drive from Wantage to Aberystwyth, Pascale had been going over the events of the last 36 hours. Most recently, the apparent disappearance of Simon.

ASH members had picked up a significant presence of travellers on the hypnotic plane around Simon's hometown the night before. At first Pascale thought they had been tracked down following the incident in the Tate. It's a very unusual skill, tracking travellers in the hypnotic plane. Only a few have ever been able to do so, so it seemed unlikely that they had been followed. Unlikely, but not impossible. And when two known members of The Enemy had appeared *en corporelle* in the town, it was time to extract Simon as a matter of urgency, hence Pascale's call.

Only they had failed to pick him up. Local volunteers had reached his house at breakneck speed, travelling from central Oxford, the Eagle and Child in fact. When they reported that Simon was gone, Pascale hoped against hope that he had decided to make his own escape and would reappear in the near future. The alternative, that he had been captured by the enemy, was also a distinct possibility. What this would mean, if true, was something that played out in Pascale's mind for the entire journey to Aberystwyth.

"You'll remember I found someone with a startling resemblance to Hugo." Pascale said with some care, cognisant of what was to follow. Isobel and Patrick nodded.

"It was quite by chance to be honest. We have been searching for the last four years, as you know, but principally on the hypnotic plane which seemed an obvious place to look given the circumstances of Hugo's disappearance."

Isobel, who had been the last to see Hugo in the material world, looked grave. Pascale hesitated before spoke.

"Go on Pascale. We are all friends here and there will be no reporting to the Council of Elders, believe me." Pascale looked relieved and continued.

"Two years ago, we also started looking for Hugo in this world. With help from ASH members in government employment, we were able to access vast databases of facial imagery, captured from all over the world. Three months ago, we got a strong hit and I mean really strong."

"How strong is really strong?" asked Isobel.

"A 100% match."

The room became electric. Isobel and Patrick were visibly stunned as the implications of Pascale's words sank in.

"So, it's him?" Patrick asked.

"Well, that's the thing," Pascale hesitated.

"Although he looks like Hugo and has the same body size and shape as Hugo, it isn't him."

"What do you mean?" asked Patrick.

"There are absolutely no signs of hypnotic energy. No echo on the hypnotic plane that accompanies him. I even took him onto the Plane."

Isobel looked up, astonished, and glanced at Patrick who barely reacted to this risky and normally forbidden activity.

"He was able to get onto the Plane and was moderately impressive in his leaps from place to place, but he's no Hugo. He even went walkabout later on his own, which was rather surprising. It's demonstrative of curiosity and a strong imagination not evidence of the kind of abilities Hugo had."

Pascale hated talking about her old friend in the past tense, but over the last four years of searching she, above all others, had started to extinguish the hope that they would ever find him alive again.

"And where is he now?" asked Isobel.

"Well, that's the thing..."

Patrick and Isobel looked intently at Pascal. Pascal felt uncomfortable and subtly shifted her position at the kitchen table, looking down into the now empty mug she held in her hands. Without looking up she said,

"He's gone. He's disappeared." She returned her gaze to her two friends and comrades.

"Either he has taken himself away, for which I wouldn't blame him given everything that has happened over the last two days, or the Enemy has taken him."

"If the Enemy has him Pascale, doesn't that suggest he could be Hugo after all?"

"I don't know Isobel. Maybe. Or maybe they just saw the resemblance as I did and decided to pick him up. If they have got him, then I fear for his safety."

"What's this man's name?" Asked Patrick.

"Simon."

"Well then. If the Enemy have taken Simon, there may still be traces of hypnotic energy in evidence. Pascale, I'll arrange for our best trackers to go to Wantage immediately. You'll need to give me the address. If there is any trace of the Enemy, they should be able to find it and hopefully give us some idea where they were headed."

"I'd like permission to leave Aberystwyth." Isobel's request was made with an emphasis that bordered on belligerence. Her tone surprised the other two.

"You know I can't grant that permission on my own," Patrick replied.

"Yes, you can. In extraordinary circumstances you can. And I don't think it comes more extraordinary than the potential discovery of Hugo Durand."

Patrick looked at Isobel in that deep, discovering way of his. Isobel met his gaze with openness and confidence.

"Very well. But try to keep a low profile, Isobel."

Isobel knew what Patrick meant. It was a clear reference to the reasons why she had been made to live in this seaside town. She swallowed any rising resentment and simply nodded her assent and thanks. She was looking forward to leaving this town, in the physical world, for the first time in 14 years.

"Pascale, I think it's time you and I went hunting."

It took a moment for Pascal to understand what Isobel meant. During the years of conflict, and in the years of unsteady peace since, ASH would routinely conduct patrols of the Hypnotic Plane looking for evidence of the Enemy. And when they found them, in accordance with the ancient agreements, they executed them immediately.

Despite their dread of a new war, the opportunity to express their grief and new hope in the pursuit of those who would wish Hugo harm, was incredibly energising.

"I think you're right Pascale." Isobel replied.

Patrick, sensing the new energy these two women were radiating, urged caution.

"Be careful. We cannot afford to lose either of you, especially in an unsanctioned engagement with the Enemy. Discretion is of the utmost importance." He looked directly at Isobel.

"Of course, Patrick," Isobel replied with the merest suggestion of the resentment she felt rising in her. Something which Patrick detected at once, of course, but chose to ignore.

Chapter 7

The disappearance of Hugo Durand was both baffling and irritating. It should have marked the beginning of the end for ASH, which in turn would have cleared the way for what *they* call the 'Enemy' to take control.

Sitting in her hyper-connected room, surrounded by a graphical representation of every internet connection known to woman or man, was Olivia Beaumont. She had worked exceptionally hard to rise to the top of the Federation of Digital Entrepreneurs, or FoDE as it was more commonly known.

In what was, ostensibly, a man's world dominated as it was by the billionaire tech boys, she had become the most powerful woman bar none. She let her boys (as she liked to call them, at least in private) think that she was so grateful, fawning even, with the merest hint of sexual availability. It was a formula as old as the sexes and, to her initial surprise, it worked still. Even on these so-called geniuses of the tech world.

To be fair, their domination of e-commerce, social media and the very engines that drive the internet, was very impressive. And although the bitter rivalry between them all was real, they recognised that a degree of cooperation was necessary if they were to gain the prize that they really wanted. Hence FoDE was born – the outward face of their secret agreement to wrest control of the hypnotic plane away from its protectors, principally ASH.

To the public eye, FoDE existed to foster responsible use of the internet, social media and, of course, artificial intelligence. This was a tried and tested strategy the world over. Whether it was alcohol companies creating a body to encourage 'responsible drinking' or tobacco firms helping smokers quit by moving them on to vaping. There was always an element of benefit to these bodies, but the real purpose was always to protect and enhance their financial and commercial interests.

FoDE followed this path by funding projects to support victims of trolling and by creating research teams to make the internet safer and ever safer, for the benefit of the world community. As well as providing help and support to developing nations. Much as a spider helps flies by spinning their deadly webs.

Whilst at the same time FoDE members were harvesting astronomical amounts of personal data in the form of messaging, posts, video, and phone calls and, from every smart device with a microphone, the actual speech of billions of people, all over the world. There was almost no corner of the world into which they could not see or hear. It was this extraordinary amount of data that spurred FoDE members on to develop their own AI programmes. No human, even given millions of years, could hope to make sense of the data they collected. With the AI creations, all things were possible.

Of course, politicians and governments had to be seen to be tackling the occasional data breech that slipped out of the boys' tight control and into what was left of a hostile media. But the control over donations to political parties and most of the media itself, ensured no real damage was ever done. A sacrificial lamb, blame focussed on China or North Korean actors, or another world pariah whether vested in statehood or something more sinister, was all that was ever needed to deflect from those that were truly to blame.

And AI was heralded as being the answer to so many problems: climate change, medical research, and freedom from the drudgery of repetitive tasks that had troubled mankind since the industrial revolution. No mention was ever made of the perils of AI and its burgeoning use in stock markets, war, illegal bioengineering and terrorism.

As a result, their power grew alongside their wealth. They were effectively out of control. A deeply corrupting force that rendered the usual instruments of democracy fundamentally useless. In many respects they had achieved what they had set out to do: ensure wealth was untroubled by democracy or the rule of law. They were the new monarchs of the world and they ruled with absolute impunity. No need for the divine right of kings, they were their own gods, omnipotent, selfish, and more than a little paranoid.

When, some 10 years ago, news began to reach the boys' ears of a new, untrammelled realm they reacted as you would expect. They wanted it. All of it. They wanted control, centralisation, commodification, and most of all the glory of being able to claim the discovery of a new realm of human existence. Perhaps, with all due modesty of course, to name it after themselves.

And so, the enormous resources of FoDE were deployed to find out more about the Hypnotic Plane.

Unusually, it took rather a long time before any information of substance was gathered. In part from having its roots in a distinctly non-technological age, and also with due regard to the threats that technology could pose to their existence and their purpose, ASH had eschewed almost all types of electronic communication. There was also, to be fair, a degree of snobbery about such inventions as the telephone. After all, ASH had been able to communicate remotely since forever. And more recent offers, such as video calls, remained vastly inferior to a meeting on the Plane.

Olivia Beaumont had made some headway, principally by using the AI models to interrogate the opened microphones and cameras on billions of devices around the world. Despite their aversion to technology, those around ASH in normal society did not hesitate to embrace the convenience of personal electronics. As a result, ASH was unwittingly surrounded by the eyes and ears of FoDE every time they ventured out into the world. The Eastern German Stasi would have been overjoyed to have access to such knowledge.

Some five years ago, Olivia had begun to piece together some interesting information (or rather her AI model had). There was a recurring reference to a number of what were described as battles or skirmishes between an organisation known as ASH and a group only referred to as the Enemy. There were no correlated news reports, hospital records, death certificates or emergency services' call outs. Olivia began to wonder if the AI model was flawed or if the information gathered was from a bunch of Dungeons and Dragons players, or other such fantasists. Then the Model began bringing forward references to the Hypnotic Plane, postulating all kinds of interpretations of what it actually was, or meant. None were convincing to Olivia until a chance conversation with a FoDE colleague who was working on a lucid dreaming project.

The idea of this project was to create something that allowed FoDE to interrogate peoples dreams and even to confect dreams that matched an individual's preferences. "Think West World for the mind!" Her colleague said.

The lucid dreaming project was designed to give people real time control of what was happening in their dreams. The potential market for selling such a service was huge, of course. Forget video games, this was a huge leap that bypassed reliance on others' imaginations.

The commercial team had already determined that the intellectual property of any lucid dreams would pass instantly and with full legal force to the business making the dreams possible. The potential for an enormous library of dreams, available (for a charge, of course) to any subscriber, all created by the subscribers themselves!

Perhaps the Hypnotic Plane was simply another way of describing lucid dreaming? Perhaps, thought Olivia, but perhaps not. Lucid dreaming appeared to be an entirely solitary affair, the words describing an experience, whereas the Hypnotic Plane seemed to describe a place. What she did take from her chance encounter was the idea that the Hypnotic Plane was accessed through the mind somehow.

When she re-interrogated the AI to ask it what the organisation called Ash was, it all fell into place. Ash became ASH and the role of hypnotists in the Hypnotic Plane became obvious. With a refocussing of her interest in hypnotism, it didn't take long to piece together the history of hypnosis and the role of early pioneers such as Puységur. Despite the relative abundance of historic information, there were no threads that led to the present day that either Olivia or her AI helpers could identify.

It was not that there was a shortage of hypnotists who were entirely visible – hypnotherapists (largely respectable) and stage hypnotists (largely not) were practising their craft in significant numbers. It was just that none of these seemed to be doing anything other than fairly routine stuff. That said, Olivia found herself being drawn to the remarkable abilities of the human brain once liberated from its conscious restrictions.

Amidst a slew of criminal prosecutions and civil litigation for malpractice and exploitation of various sorts – mostly involving sexual assaults and then financial exploitation – there was one incident that Caught Olivia's attention, via the industry of her AI, of course.

Police computers in Scotland, in common with almost all of the rest of the world's data, relied upon FoDE's good offices for its storage, retrieval, and processing. Naturally Olivia's AIs had instant and full access to all of it. Having focussed initially on prosecutions, Olivia now directed her Ais to any and all intelligence reports, complaints, Officers' observations and even pocketbook entries. One particular incident caught her eye.

Most complaints were from women, having been exploited by men in one way or another. This incident was a reversal of that convention, and by some measure. 14 years ago an unlikely number of young men had made a complaint to police in Edinburgh, following what they described as a drunken night out that ended up with them engaging in sexual acts 'against their will' with a sole woman, a few years their senior. Claims of mind control made by the young men in question were given short shrift by the police, who suggested that any 'mind control' was more likely to have come about as a result of the influence of Messrs Glenfiddich, Balvenie and Laphroaig. And the very fact that young men under the influence of this trio (which, on reflection by the senior investigating officer, sounded like a particularly upmarket firm of lawyers) would make a complaint about being coerced into sexual activity with a single female against their will was treated with a degree of scorn that was reflective of both the times and the probability of such an event occurring.

So it was that the woman in question, one Isobel Fernandes, was briefly asked to attend the police station in Gayfield Square to 'clear up some outstanding complaints' as the officer who contacted her delicately put it.

The interview lasted a mere 20 minutes and, but for a recent crackdown on poor record keeping by senior officers, the detective constable who had been handed this complaint wouldn't have even bothered to make a written record. Instead, she did. And in sufficient detail that, nine years later, Olivia Beaumont would have the first crumbs of a trail that would lead to what appeared to be a major breakthrough.

Chapter 8

The journey back from Aberystwyth was uncomfortable, if enjoyable. Patrick still smarted every time his motorbike hit a bump in the road, and the bruises he had sustained in his misplaced attempt to rescue Isobel (from the door frame as it turned out) cried out for a few days' rest. Isobel had tried persuading him that a course of rest was the best for him. He had agreed without much resistance but they both knew that as soon as she and Pascale had left the little house in Chalybeate Street, he would likely be on his way. And so he was.

As Patrick navigated the winding, climbing road towards Llangurig (his ancient, black, BMW K75 rewarding his expert riding) he experienced the kind of detachment and calm that can normally only be achieved through narcotics or meditation. Replaying the events of the last few days, he was deeply troubled.

Firstly, Pascale had kept the potential discovery of Hugo Durand to herself, secondly the attack on Isobel in the Old College Library and then finally the apparent abduction of the man known as Simon from his home in Wantage.

Long experience and wisdom had taught Patrick not to try too hard to solve the puzzle forming in his conscious mind. Let the puzzle appear and then best to send it to the Committee Upstairs, as Patrick referred to his unconscious. Sometimes the answer came back quickly, and sometimes it took many days. He could never tell how soon, or not, an answer would arrive. The circumstances were almost always the same, however: the answer would arrive unexpectedly. Not matter how hard he tried to anticipate its arrival, it made no difference. One moment there was nothing, the next he knew.

In the meantime, he was enjoying himself. The three-cylinder engine was smooth, and the gearbox was slick. He was handling the machine perfectly, shifting his weight and judging each corner precisely. As he approached a long, long right hand bend some 15 miles outside of Aberystwyth and about a mile before Elvis Rock, he sensed danger long before would have seen it.

Without stopping to think, he scanned the road for an exit route. There was none. Instead, he executed an expert U-turn in the road and demanded all the power that was available from his 75BHP bike as he raced back the way he had come. Glancing briefly in his mirrors he saw nothing except the empty road behind him. For an instant he questioned whether his perception of danger was correct, or if the bang on the head had affected his instincts in some way. He knew better than to doubt his perception of danger.

In little more than a mile and a half he was passing Dyffren Castell and the opportunity to turn off the main road presented itself. Patrick took the left turn and thundered towards the village, Pontarfynach, and Devil's Bridge. This way he could head back to Aberystwyth and the relative safety of Isobel's home. Assuming he could make it that far.

He decided he should ditch the bike, as much as it pained him to do so. He headed towards Devils' Bridge station, one end of the Vale of Rheidol Railway. There was room to park his bike outside the Two Hoots café, which he did, and he carefully took off his helmet and gloves, replacing them in the panniers once he had removed his bags. For all intents and purposes, he now looked like a tourist, albeit one with more luggage than might have been expected.

"You can leave that round the back if you like," said a friendly mountain of a man, and indicated a closed gate at the rear of the café.

"Perfect, thanks. I might be a day or two in Aberystwyth. Is it ok to leave it with you?"

"Of course. We bikers must stick together!"

With that, Patrick pushed his bike around the back of the café where it would remain entirely out of sight. He also pondered what kind of bike the café proprietor must ride. He guessed not a Monkey Bike: Honda's very small, 125cc funster.

Patrick decided to secrete himself in the café, bags under the table, and see what happened. Taking a seat at the back with a clear view of the windows and door, he ordered tea and lemon cake and sat down to wait.

He was unsure if he should access the Hypnotic Plane while he waited. Although he would retain some awareness of his immediate surroundings, they would be compromised as he travelled on the Plane. Patrick decided to wait and instead focus on reducing his visibility.

Visibility reduction was a technique well known to many warriors and spies over centuries. Whilst not actually becoming invisible to the eye, the technique focusses on reducing one's presence, one's apparent energy. Accomplished practitioners can almost disappear and certainly never stand out in the way that someone full of nervous energy is likely to do so.

Patrick focused on breathing slowly and carefully, and on effectively turning down the dial on his presence and energy. He allowed himself a degree of satisfaction when the young man from whom he had ordered his tea and cake had difficulty in finding him to bring him his refreshments.

"Oh, there you are," the young man said.

"Thanks. Can you tell me the time of the next train to Aberystwyth please?" Patrick asked.

"On the half hour, every hour until 4.30pm."

After thanking the young man for the information, Patrick settled in to enjoy his tea and cake, and to keep a weather eye on the door and surrounding areas visible through the windows.

Free of any immediate peril, at least for the moment, a creeping sense of dread came over him. What about Pascale and Isobel? Did they travel the same route, and if they did, did they get the same sense of danger he had and more importantly, are they ok?

He had intended to stay at the station and catch the last train of the day, but his concern for his friends made him reconsider his plans. The next train was due to leave almost immediately. Patrick grabbed his bags and exited the café rapidly. The proprietor was startled to see him move so quickly, having come out of nowhere from his perspective. Despite shouts from the guard on the platform, Patrick opened the door of a moving carriage and leapt aboard. The few passengers in his carriage looked up, some disapprovingly, and then returned their gaze to the unfolding countryside around them. Patrick looked back at the station and saw an incongruous group of four or five men get out of a large SUV and start fanning out across the car park searching for something. Presumably him and his bike. It was not the first time serendipity had intervened to keep Patrick safe, he thought. And neither would it be the last.

*

Just as the diminutive steam engine pulled slowly away from the platform, Isobel and Pascale were making their way at speed towards Rhyader, some 30 miles and an hour's drive from Aberystwyth. No drama on the route and no sign of any danger.

The atmosphere in Isobel's car was relaxed, even joyous. The two women aware of their own release from restrictions that had been placed upon them for many years. Isobel, free to leave Aberystwyth was feeling elated, despite her deep affection for the town. And Pascale felt a rising of homicidal intent that she had kept suppressed for so many years since Hugo had disappeared. She regarded his disappearance as creating a debt which had to be repaid, and preferably with death to the Enemy or whoever had made him vanish four years ago.

Driving in silence, they watched as the rugged mid-Wales scenery rushed past. Isobel turned to Pascale,

"Do you really think this man is Hugo?"

"I do."

Isobel refrained from asking any more questions, but the doubt hung around the car, unspoken.

"Simon looks exactly like Hugo, and there are certain characteristics that they both share."

Isobel kept silent.

"He took to hypnosis quickly, he's quick to frustration and he finds me attractive..."

Isobel raised an eyebrow involuntarily, unseen by Pascale.

"And how do you know that?" Isobel asked, wearily.

Pascale briefly took her eyes off the road and looked at Isobel.

"I didn't fuck him, ok?"

"Ok."

A brief silence was broken by both women laughing out loud.

"Well, I know what you're like, Pascale-"

"You know what *I'm* like! Let's look at our track records, shall we?"

An awkward silence rose up like a wall between them until they both laughed so hard that Pascale almost had to pull over.

"I did think about it, to be fair. And so did he, clearly."

"Clearly?"

"I spent half the night with a somnambulant erection poking in my back. It was all I could do not to turn round."

"If that was Hugo, he would have initiated something more, surely?"

Isobel's eyes began filling with tears as she recalled the passionate, on / off relationship she and Hugo had enjoyed for so long. What would she have given to be reunited with him.

"Yes. You're right. I suppose that was my way of testing him. But even so, I still can't be sure it's not Hugo, or not partly Hugo at least. Oh, that makes no sense!"

Isobel placed a soothing hand on Isobel's leg and gently squeezed. Like almost every adult human, she understood the emotions of loss and longing. She also understood that they never really leave you.

Lovers and friends leave their mark indelibly, for better and worse. Scars and adornments carried forever. Isobel of all people knew this, and age and wisdom (in part brought about by her lengthy exile in Aberystwyth) allowed her not only to accept these scars and adornments, but even to celebrate them as signs of a life well-lived. Much like the Japanese art of Kintsugi, where broken pottery pieces are put back together with gold, celebrating flaws and imperfections.

To say that this was empowering was an understatement. Just as Pascale felt a rising sense of violent intent, Isobel felt a wave of controlled power and self-assurance as she re-entered the wider physical world from which she had been excluded for so long.

"I really want it to be Hugo, and I'm worried that's clouding my judgement. The first time I met him, in a dingy pub in Oxford, it was all I could do to retain my composure. As I got know this 'Simon' I became less sure he was Hugo. It was as if something was missing, like Hugo had evaporated, the real man having faded to the point of invisibility. Still going through the motions, breathing, talking, but just not the man I knew. Or thought I knew."

"And now he's disappeared." Said Isobel.

Chapter 9

"Can I just ask you one thing? Why are we talking in the shower?"

"Turn it on, then they can't hear you." Said Iago, directly to my mind.

I did as he asked, the falling water narrowly avoiding his beautifully smooth and glossy coat. He walked in an arc towards the open end of the walk-in shower and then stopped and resumed his seated position.

"Simon, I'm sorry you've had to endure the events as they've unfolded over the last few days. It was never my intention that you should have suffered as you now have."

"Hang on a minute," I said, "You're a cat. I'm a human – your owner in fact – and you're speaking to me as if you're in charge. Not only that, you're dead and have been for the last four years!"

"In a way, yes. But also, no."

Iago let the words in my head sit there for a while. A silence hung between us. I lifted my hands to my head until my elbows were in front of my face, and I slid my back down the shower wall and ended up sitting down, knees raised, facing Iago.

Between my elbows, I could see Iago regarding me with what passed for a kind of feline pity. Like the normal scorn that cats reserve for most humans but dialled down a bit.

"Perhaps I should let you ask me some questions," he said.

"Ok. For one, who are you? I know you're not my cat, Iago, because he is dead. So, who are you?"

"I am the mental projection of who you *really* are. I, or rather we, have chosen Iago as the object upon which we have made these projections."

"That really isn't helping," I said in reply.

"Ok. To put it simply, I am you."

"You're fucking not. I don't lick my arse, eat mice – raw or cooked– and I definitely don't shit in the garden."

"Ok, ask me another question."

"Why are you here?"

"Because you're here. Next"

"How come I can hear you in my head?"

"Because I am in your head. Next"

"Why won't you leave me alone?"

"Because *I* am *you*. Next"

"Then who the fuck am *I*?!" I shouted, before bursting into a flood of tears.

I lowered my arms into my lap and wiped away the tears on my face with the back of my hand. I hoped that Iago would be gone, but he was not. He was still sat there, implacably, immaculately. Before long, I heard his voice in my head again.

"Let's start at the beginning," his voice said, though in a kinder and less urgent tone. I straightened, wiped my eyes again and gave him my full attention.

"Four years ago you and I separated. Before that, we were a single person. I know this is difficult to comprehend, but please bear with me. Your – our – real name is Hugo Durand. The reason we had to separate was to hide my hypnotic abilities, I had to take them away from us and project them onto something else. The only thing available to me at that time was our cat, Iago."

"But Iago died four years ago," I protested.

"Yes, I know. And I'm sorry."

"Why are you sorry?" I asked, with a rising sense of anger.

"Because the projection onto Iago killed him in the end."

"So how come he, you – we – are still here? And what do you mean by 'in the end'?"

"The projection onto Iago, and his subsequent death, meant I could only manifest on the hypnotic plane. At least that's what I thought..."

"Which is why you come and go..."

"Exactly."

"So how come I can see you and others can't?"

"Because we're the same person, I guess. And actually, they can."

97

Hugo paused.

"In the last two years I've found I can, more or less, manifest in the physical world, directly from the hypnotic plane. This does have certain advantages, not least of which is that no-one is suspicious of a cat hanging around in the physical world."

I was far from reassured by the 'conversation' I was having with Iago/Hugo/me. If I am him, then who am I? And what exactly is going to happen to me if he takes me over?

"I understand all of your concerns. I just don't have any definitive answers for you at the moment, sorry."

"So, in the meantime, what the hell am I supposed to do – I'm being held here against my will, wherever here is, being drugged and interrogated and finally talking to a dead cat!"

"Leave it with me. And try not to say anything to anyone – " Iago disappeared almost as soon as Hugo's words had entered my mind.

*

I gingerly got to my feet and took advantage of the shower that was still pouring its near perfect column of gently aerated water from ceiling to floor. I had to admit to myself that it felt good to feel the water gently massaging my shoulders, neck, and back. After a while I returned to the bedroom and flopped down on the bed. The very comfortable bed...

*

"Simon, wake up."

I opened my eyes.

"Simon, wake up."

There was a woman standing some two to three metres away, holding a clipboard and wearing a white, pristine, lab jacket, with her back to the picture window. It was sunny outside and my attention became focussed on how green the grass was –

"Simon. Pay attention."

My eyes flicked towards the woman. Our eyes met for a moment and I noticed the merest flash of fear, before she regained complete control. Something she was not lacking, I thought, as I studied her demeanour.

Without moving I said "What?"

"You are required to get dressed and then to come with me. I have brought you some clothes to wear. I will be back in three minutes."

Placing the clothes at the foot of the bed, she turned around and headed towards what appeared to be the white, pristine wall. She paused for a moment and an opening appeared, through which she swiftly departed. The opening closed behind her leaving a barely perceptible outline of a door of some kind.

I sat up, scratched my head and thought about taking another shower. I hesitated. I was not ready to have another conversation with Iago and our recent discourse had left me reluctant to go near it.

"Get over yourself," I said to no-one in particular, and crossed the room to freshen up.

In approximately five minutes I was ready, to the obvious irritation of the woman who was waiting to escort me to, well, somewhere. She handed me a soft, silky hood.

"Put this on please," she said. I obliged. Perhaps showing some compliance would obviate the need for drugging me. I was led down a corridor, as far as I could tell from the acoustics, and then outside. I felt the sun on my hands and through the hood, along with a slight breeze. It was warm, very warm. I was then guided, not bundled, into the back of a car. The air conditioning and cool of the seats was striking. I felt someone put a seatbelt on me – how touching – and then the vehicle moved away. I was aware of someone in the seat in front of me and also in the one behind. Nobody spoke and I was fine with that. I had much to think about.

*

"Simon."

I groaned inwardly as the familiar head-voice of Iago summoned me from my thoughts.

"What?"

"We're being taken to see someone. It's someone I – we – used to know and were very close to. You may or may not recognise her but if you do, I don't want you to show it. Not in any way. Do you understand?"

"Yes," I replied. "And who is she, exactly?"

"It's honestly better for you not to know, at least at this stage. We'll be stopping shortly, and they'll lead you into a garden where you'll meet this person.

"How do you know this?"

"I can still travel on the hypnotic plane and as I said I can now manifest physically. While you've been incarcerated, I've been piecing a few things together."

"That sounds ominous."

100

"Enough for now. And remember what I said."

Bang on cue, the car was drawing to a halt. I could hear the sound of tyres on gravel as we drew to a halt. Still no-one spoke inside the car, but I could, perhaps, just sense the trepidation – or was that fear – of the other occupants.

I felt a hand unbuckle my belt and heard the sound of the front car doors open and close, accompanied by footsteps on the gravel. My door was opened. A gentle but firm hand took me by the upper arm, another was placed on top of my head, presumably to protect it from being knocked as I stumbled out of the car.

As I straightened and flexed my back and neck, I could feel the sun and perceive its strong light and heat, even through the hood which was still covering my head. I was led, gently across the gravel and then, as the sound and textured changed, onto some grass. Perhaps another 50 steps and we stopped. I could feel a breeze now and the faintest sound of waves. A definite smell of the sea washed through the hood. Wherever I was, it was clearly a garden of some size and its proximity to the sea suggested a degree of luxury and wealth.

We stopped and my right hand was guided to a chair behind me, presumably to reassure me as the indicated, through control of my other arm, to sit down. The seat was warm and unyielding and the back somewhat upright, though not uncomfortable. I placed my hands in my lap and waited. I felt oddly calm, all things considered.

As I listened to the sound of the sea I heard another sound. The faint tip-tap of fingers upon a keyboard. The sound came in groups, as if the person using the keyboard was composing something or responding to emails. Other than that, I could make out no other sounds that could provide me with any more intelligence.

After a while, I began to feel somewhat foolish, sat as I was with no restraints on my hands – or anywhere else for that matter – whilst sporting a hood. I considered taking off my adornment. What's the worst that could happen, I asked myself. I had no idea and it was certainly not something for which I was prepared.

With one hand, I reached behind me and pulled the hood over the front of my head and off my face. The bright light made me squint for a moment or two during which time I did what I could to reinstate my hair to some semblance of normality. Initially I was struck by the view – we were sitting atop some kind of cliff or raised area and reaching out to the horizon was the sea. It was a beautiful day and for a moment I simply experienced what was in front of me with no thought to disturb my presence and connection to nature.

"Aren't you going to say hello?" Asked a voice to my right.

I looked across and saw a woman, still typing, and looking at the screen of the laptop in front of her. She was wearing a sun hat that partially obscured her face. As if sensing my gaze, she stopped typing, paused, and then without removing her hands from the keyboard, lifted her head to look at me.

"Who are you?" I asked.

I didn't feel like observing the usual social niceties at this point, given the route by which I had arrived at this place.

"Ah, now there's a question," she replied and returned her attention to her laptop.

I studied what I could see of her face. I couldn't summon up any memory of having met her before but as I looked more deeply at her I felt the merest mental sigh of recognition, somewhere deep in my consciousness. As if she sensed this, she turned her head once more to face me. This time she stopped typing, closed her laptop and placed it on the table in from of her.

"The thing is, Simon, that I am a little perplexed. You see I've been watching you for some time. You do bear an uncanny resemblance to someone I used to know, who I would very much like to see again for my own rather personal reasons. But despite your physical resemblance, you really aren't even a shadow of who he was as a man."

I have to admit this stung somewhat. Especially as that man was now manifested as a cat.

"I can see that irks you Simon. Perhaps there is a trace of – "

She broke off before speaking his name out loud. I sat and said nothing, looking as impassive as I could. She turned her gaze towards the sea, scanning the horizon for something or some thought of what she would say next. Then, as if settling on what that might be, she turned slowly to look at me. Her face had changed from relatively benign to almost inhuman. It was extraordinary and terrifying. As WB Yeats would have it, her gaze truly was as blank and pitiless as the sun.

"If you won't or can't tell me what I need to know, then I will do what I must to encourage your friends in ASH to come and find you. Do you understand what that means, Simon?"

"No, I don't," I was starting to feel deeply uneasy.

"If you are who I think you are, even just a tiny part of you, then I think your friends will do anything to help you, to find you. And I can help them do that or rather you can."

103

Seeing an opportunity for some kind of redemption with this soulless creature in from of me, I asked

"How's that?"

"By suffering Simon. By suffering so much that your very soul cries out in pain and anguish across the Hypnotic Plane to summon them to your assistance."

I felt as if the blood was draining away from my extremities, I felt light headed and most of all I felt afraid. For the first time in my life I felt really afraid. Before I could speak I felt a hood being place over my head once again. I was pushed forward and two zip ties were roughly and painfully tightened around my wrists. Next were my ankles. The plastic dug into my skin and made me wince. I was then carried horizontally. For a moment I wondered if they were going to throw me over the cliff. But the sounds of feet on gravel suggested otherwise. The next thing I knew I was being manhandled into what I realised was the boot of a car. I felt a sharp jab in my neck and then I fell into unconsciousness.

Chapter 10

Patrick couldn't help but be amused. He knew ASH were somewhat Luddite in their view of technology, but to be arriving in Aberystwyth on a steam train well, that was way beyond the twenty first century ASH's expectations. Truth be told, the morning's adventures had been enjoyable. And rejuvenating. Patrick had never looked his age, but now he felt as though the years were being discarded, much as a snake sheds its skin, to reveal a new, shiny, and vigorous version of himself.

As the train approached Aberystwyth, he reflected on the shadow war ASH had been fighting since the Enemy disappeared four years ago – along with Hugo Durand. Maintaining vigilance was exhausting, and not just scanning the horizon for external threats.

For the last 18 months, Patrick had sensed something malevolent within the organisation itself. Just the merest suspicion at first, borne out of instinct and intuition rather than real world, empirical fact. But Patrick had learned long ago to trust his intuition and not to suppress feelings for which immediate supporting facts were unavailable.

The train began its slow approach into Aberystwyth. Just ahead a line of tourists stood on the platform waiting to board the train for the return to Devil's Bridge. A mixture of cyclists, hikers and seaside holiday makers reflecting perfectly the tourist demographic of this deceptively charming little town.

Patrick scanned the platform and, as far as he could, the station beyond the ticket check (not in operation) and entrance from the street outside. He could see no apparent threat and could not sense one either. He decided to make his way back to Chalybeate Street, a very short walk from the station, and then decide what he should do.

Walking towards the house, Patrick started to feel uneasy. As he approached, he decided to walk past, glancing to his left as he passed the front door, he saw that it was, ever so slightly, ajar. He ducked into the wholefood shop next door, nodded a casual greeting to a couple chatting at the till, and secreted himself between a row of tall shelves offering the full range of seeds, nuts, grains, and remedies that would be expected.

He picked up a bag of organic, milled, flax seed (actually one of his favourites as it helped him sleep, or so it seemed) and began to read the blurb on the labels. At the same time he used his formidable hypnotic powers to enter the hypnotic plane, specifically the house next door. He visualised the small bedroom in which he had had a brief period of recuperation, and almost instantly, found himself there. It was a god job he hadn't chosen the kitchen. In the kitchen, on the hypnotic plane, were two men and a woman who Patrick could see, just, through a small opening in the bedroom door.

"I thought this was supposed to be our big chance to deal with Patrick and his girls. So where the fuck are they?"

The words were virtually spat out like venom from a middle aged woman, perhaps late 40s, clearly dressed stylishly, noticeable even in the hypnotic rendition of her physical form.

"Like I said," replied a smallish man, "He didn't appear on the road to Llangurig, so our ambush was ineffective. And as for the girls, they've clearly left as well."

There was enough of an edge to the way he said these words for the other man, larger, older, with a thin face and goatee beard, to look uneasy. Concerned even.

"Olivia, we're onto this and I'm sure we'll track them all down soon. Just be..." He trailed off mid-sentence, aware that asking Olivia Beaumont to be patient was unlikely to have any such effect.

Instead of venting her anger on the two men, Olivia simply stared at them, full of fury, and then metaphorically turned on her heel and left. Patrick knew this was his chance. Even in the hypnotic plane, everyone leaves a trail albeit ever so slight and very short-lived, and Olivia Beaumont was no different. The best way to describe it is as a very subtle con trail such as jet aircraft leave in the sky. To the trained eye it is possible, just, to track. Patrick had no difficulty in doing so.

Like Theseus following Ariadne's thread, Patrick followed Olivia's trail. Only on this occasion, rather than to escape the Minotaur, Patrick was keen to enter the equivalent of the labyrinth at Knossos.

Although travel through the Plane is incredibly fast, Patrick started to recognise landmarks as they sped their way back to where he assumed Olivia's body remained. They passed over the Cambrian Mountains, Gloucestershire and on towards the Cotswolds. Soon enough they were speeding over Oxfordshire and Oxford itself. The M40 was an obvious landmark until they started to pass over the outer edges of London with the familiar yellow-brown sulphurous dome that covers the city, like an unhygienic cake cover, appearing in view.

Not surprising, Patick reflected, that Olivia came from London. But the direction they were taking was starting to make him feel uncomfortable. From the outer edges of Chiswick he sensed they were on a direct line that would intersect the Strand and then, perhaps John Adam Street.

More importantly, perhaps, the destination could be number 8. Patrick checked that his intuition was not being corrupted by a sense of paranoia. He really couldn't tell. As they sped onwards on the same straight course, Patrick felt more and more uneasy even to the point of nausea. As they approached John Adam Street, Patrick hung further back, and it was a good job he did so. Olivia Beaumont came to the equivalent of a screeching stop before whipping round to see if there was anyone else in the vicinity. Patrick had managed to conceal himself just in time. When he dared to look out from his concealment, she was gone along with any signs of a trail.

Patrick's mind was racing. Has she gone into number 8? If she has, what does that mean. The implications were beyond even his worst imaginings.

*

When Patrick returned to his body in the health food shop he estimated that a little over one minute had passed since he had taken the rather unusual step of leaving his physical self in a public place. With a small, almost imperceptible, jolt Patrick arrived back. He gathered himself for a moment and then carefully looked up and down the aisle to check if his odd, unmoving presence had been noted. It had not. The couple at the till continued the conversation in which they were engaged when Patrick had left. He replaced the flax seed on the shelf and left the shop.

With a great deal of care, Patrick approached the front door of Isobel's small terraced house. The front door was now closed, though not locked. He gently pushed the door, grateful that its hinges were silent, and swiftly entered the hallway. Closing the door gently behind him he stood and listened for the sound of any other occupants. He heard nothing. He silently made his way through to the kitchen and having satisfied himself that he was alone, did what anyone would do in the circumstances: he filled the kettle and then made a nice pot of tea.

*

Patrick sat in the kitchen and thought deeply. He had sensed that the Council of Elders was not to be entirely trusted some while ago but who was this Olivia, why had a trap been laid for him and, Isobel and Pascale, and why did Olivia disappear into number 8 John Adam Street? The address had been used by ASH for more than two hundred years.

He knew well that during the French Revolution, Puységur had established contact with the newly formed Society for the Encouragement of Arts, Manufactures and Commerce and some enlightened members (later known as Fellows) gave shelter to Puységur, his ideas, and followers. As a matter of safety to begin with, ASH held meetings in John Adam Street. Over the next 270 years the knowledge of their presence remained a closely guarded secret known only to a handful of Fellows and staff. It was rumoured that King Edward VII (who granted the use of Royal in the shortened name, the Royals Society of Arts) was a competent hypnotic traveller and practitioner. Indeed, it was his inappropriate use of hypnosis to seduce countless women, that led ASH to introduce some immutable laws for its adherents to obey. And which had led to Patrick's friend Isobel, being sent into exile in Aberystwyth.

Over the centuries, other Fellows were either already members of ASH or became so, after careful vetting. The list of distinguished international actors was impressive, to say the least: Charles Dickens, Benjamin Franklin, Stephen Hawking, Karl Marx, Adam Smith, Marie Curie, Nelson Mandela, David Attenborough, Judi Dench, William Hogarth, John Diefenbaker, and Tim Berners-Lee.

Patrick counted himself lucky to have met some of these extraordinary women and men. Could any of them really have betrayed ASH, let alone a member of the Council of Elders. Patrick trusted his intuition. And once again he was being proved right to do so.

Chapter 11

As they drove on through the Cambrian mountains which gently gave way to views of the Malvern Hills and then the outer reaches of the Cotswolds, the two friends each silently contemplated the meaning of recent events.

For Isobel, being free to return to the wider physical world was like taking a deep breath: exhilaration and satisfaction in equal measure. She felt a renewed sense of purpose and even vigour returning to her. Since the incident in the Old College Library, Isobel had a feeling akin to waking up after a long sleep. That part of her that had been so distinguished in battles on the Hypnotic Plane was stirring once more. Of course, Isobel was conscious of her increasing age but just as Patrick retained a remarkable vigour, so too could she. The frustrations and sadness at having been in physical exile for so long were starting to fuel a rage, even hatred, that she could now direct to the Enemy.

Pascale's contemplations were somewhat different. When Hugo disappeared, she had many other losses to deal with: of friends and comrades who were lost in the price of victory. But over the interceding years, during her hunt for Hugo, her love for him and the sadness of his loss, had competed for the head space she needed to conduct a competent and thorough operation. Hope for operational success was inevitably intertwined with a longing and hope for a reunion with her lover. At times, she reminded herself of the terrible rows and glorious reconciliations they had suffered and enjoyed over the years, lest her view of Hugo became too idealised. But the alchemy of love, absence and longing, burns brightly in the crucible of the heart. Pascale so wanted Simon to be Hugo. Even the facsimile of Hugo that was Simon was a comfort. Whatever the truth, Pascale was determined to discover it.

"Shall we stop for a while?" Isobel asked.

"Yes." Pascale replied, "I know somewhere near here."

Within five minutes the two friends were driving over a cattle grid towards to the top of Crickley Hill where a café with views of the Cotswold Area of Outstanding Natural Beauty, as well as a decent cup of coffee, could be had.

The car park was relatively full. Unsurprising given it was nearly lunchtime. The full range of Land Rover's opulent if unreliable range of vehicles was on show, with the occasional interloper in the form of a Mercedes or BMW 4x4. Not one to normally notice these things, Pascale was aware of how incongruous her Ford Focus looked. A car that would never merit a second look in the urban or suburban environment, here it was the closest it would ever be to standing out.

Making their way up the steep path from the car park to the café left them both a little short of breath. Reaching the top and turning to take in the view was more than ample compensation. The countryside stretched out before them and they were united in appreciation without thought or speech for a few precious moments.

"What is it? Can you sense his presence, out there?" asked Isobel while both women continued to take in the view.

Pascale appeared troubled – her senses were alive and prickling. She looked around her with excitement and consternation.

"He's here."

"What? What do you mean?"

"I can sense him really strongly, he's here somewhere."

The two friends scanned the areas around them – the café, tables outside, the car park below. No-one nearby had the merest resemblance of Hugo. And yet, Isobel was drawn towards one table in particular. There was no-one even at the table, not human anyway. Just a rather sleek looking black cat.

"He's there,"

Pascale indicated the cat, alone in the sun, sitting on a café table. Isobel followed her gaze and looked at the cat. Really looked at the cat.

"Christ..."

While Isobel was beginning to sense Hugo's presence, Pascale had already started walking towards the cat, seemingly transfixed.

"Pascale, wait –"

Isobel, ever alert to the deceptions and traps of the Enemy rapidly scanned to area again and used all her sensing powers to detect any other presence. She visibly relaxed. There was none.

In the meantime, Pascale had reached the cat and was standing in front of it. The cat regarded her with a kind of detached amusement while she fixed the cat with the kind of stare reserved only for those we love or for those we hate. Perhaps in this case it was both of those things.

Isobel walked upon behind Pascale and stood behind her looking over her shoulder.

"What should we do?" Isobel asked as she turned around to look at her friend. As she did so, the cat jumped down form the table and crossed the seating area heading in the direction of the car park.

The other customers had begun to notice the two women now, behaving a little oddly with such a focus on this cat. A café worker stopped and said,

"Is it yours? I've never seen him here before this morning and I wondered if he was a stray."

As she spoke, the cat disappeared down the footpath towards the car park.

"I'm not sure," said Isobel. "Maybe."

"She thinks so!"

Pascale had followed quickly after the cat and had also now disappeared from view.

"I'd better follow her, bye." And with that Isobel set off after her friend. As she reached the top of the path, she looked down to the cars below. Sat on the bonnet of Pascale's car, was the cat. He was looking back at Pascale who was making her way towards him. Isobel laughed out loud at the absurdity of the situation. Pascale looked briefly over her shoulder to see what Isobel was laughing at before reaching the car, where she stood and stared at the creature casually planted on her car.

By the time Isobel had caught up with her, Pascale had unlocked the car and opened the back door. Before she had time to wonder why, the reason became apparent. The cat jumped off the bonnet, made his way to the rear of the car and hopped onto the back seat. Pascale shut the door and opened the driver's door. Pausing she looked at Isobel who was staring at the scene in front of her, planted to the spot.

"We need to get out of here," Pascale said as she got in the car, shut the door and started the engine.

"Yes we do," Isobel replied quietly. She got in the car and Isobel drove out of the car park back towards the main road.

*

As they made their way, two humans and a cat, away from Crickley Hill and onwards towards Burford, silence filled the car. The two women were trying (in their own ways) to make sense of the current circumstance.

Pascale had been searching for Hugo for years. And having found his double, in physical terms, he turned out not be Hugo. And now, driving along with a cat on the back seat, she feared for her sanity for all her hypnotic instincts told her it was him, despite her intellect telling her otherwise.

"Thank you for trusting your intuition, Pascale. It's good to see you."

The two women turned to look at each other, sharing their astonishment and looking for confirmation of what they had just 'heard'.

"How can I be sure it's you?" Asked Pascale, not yet ready to use his name.

"I think you know already that it's me. But if you're looking for confirmation, I'm sure you can think of something to ask me."

Pascale could indeed. And all of them very personal. She was not sure if she wanted Isobel to hear any of the questions that immediately sprang to mind. While she was grappling with what to ask, Isobel spoke up.

"What is your mother's name?"

"Marine."

"What is Pascale to you?"

"My friend, sometime lover, my comrade."

"Where do I live?"

"Aberystwyth, at least that's where you were confined to after-"

"Yes alright," Isobel cut across Hugo before he had a chance to humiliate her. This was Hugo alright, and not just from the knowledge he displayed.

Pascale then spoke up. "Who is your father?"

Hugo didn't answer for a long time.

"I don't know. I've never known," Hugo added in clarification.

Pascale gripped the steering wheel even tighter and stared at the road ahead. Large tears filled up her eyes and rolled down her cheeks, falling onto her lap. Hugo had pulled some weird, charming and even romantic stunts over the years. Pushing the limits of what could be achieved with his prodigious powers time and time again. But this, *this* was something else.

Sensing she was about to lose her composure entirely, Pascale pulled into a layby at the side of the road. She stopped the car, pulled on the handbrake, turned off the engine and undid her seatbelt. And then she wept. Long sobbing tears filled the silence in the car. Next to her, Isobel looked down at her hands, now neatly folded in her lap. If Pascale had been able to see through her tears, she'd have noticed Isobel's eyes were wet too. A profound sense of grief, relief and frustration filled the car.

Hugo deftly jumped from the back seat onto the arm rest and then insinuated himself onto Pascale's lap. He began to purr. Pascale looked down and instinctively began stroking him, taking comfort in doing so. Hugo lifted his head, demanding it be stroked in the way cats do. And of course, Pascale obliged.

Isobel regarded the scene to the side of her with mixed feelings, to say the least. There was something utterly bizarre, intimate and entirely normal depending on the perspective her observations took. In any event she started to feel more and more uncomfortable as her perception settled on 'intimate'. The reconciliation of lovers is not for others to witness, especially in such close quarters, but when they are not of the same species it became, for Isobel, quite unbearable.

"I hope you haven't got fleas, Hugo." Isobel said out loud in an attempt to break up the lovers' reunion.

Hugo turned around sharply, while Pascale began to laugh. Gently at first, building in intensity and finally erupting in a crescendo of belly laughs which in turn transformed into anger.

"What the fuck happened to you!" Pascale shouted.

"It's a long story," Hugo replied.

"Then I think you'd better start telling us, puss." Said Isobel, composure regained and with just a hint of malice.

"I will but not here, it's not safe."

"Where then?" Demanded Isobel.

"Wantage."

And with that, Pascale wiped away her tears, regained her focus and looked down at the cat sitting on her lap looking up at her.

"You, in the back." She said, with a nod of her head in the direction of the back seat. There was more than a sense of making the most of her physical advantage over Hugo, signified by the slight, ever so slight, smile that appeared on Pascale's lips. Hugo jumped onto the back seat and Pascale checked the rearview mirror – first for her appearance, then Hugo and finally to check the traffic behind her as she buckled up, started the car and got ready to drive away.

"You know, I've always wanted a pet, Isobel. Perhaps this could turn out rather well."

"Fuck you," said the rather cross looking cat on the back seat.

As they travelled on, largely in silence, the picturesque Cotswold towns of Fairford, Lechlade, and Faringdon came and went. Hugo felt a growing sense of anxiety as he contemplated the story that he needed to tell and the information he needed to impart. He also felt anxious for the physical suffering his disembodied self was going to have to endure in the coming hours and days. Whether the connection between them would mean that Hugo, as a cat, would feel some of that suffering was unknown. Inwardly Hugo shrugged, resigned to the fact that he would find out.

As the car passed over the railway line at Challow Station, Isobel asked,

"Where in Wantage do you want me to park up?"

"I'll tell you when to stop," the silent voice of Hugo replied.

Pascale continued driving: past what was Segsbury School, over the Camel Crossroads and past the Lamb Public House.

"Stop on the right, in front of the mill."

The old flour mill that recently ceased trading after more than a hundred years, was an impressive three storey building that extended way back from the road. Apart from some apartments built in redundant space on the town side going up the hill, the mill had remained empty for some time.

Pascale stopped, facing the mill and turned off the engine.

"Now what?" Isobel enquired.

119

"We go inside," Pascale replied.

"Yes."

The two women got out of the car, attracting little attention from the passing traffic and pedestrians. Hugo was let out of the back and he quickly slipped out of the car and trotted towards the mill building. Skirting the frontage, he turned round the corner to the path that went alongside the building and also the mill stream. As they followed, they could see a gap in the chain link fence up ahead, just big enough for them to clamber through, which they did.

They were now standing in the abandoned yard. An HGV trailer with Wessex Mills proudly written across its side was the only indication of recent activity. Abandoned or unused industrial sites always carry a sense of pathos, even regret, and this was no different.

Hugo trotted on at some pace, past some old bins and towards the broken door of what was once the Goods Inward office. Slinking past half-open door the door Hugo disappeared inside. Pascale was about to follow him when she felt a strong pull on her right hand.

"Are you sure about this," asked Isobel.

Pascale turned to look at her friend and stopped for a moment of contemplation.

"Yes," she replied and, disengaging from Isobel's grip, slipped quietly inside.

Chapter 12

I started to regain consciousness. That hand, pulling me out of the warm waters of a tropical ocean was there again, only this time I had no expectations of anything so comfortable as a walk along the landing towards the toilet.

I noted I was lying down. And then, with increasing dread, I noted that my ankles, thighs, waist, chest, neck and head were all restrained, tied down to whatever I was lying on. The little movement I had of my head was confusing. It felt like I had a pony tail, and it had been a very long time since that had been true. More wriggling left me with the distinct impression that there was something like wires coming out of the back of my head, towards the top. By pushing my head backwards, I could feel that they were connected to my scalp. I felt queasy.

I'd kept my eyes firmly closed during this deeply worrying realisation. A childish habit, perhaps, of wishing myself somewhere else. Gingerly I started to peer through my very slightly open eyes.

Ceiling tiles. Bright, white LED lighting. I had no vision or sense of anyone else being in the room. To the extent that it was possible I relaxed slightly and scanned my now fully open eyes around the limited view I could achieve. I saw no-one. To my left was a large window, like those in an x-ray department designed to keep the operator away from whatever hazard the patient was exposed to. And whilst the intentions of a radiologist were to assist the patient, I had no sense of that being the case in my current situation. I remembered the phrase used by the woman I had just met and I felt terrified once again. I vividly remembered her threat to cause me 'suffering so much that your very soul cries out in pain and anguish across the Hypnotic Plane'.

I tried to resist the rising sense of panic welling up inside of me, testing the strength of each of the bonds that secured me to where I was lying, more a table than a bed. I heard the sound of approaching feet and a door handle being turned so I stopped, rigid in fear, in the childish hope that if I lay perfectly still they might not find me. This really was like being a child, besieged by night terrors, staying perfectly still in his bed.

I caught glimpses of someone walking around me. They were dressed in scrubs with a mask and blue gloves. They were definitely choosing to not look at me, rather checking the installation that surrounded me. No reassuring smile or enquiry as to how I'm feeling. Instead, I imagined our exchange as something like this:

"How are you feeling?"

"Scared."

"Yes, you should be. And it's going to last a long time, this unbearable suffering."

"Oh. Is there a risk of dying?"

"Very much so!"

My imaginings were interrupted by a disembodied voice over a loudspeaker.

"Hurry up and finish, then get out."

I recognised the voice of the woman I met in the garden near the sea. The attendant (such a benign word to use!) scurried around and then made a beeline, presumably for the door, as they disappeared from my sight. I heard the door click shut.

"Hello again, Simon. I trust you had a comfortable journey even in the boot of my car. Well, one of my cars anyway."

I said nothing. Not out of defiance, I just had absolutely no words to give.

"What comes next is going to be a bit of a discovery for all of us. I'm sure this won't sound very reassuring, but we've never actually done this before. Not that I want you to be reassured, quite the reverse in fact."

She stopped speaking for a while, although I could hear the sound of her breathing as she continued to keep the channel to the speaker on. I sensed that she was expecting me to say something. Instead, I felt oddly calm, relatively speaking, and I heard the microphone click off. I began to realise that my silence or rather my growing sense of absence was giving me just a tiny bit of power over the situation. Psychiatrists might have called it dissociating but whatever it was, it was welcome. The microphone clicked back on.

"Ok, well here we go. In a moment you will lose consciousness. Not the pleasant option you might imagine it to be, I'm excited to tell you. Instead, you will enter the world of dreaming. We've been experimenting with lucid dreaming for some time, harvesting actual dreams from our volunteers. Sounds delightful doesn't it? Some of them are, for certain. And some of them are absolutely filthy – I'm astonished at the range of sexual perversions people dream about – but before you start getting a little stiffy in anticipation, we've saved a special category of dream for you. Can you guess what they are?"

I was way ahead of her.

"Nightmares! Oh Simon you are going to suffer the most awful, gut wrenching, heart breaking and terrifying nightmares that our volunteers could produce. We worked so hard to get them to create these fearful things – regression to real events (who knew PTSD was so useful?), hallucinogenics, and perhaps a little bit of good old fashioned physical abuse. But listen to me waxing lyrically about them. We must let you see for yourself. Enjoy! Or rather, don't enjoy."

The microphone clicked off and the lights in the room dimmed. For a moment I could make out the silhouette of the people behind the large picture window before their lights dimmed and they faded from view.

I decided to try and concentrate on my breath. Counting each in and out breath, to keep my mind occupied and even to keep the nightmares at bay. I began to feel a strange sensation radiating across my scalp. Presumably they were doing something through the wires that were bunched up at the back of my head. Without warning, I felt like I was falling backwards at a tremendous rate. It's a feeling we all get from time to time when falling asleep

– perhaps that's why it's called 'falling' – only this went on for what seemed like ages. My fall gathering pace as I instinctively braced myself for some kind of impact. So much for breath counting.

My fall continued until it stopped as suddenly as it had started. It was pitch black now. Unsure as to whether I was still on the table or experiencing the dream, I tried getting up. I was able to do so. Therefore I must be in the dream. Before moving I returned to my seat. I sat still and listened. I could hear a faint scurrying noise in one corner of the room, like claws on a polished floor. By my right hand I felt something like breath. I did – something was sniffing me. Instinctively I withdrew my hand across my body before swinging it back with great force and giving whatever it was a resounding whack with the back of my hand. I felt it crunch beneath the pressure and a gentle thud as it landed some distance away. Almost immediately I heard more scurrying only this time it seemed to come from all around me. I could only guess at the number of things, but there were many. Already too many to bat them away, I thought.

As I sat still, petrified, I started to hear the beat of small wings, more of a buzzing really. I imagined that whatever these creatures were, they were beginning to take to the air around me. I could feel the hairs on the back of my neck standing up with fear. The next thing I knew was a rushing sound and something brushing fast, really fast, past my face. I raised my hands to try and defend myself and as I did so I felt a sharp, painful scratch on my shins. This was swiftly followed by a scratch across my face. I put my hand to my cheek and I felt something warm and wet. Without thinking I put my wet fingers to my mouth. I regretted it instantly as a taste something akin to very strong acid mixed with dog faeces overwhelmed my senses. Not that I'd ever tried either, you understand, but that was precisely what my brain was telling me I had tasted.

I started to feel more sharp scratches – cuts really – across my face. As I covered my face with my hands the intensity increased. Now on the backs of my hands and soon across my arms and stomach. I could feel my clothes began to fall off me, shredded under the savage attack. My shredded clothes were wet, presumably with blood and that awful liquid. I was in so much pain, unbelievable, intolerable pain. I was about to cry out, despite my best efforts to avoid doing so.

Then it stopped.

I heard a voice, her voice.

"How are you enjoying nightmare number one, Simon? It was my idea to modify it so that you'd start off in the dark. I wanted you to imagine what it was that was cutting you, ever so slowly and painfully, to pieces. Shall I turn up the lights Simon, do you want to see what I've sent to play with you?"

As the blackness started to lift, ever so slightly, I began to make out a faint outline of something around 20 centimetres long and insect shaped. I closed my eyes, preferring to not see the horrific creatures that continued buzzing around me, circling me with malicious intent. Every time I tried to shut my eyes, it was no more effective than blinking – I could still see.

"You'll have to do better than that my darling."

The blackness continued to retreat and I made out very clearly flying things that strongly resembled hornets or wasps but with what looked like three or for sharp protuberance coming out of the end of the abdomens.

Something reared up from my childhood – a voice that told me to,

"Sit still and they won't bother you mon chéri. Try to imagine them flying away."

The voice was so familiar and so comforting. A French accent, for sure, but not so strong. It wasn't Pascale either. I sat as I was told. Quite still and, as far as I could, clam. I placed my hands in my lap. As they started to fly around me, I imagined them losing interest in my presence. It didn't work – the sharp and painful attacks continued, albeit with less ferocity. The less I feared them, it seemed, the less they attacked. It was incredibly hard to keep fear at bay just by being still and imagining them leaving. I decided to see if I could engage my imagination still further.

Instead of the sharp pain of a cut and then the sting of the dog-faeces acid, I imagined the sensation would be like being tickled instead. As another wave of insects came towards me, it still hurt like hell. I wondered what my face and body would look like after this, if there was an 'after this'.

That single thought tore down the curtain of this dream and I realised that there was no damage being done to my actual, physical, self at all. It was all in my mind. Moreover, it was being placed in mind like some awful intrusion, a burglary if you will. I became angry and indignant that anyone could do such a thing.

"Fuck you!"

In my imagination, I shouted as I stood up from my chair. I brought forth great spouts of liquid fire coming from the ends of my fingers, a manifestation of my current rage. I reached out and pointed my hands towards the fearful insects. As insect met flame, they dropped like ash from a bonfire, onto the ground around me. I seemed to be gaining the upper hand. As more insects appeared, I even started to enjoy myself. It felt like a video game, and one over which I was an accomplished master. That was my imagined skill, and it worked.

Suddenly I was back in the room (game over, I thought to myself, unable to suppress a grin). I was once again secured to my table. Only I wasn't, of course. To prove the point, I imagined myself floating, table on its end, around the room, and found that I could. I began to enjoy myself. Banking into sharp turns and zooming parallel to the longest walls. Brilliant!

"Very impressive Simon,"

Said the woman over the dream's loudspeakers.

"I'd begun to wonder whether you truly are the person I've been looking for, but now I know that you must be. Such talents, so carefully hidden. Until now, at least"

I had no idea what she was talking about. Well, almost no idea. In fact, the faintest glimmer of a recollection began to light my way back to memories I had long forgotten or suppressed.

"Hidden, but maybe not by you?"

She asked with an enquiring, thoughtful tone.

She was clearly onto me. Or rather us, or me and the cat. I felt distinctly exposed. I was the one out of the three of us that had least knowledge of what was going on. No, wait. It was memory that was lacking here. Before I could develop my train of thought, she spoke again.

"You need to go back to your room now, Simon, while I decide what I'm going to do with you."

Everything went dark again, and I passed out of conscious unconsciousness. When I awoke, I was back in the white room with the large picture window.

*

It was daytime, presumably near midday given the absence of shadows, and it was quiet. Ever since my abduction from The Wheatsheaf, I had lost all track of day and time. Even location. I knew I was somewhere warmer than home but that hardly narrows it down.

Unsure if I was still being held in a dream-like state, I tried various imaginative feats. None worked.

I started to consider the events of the last – what, days, weeks, months even? My time at The Wheatsheaf was set out clearly in my memory from the day I moved in. Trying to reach back further than that had always been difficult, other than my early childhood which I could recall in disjointed images and sounds. The bits in between – work, marriage, children, divorce were so hazy as to be almost invisible, like watching something through almost closed eyes. I had put this down to the trauma of family break up and had happily suppressed whatever fragments of my memory remained as a coping mechanism.

But what if what Iago said was true? I had hoped that his manifestation was just a symptom of yet another mid-life crisis, but that was seeming less and less likely, given all the other extraordinary things that had happened to me.

I decided to see if I could meditate, and through that level of relaxation, try and remember more than I had previously cared to.

Lying on the pristine bed, I closed my eyes and turned my attention to my breathing. Simply counting breaths, in and out, had always been the simplest way for me regain some inner equilibrium. Count to ten, then back to one again. Over and over and over again until I am able to detach from my thoughts. Detach and let them drift past like clouds in the sky. I lost any sense of where my body was, the individual parts, just a vague impression of my physical form. I felt relaxed for the first time since I finished that run of End Game at the Old Fire Station Arts Centre, whenever that was.

I turned my focus onto the past. I imagined an old fashioned film projector in a cinema projection booth running a reel of my life backwards. Starting from now. My recent experiences seemed so ridiculous, so unlikely, as I began to see them running backwards. My quiet, if largely boring, life came into focus. Consultancy work, plays, occasional outings to the pub or a restaurant, carrying out renovations after moving into the Wheatsheaf. The day of the move even. And then, nothing.

I tried to remain patient, but it was like trying to open a locked door when you don't have a key. To try and force a way through, metaphorically, would only end up with me losing this meditative state to adrenaline and back to my physical form.

I returned to my breath counting, quickly regaining any of the thought-detachment I had lost. If my intuition had suggested a locked door, it was probably a good image to work with. For a few moments I let my mind wander, to see if I could picture this imaginative door.

It was vivid. Plain white in colour, no panels just a slab front with a steel door handle above a Chubb style keyhole.

I decided to imagine that I could pass through solid objects, to easily transcend the physical limitations of the door. Memories of the film The Men Who Stare at Goats briefly entered my head – the scene where an army officer decides he can pass through walls – and the comedic failure to do so (despite a lengthy and speedy run up, I might add).

Stop it! I said to myself. (I am so easily distracted).

Returning to the door in front of me in my imaginative state, I tried gently pushing but was met with equally gentle resistance. I tried the door handle – no luck. I then stood in front of the door and tried to simply imagine it away, make it dissolve. Whoever had blocked access to my memories with this locked door, had done a good job.

I spent a few moments regaining my composure and state of deep relaxation. I conjured up the door again in my imagination.

What if I imagined a key, I thought to myself. I did so, fairly easily. Inserting the key in the lock and gently turning clockwise to release the door, hung on hinges to my right. My effort met with firm resistance, not even a hint of movement or engagement within the lock mechanism deep within the solid door. I tried again, imagining a different key this time. Still no good. Then I created a whole bunch of keys – 20 or more. Surely one of these will work! But no. I became exasperated, imagining a new bunch of keys over and over, trying to force the lock to turn. Eventually, an objective view of the futility of my efforts prompted me to stop.

As I reflected on the blockage to accessing my memories, I wondered if this was one I had created or one that had been imposed on me by someone else. Iago/Hugo perhaps? If he had really projected himself/us into my poor cat leaving behind an unconscious and uninformed remnant of who he was, would any memories remain? Or would he be able to take them away, so to speak? If he had taken them away then there was no point to having this door in the way, and if it was my imaginative door then I could surely open it. I started to wonder what lay on the other side. What was it that I/we were not wishing to see, not wishing to confront, I wondered.

I stood back from my imagined door and contemplated it again. It was certainly solid and clearly immovable without the right key. And without that, I could see no way of passing beyond it.

Chapter 13

Patrick was on the train back to Devil's Bridge, his bags on his lap. Armed with the knowledge that ASH seemed to have been compromised, he decided to make a beeline to John Adam Street once again. Only this time he would do so en corporelle. He reckoned he could safely assume that no-one knew of his recent hypnotic plane visit to the RSA's home, and that therefore he would be reasonably safe.

The train trundled along the valley. Patrick made the most of the hour it took to arrive at Devil's Bridge. He admired the scenery and relaxed deeply, gathering his mental and physical energy, in anticipation of whatever may lie ahead of him.

Accompanied by a resounding hoot from the little steam engine that pulled the carriages into the Devil's Bridge station, Patrick climbed down from the carriage and emerged from a cloud of steam as he walked towards the café. Still on high alert he scanned the clientele through the café windows. Content with the apparently benign nature of the customers sat in the café he ventured inside.

"Back so soon?"

A friendly voice intoned from beyond the counter. A voice that was soon joined by the proprietor who had offered Patrick safe storage for his motorcycle.

"Ah, yes, I'm afraid so,"

"You can't resist getting back on the bike, can you? I don't blame you, the A44 between here and Llangurig is a wonderful ride, as long as you don't get stuck behind any traffic."

"Exactly," Patrick replied, grateful for the explanation of his rapid return that the large man had provided for him.

"I find that the best thing for overtaking is to just wind up the engine, squat behind the tank, get on the other side of the road and hope for the best!"

"Well, that's one of doing it. I suspect my riding is a bit more sedate than yours." Patrick added, "May I ask what you ride?"

"A Honda," replied the proprietor.

"Which one?" asked Patrick.

"A Monkey Bike," he said with the most enormous grin.

*

Back on the A44 to Llangurig, Patrick was still chuckling to himself as he began to find his flow through the many twists and turns on the road. Riding a motorcycle is almost meditative sometimes, he thought to himself, demanding total presence and the exclusion of all other intrusive thoughts.

The smooth triple cylinder engine took the journey in its ample stride and all too soon Patrick found himself approaching Oxford. The roadworks were still underway (when weren't they) but he threaded the slim machine, even with panniers, through the traffic with ease. This was the best thing about motorcycles, Patrick thought, travelling easily when other people were stuck, going nowhere. The parallel between motorcycles and travel on the hypnotic plan was not lost on him.

Soon enough, Patrick was within the great circular grip the M25 seemed to exert on a steadily expanding London. Before long, Patrick was riding down the Strand before turning right into John Adam Street. He rode, as slowly as he could without being conspicuous, past number eight. Searching with his eyes and his hypnotic senses, nothing seemed amiss. He rode on to Adelphi Terrace and parked his BMW in the motorcycle bay, conveniently under cover.

It was not unusual for Patrick to appear at the entrance and reception to John Adam House, and today he was greeted as he usually was. Even his appearance in his riding gear was not unusual. Having retrieved his membership card from his pocket, Patrick scanned the card and walked into the main building. He made his way downstairs towards the vaults.

These days, the vaults were often hired out as a venue for all kinds of events. Unbeknown to most of the hirers and RSA staff, there is a separate doorway that provides access to the Thames, from where supplies were originally offloaded. Since ASH took residence, however, a sizeable part of the offloading area had been enclosed. Although the presence of ASH was known to a few RSA fellows (who were also members of ASH, of course) the vast majority were entirely unaware of their presence.

Patrick opened the ancient, heavy oak door that led to ASH's rooms. A long narrow corridor led from the door to a single desk. On the desk was a single lamp, angled downwards. The face of a woman behind the desk was illuminated from the reflection of the lamp. She was looking down, attending to some matter or other. Only when Patrick has reached the desk, stopped and had waited for a good twenty seconds did she look up.

"May I help you, Patrick?" She enquired.

"Yes, you may Janice. I need to talk to the other members of the Council of Elders."

"I see. I understood you had given your apologies for today's Council meeting?

Patrick was genuinely taken aback by this new intelligence.

"I did not." He said, trying to keep his rising anger in check.

Janice looked confused and then concerned, and checked the papers in front of her, as if scanning a list.

"This is most irregular. I apologise Patrick. They've only just begun the meeting, some... "

She checked an ancient clock on the wall, by tradition always showing the time in Paris.

"Eight minutes ago. In the Council Chamber."

Before she had finished, Patrick had set of at speed along a corridor to Janice's left, turned right, climbed a flight of stairs and finally stood before a relatively small but very heavy door. He listened intently but could make out no sound at all, no doubt by design of the original craftsmen. He decided to enter immediately.

136

As the door opened, the assembled Council of Elders, to a woman and man, looked round in silence.

"Hello Patrick. Well don't hang about, come in and seat down. We've only just started," the familiar figure of Antoine broke the silence.

"I thought you said you weren't coming." He added.

"I did not," said Patrick, gruffly.

As Patrick's eyes adjusted to the gloom, he began to recognise the other Council members. The chair that Rebecca would normally occupy was empty, having crossed Patrick at the last gathering, she had decided to step down.

"As I was saying, we are gathered here at this extraordinary Council of Elders meeting to elect a new member of the Council. As président of the Council, it falls to me make the nomination."

Patrick was, unusually, taken aback. Election of a new member usually took weeks if not months. Rather than nominations from the existing ASH members, a subcommittee of the Council would meet to carefully consider potential candidates before vetting each one in detail. The vetting process alone took a long time.

Patrick began to feel uneasy that he had, unwittingly, been played in helping to create a vacancy in the first place. A vacancy for which the conspirators, at present unknown, had been planning to fill with a candidate of their choosing. Despite feeling very uneasy about the present proceedings, Patrick decided to not do anything just yet and instead to let matters play out.

"Now we are finally all gathered together, let us get on with the business at hand. As you all know we have had a vacancy for a short while on the Council since Rebecca, well, left us."

All eyes of the remaining Council members turned their gaze towards Patrick. Patrick scanned each member for any suggestion of malign intent. No doubt prepared for such an eventuality, he found none. Just studied neutrality.

"Normally, we would have commenced our search for a replacement, and after some time we would have created a longlist of potential candidates. In turn, after much deliberation and vetting, we would have agreed on no more than three. A final appointment meeting would then make its selection."

"Indeed," said Patrick, powerfully and with obvious irritation.

"But these are not normal times." Countered Antoine. A rising murmur of approval went around the chamber.

"Since we heard from Isobel in... the place she lives, there have been more attacks. Four in fact."

"Why were we not been informed of these attacks as soon as they were reported?" asked Patrick.

"You were." Replied Antoine. "Along with your invitation for this meeting. We even spoke on the telephone."

"I received neither and I wish to raise a point of order."

"Thank you, Patrick, your point of order has been noted and now by the power vested in me as président we shall continue."

Antoine had clearly been expecting such an interruption and was well prepared for it. Sensing he was losing any status, Patrick interrupted once again.

"Noting my point of order is not sufficient. I want to know why I was not alerted to either the attacks or the fact that this meeting was taking place."

"I understand from colleagues that you were, shall we say, indisposed recently? A little trouble with your head I understand."

Antoine couldn't prevent a small grin from appearing on his corpulent face. Something he tried to cover up with a handkerchief, as if he was wiping away some smear of food from the corners of his mouth.

"Perhaps that affected your memory?"

Patrick was a master at keeping his composure, but even his ability was being stretched to the limit. Focus on the details, not the emotion, Patrick said silently to himself. Clearly, he had been seen in Aberystwyth and even his accident outside Isobel's house had been observed or at the least reported on. Now the ambush made more sense, and this new knowledge drew a clear connection between Antoine and his would-be assassins. He decided to dial down his outrage.

"Well, Mr Président, that may be so. In which case, perhaps the Council can humour an old man and give me some of the details of these four attacks?"

"Oh really, can we just get on with the substance of the meeting?"

"If I can just ask for the indulgence of the président on this point, I would be most grateful."

Patrick was not used to being so obsequious, and it really didn't suit him. On this occasion he was convincing enough, however.

"Very well," Antoine sighed. "Fay, can you appraise Patrick, again, of the recent attacks."

"Of course. One occurred in North America, another in Australia, a third in East Timor and the fourth in Patagonia. There is nothing that seems to have connected the attacks and the only thing they had in common was the lack of skill of the assailants. And the fact that the intended victims were all First Nation people."

Patrick immediately made the connection between these ineffective attacks and the one Isobel endured in Aberystwyth. He said nothing.

"It seems to me," said Council member Claire, "that the Enemy is back. Probing our defences, and those of our allies, our skills and readiness, is a familiar tactic. Find a weakness in one area or another and then pile in. Very Russian, as it happens."

The other Council members, other than Patrick, murmured their agreement. To Patrick it made no sense. Probing defences and readiness *was* a tactic of the Enemy, but it normally involved using well-trained attackers and in large numbers, such was the profligacy and disregard for loss of human life of their commanders. Patrick held his silence.

"Thank you, Fay and Claire, which is precisely why we need to ensure the Council is fully staffed and, indeed, strengthened, with a new appointment."

Both women applauded Antoine, making Patrick's apparent intransigence all the more obvious, as he did not join in.

"So, we are finally back to the business of the meeting. Although not a member of ASH, the Council and I, have

140

taken the unusual step of making this nomination in recognition of the outstanding track record in business and the world of technology achieved by this nominee. They are, however, an existing and distinguished fellow of the Royal Society of Arts, albeit one whose modesty means that fame and notoriety have been largely avoided. Such discretion recommending them powerfully in its own right. Therefore, to restore our number and significantly improve our strength, may I formally make the nomination. In common with our custom and practice, we ask the nominee to be shown into the chamber."

Patrick was astounded. Only once had a non-ASH member been elected to the Council and that had not ended well at all. One Magaret Hilda Roberts, on that occasion. Everyone in the chamber knew of this near disastrous appointment, and yet they were here again.

"This is completely unacceptable," Patrick growled, loudly.

Antoine, similarly irked, replied, "Oh really you are impossible. We have spoke about this and, until now, you and I were in complete agreement."

Patrick's head was spinning. Were his faculties really affected by the whack on the head he had caused himself to suffer? It made no sense at all. Even Antoine would not tell such brazen falsehoods in open session of the Council. Whatever was going on, Patrick had been outmanoeuvred and he knew it. All he could do was watch with increasing alarm as the side door to the chamber was opened and a steward called out down the corridor for the nominee to the Council of Elders of the Ancient Society of Hypnotists to step forward. This was a

141

turn of phrase the Steward momentarily regretted as the nominee entered the room in her electric wheelchair.

"Nominee, do you enter this chamber in truth and humility seeking to serve the Council of Elders faithfully, loyally and courageously and to abide with all laws of the Ancient Society on pain of expulsion, elimination of powers and the imposition of a hypnotic lock for all time?" Antoine theatrically intoned.

"I do," replied the woman in the wheelchair.

"By the power vested me by the Council of Elders and all members of the Ancient Society of Hypnotists I appoint you as a member of this Council, Olivia Beaumont."

*

From the moment Olivia Beaumont rolled into the chamber, Patrick was struggling to make sense of what was happening. Who the hell was this woman and what, exactly, was her plan? At least he now had a name, assuming it was her real one, and he could begin to piece together what had happened and hopefully work out why.

Patrick wondered how Isobel and Pascale were getting on. It was time to find out and to pool their respective knowledge. Once they had a clearer understanding of what Olivia and the other Council members were up to, they could start working on a plan. Until then they were just stumbling around in the dark.

Patrick pulled on his helmet and gloves as he walked along the street towards his motorcycle. Thoughts were cascading through his head, none of them particularly useful, he acknowledged to himself. Time for the committee upstairs to do some work, he mused.

Patrick often referred to his subconscious mental processing as the Committee Upstairs. The Committee had served him well once he had learned to trust it. He would simply pose a question and wait for the answer to return. Sometimes it would take a few minutes, sometimes days. But return it would.

Pressing the started button, he paddled his BMW backwards out of the parking space, and with a check of his mirrors and a glance over his shoulder he set off.

He was unsure where he should go, but before he even got to The Strand, the Committee had provided him with the answer to that question: Wantage, it said.

Chapter 14

The smell of the old mill was powerful and somehow comforting. It evoked memories of a childhood kitchen, warmed by the oven that had been lit in anticipation of baking the bread her family had enjoyed. Not surprising, perhaps, that the smell of flour was still in air after nearly two hundred years of milling.

Pascale took time for her eyes to adjust to the relative gloom of the interior. No such pause was required for Iago who had slinked on ahead of her and was now, silently, calling her to make her way into the depths of the building beyond. Pascale looked round to see if Isobel had followed her inside. She had not.

Pascale trusted Isobel's judgement, but the call of Iago and the possibility that it was Hugo, was a strong draw. They had had a longstanding on-off love affair, mostly off in recent times, but the embers of that fire were still alive if only just.

The problem, as Pascale saw it, was Hugo's enormous ego. Yes, he was the most talented ASH member of his generation and perhaps greater than that. Yes, he was an outstanding combatant. Yes, he made her laugh. Yes, she found him deeply attractive (at least in human form). But, and here it was, he not only knew all these things to be true but metaphorically paraded them around like medals, constantly looking for attention, affirmation and recognition of his superhuman status.

Pascale *hated* this about him and probably hated the fact that she was still attracted to him, despite his manifest flaws, even more.

As she stood in the darkness wondering what to do, she heard the sound of the outside door behind her opening. Without turning round and with the slightest movement of her head she said,

"Isobel?"

"Who else did you expect it to be, the fucking postman."

Pascale turned to face her friend. Both understood the significance of Isobel coming into the mill, albeit reluctantly.

"Thank you"

"Come on, let's go and see what Puss in Boots wants."

Pascale let out a half-choked laugh as both women ventured further into the mill in pursuit of Iago. Moving beyond the goods inward reception area, they found themselves in a long corridor running parallel to the outside wall of the building. Off the corridor on the left were a series of doors which led to the production line for the flour itself. At the end of the corridor there were two stair cases, one up and one down. Iago was waiting at the top of the descending stair case. Once he was sure that the women had seen him, he turned and disappeared down the stairs.

Arm in arm, the women walked unhurriedly along the wide corridor until they reached the top of the stairs.

"Ok?" asked Isobel.

"Yes. And thank you."

With her free arm, Isobel gave Pascale's upper arm a squeeze of comfort and reassurance as she looked warmly towards her friend. They both understood the meaning, the expression of solidarity even sisterhood. Whilst they had never been best friends, their comradeship was never in doubt and the shared experiences of conflict and struggle created a deep bond of loyalty.

In single file now, they start to go down the stairs. A half landing and turn meant they were now facing back towards the rear of the mill and traversing another long corridor. Iago was waiting about halfway down.

It was gloomier now and the bare walls were starting to show signs of damp, the soft clay bricks beginning to crumble, small piles of failed lime mortar accumulating on the bare wooden floors.

"Follow me," Hugo silently said as he disappeared through a doorway.

As the women turned into the room beyond the doorway, they faced a grimy window, high above the eyeline, which more or less illuminated the room. It appeared to be an administrative office of some kind. A few desks around the room, with just enough room between them to place office chairs. They both sat down as Iago hopped up onto a desk and turned to face them.

"I think you'd better start explaining," said Isobel.

"Yep," added Pascale.

*

"There's a reason I brought you here, apart from the fact that this is where I live in the physical world, or rather where Simon lives in the physical world.

Wantage, I discovered, has a rather interesting history not just that which has been documented but also in the hypnotic realm. You won't have missed the large statue of King Alfred in the square, and you'll no doubt have some knowledge of the role he played in defeating the Vikings, subsequently making peace with them and ruling the greater part of what is now known as England."

Both women bristled as he mansplained in typically patronising terms the history of the only English King to be given the epithet of Great. Containing their irritation, as women have so often done, in the interests of advancing the story, they simply gave Iago a look that would make any sensitive human being (or cat) a clear message of displeasure. Hugo continued seemingly without any reaction,

"There is some evidence to suggest that Alfred was not only a successful warrior, scholar and ruler, but that he also developed certain other abilities."

Hugo paused, looking for a reaction or some kind of congratulatory approval. The women looked at him with as much neutrality as each could muster. If a cat could appear disconcerted, or at least a little put out, Iago failed to show it. Unabashed, Hugo went on.

"There is a scholar, Rosemary Harker, who specialises in the life of King Alfred and before the last conflict and my transformation into Iago, I developed a friendship with her."

Both women knew what Hugo's friendships with women, and sometimes men, generally entailed. Isobel gave Pascale's hand a fortifying squeeze as Pascale sat looking, as best she could, impassive.

"Her research is deeply impressive. Of course she was familiar with all the usual stuff – the Anglo-Saxon Chronicle and Sir John Spelman's biography but she also travelled to Rome, to the Vatican in fact. Alfred had visited Rome and even had an audience with the Pope when he was five years old. Anyway, my scholar friend was granted access to the Vatican Library. She spent countless hours days and weeks searching for a record of his visit but found very little, other than some confirmatory entries in an early papal record of official meetings."

"Is this story going somewhere?"

"Yes Isobel, it is." Hugo replied with obvious irritation. He and Isobel had never really seen eye to eye. Perhaps each recognised in the other traits that both found uncomfortable to acknowledge in themselves.

"Anyway, her scholarship was largely unsuccessful until one day, in a reading room at the Vatican Library, a fellow scholar sat down beside her. He surreptitiously passed her a note that simply said, 'follow me'. Rosemary is not a faint hearted person at all but even she considered the wisdom of following the note's entreaty. In the end, as the author of the note threatened to disappear as he walked away, curiosity overcame her and she swiftly stood up and, with as much of a casual air as she could manage, followed."

Iago heard a noise outside, the benefits of the physical form of a cat granted him exquisite hearing. His ears turned, followed by his head in the direction from which it came.

"What is it?" asked Pascale.

"Wait," Hugo replied. "Sometimes a security guard makes a cursory patrol of the building. We should really go. Follow me."

With that, Iago gracefully jumped down from the table and rapidly made his way out of the office door.

Pascale and Isobel exchanged a glance and quickly followed. Iago had made some distance down the corridor before he turned into another doorway, much lower this time. The women had to duck to pass through, finding themselves in a low passage. Iago's excellent night vision allowed him to pass along what was effectively an unlit tunnel with ease. Not so the two humans who tried to follow. Isobel looked over her shoulder to see the distant beam of a flashlight crossing the doorway, before it disappeared. The security guard's patrol was cursory indeed.

Pascale took out her phone and turned on its torch. The feeble light was more than enough to light their way along what was a twisting and turning route that was steeply ascending. The walls comprised brick and stone, alternating and interspersed with no apparent plan or order. They hinted at various repairs and renovations that had been made over the centuries in whatever materials came to hand.

Turning a corner, they caught up with Iago. He was sat in what was a round space about five metres in diameter with a high, vaulted ceiling. Off this chamber, there were

149

five doorways including the one through which they had just arrived.

"Wow, where are we?" asked Pascale struggling to catch her breath.

"We're in Alfred's tunnels," Hugo silently replied.

"Who's Alfred?"

Pascale and Iago turned to look at Isobel.

"What? I don't know who he is, ok?"

"I think Hugo is referring to Alfred the Great. You know, the King?"

Isobel looked a little embarrassed before she replied,

"Well, yes. Obviously. The King. Alfred. I mean who else could it be."

Pascale tried to cover the enormous smile that was forming on her face, deeply amused at her friend's discomfort.

"So what now?" asked Isobel, trying desperately to move the attention away from her embarrassment.

"I'll continue my story if I may," Hugo replied.

"Will it take long?"

"As long as it takes, Isobel."

With that Isobel sat down on the floor with her back against the stone arch of one of the five doorways. Her expression was very clear, as in 'get the fuck on with it then'. An expression that was not lost on the other two.

"So, Rosemary has decided to follow this scholar, the one who passed her the note. He had almost passed out of sight and Rosemary had to walk at a rapid pace to catch up. Passing line upon line of shelves filled with ancient manuscripts, she turned to look down each one, in search of her mystery scholar. Just as she thought she may have lost him, he appeared in front of her. Rosemary started, but quickly regained her composure. The scholar leaned forward and for one uncomfortable moment she thought he was coming in for a kiss. Instead he whispered:

"What you seek is in the palimpsest collection," and he passed her another note with a location and shelf number.

With that he quickly disappeared."

"What's a palimpsest?" Pascale enquired.

"It's basically velum that has been reused," Hugo replied

"I don't understand."

"Velum was expensive to produce, right," Isobel interjected, "and it was often cleaned with milk and oat bran to replace the original markings on it and then used again. Only the original marks eventually become visible again, sometimes after decades or even centuries."

"Exactly right," Hugo silently concurred. "In this case, the Vatican Library had no idea that some obscure scrolls actually contained some extraordinary Anglo-Saxon writings, specifically about Alfred and his magical abilities."

It took only a moment for Pascale to realise what Hugo was communicating.

"You mean he could travel, on the Hypnotic Plane?"

"Exactly. The palimpsest manuscripts Rosemary was directed to contained lengthy narratives of how he could walk about the land unseen, like a ghost, yet seeing all around him whilst his body lay asleep, protected by only his most trusted guards. And he used that ability to gather intelligence and information about his enemies, the Vikings. It's one reason why he was so successful in battle.

Anyway, once she had read the palimpsest scrolls and taken copious notes, she contacted me and we went over them together."

"I bet you did," muttered Pascale under her breath.

Despite Iago's outstanding hearing, Hugo decided not to respond. Largely, of course, because the sentiment that Pascale was so resentfully conveying was an accurate assessment of his and Rosemary's sometime relationship.

"Aside from descriptions of Alfred's travels, the scrolls also made reference to two other matters of great interest."

He paused, once again looking for the attention he craved. Isobel was affectedly looking at the floor while Pascale was looking at Iago, trying to contain her interest and awe. Seeing no more admiration was forthcoming, Hugo continued.

"Firstly, were these tunnels. The five doors lead in different directions. The first from the flour mill whose site has had some kind of mill on it since the fourth century, the second over there which leads directly and appropriately enough to the cellars of the King Alfred's Head pub, the third leads to what was the original palace and birth place of Alfred in what is now Grove Street, and the fourth leads to the crypt of what is now the Church."

"Which leaves the fifth," Isobel said out loud despite herself.

"Yes, the fifth."

"Well come on then!" Pascale implored.

"The fifth was a bit disappointing at first. A dead end at initially. But as is started to look around I saw some markings on the floor. They were hard to make out but with a little clearing away of the dust and detritus I could make out some letters."

With this, Iago started to draw out some lines on the floor with his paw. Hard to see in the dim light, when he had evidently finished, returning to sit down and lick his paw clean, Pascale turned the torch of her phone to illuminate what he had just inscribed.

It read:

AELFRED MEC HEHT GEWYRCAN

Iago looked from one woman to the other, apparently pleased with himself.

"So what does it mean?" Pascale demanded.

"It means, Alfred ordered me to be made."

"You're full of surprises, Isobel." Said Hugo.

Isobel let out a 'huh' as she continued.

"I've seen that phrase before,"

"Go on,"

"It also appears on the most valuable relic from the period – the Alfred Jewel."

"Exactly!" Hugo exclaimed silently.

"What's the Alfred Jewel?" asked Pascale.

"It was ploughed up in a field in Somerset in the late 1700s and it's actually really beautiful, made of gold and enamel. I think that it was meant to hold a pointer or something to help people follow text in books."

Hugo snorted.

"I'll come on to that," he said "I cleaned the area around where these words were inscribed and I could just make out a rectangular edge, like it was a box set into the floor. There were no rings or loops with which I could pull it up. I tried inserting my fingers in the gap, but it wouldn't shift one bit. So I did the obvious thing."

"You tried to shag it?" Pascale tried to look serious as she said this but instead fell about laughing, joined with some enthusiasm by Isobel.

"Ha fucking ha. No, I used my hypnotic powers to raise it out of the ground. Which makes sense of course – why would Alfred use a conventional lock to keep the box secure when he could use a physical hypnotic lock? Ingenious but I worked it out."

Simultaneous eye rolling by the two women did not go unnoticed, but Hugo continued.

"And once I'd got the box out of the ground, opening it was fairly straightforward. The lock was on the inside, so I just projected my hand inside the box and released the mechanism. Do you want to know what I found inside the box?"

"Yes!" the women shouted in unison.

"Then I'll show you."

The box started to vibrate and then slowly became raised above the void in the ground it left behind. Iago nudged the box to the side with his paw. The box was made of what looked like lead – certainly very dull and with a number of marks and dents to indicate the softness of the metal. It was entirely featureless with no obvious opening or lid.

The box settled on the ground and after a few moments emitted a definite click, whereupon a lid, hinged on the long side of the box, moved a few millimetres upwards. Everyone stared at the box. It felt like a significant moment.

"I guess we should open it."

Both women hesitated until Isobel reached forwards and gently raised the slightly open lid. She and Pascale leaned over the box to survey the contents. What they saw was another box, this time made of much finer metal, silver guessed Pascale, and on the top was an inscription:

Þā mihta þāra digelra eardas licgaþ binnan þissum boxe. Hīe þe hīe brūcaþ, sculon þone ceap forgieldan

"What does that mean?" Pascale peered at the box as she interrogated Hugo.

"I'll Google it," said Isobel. She took a picture of the inscription but found she had no internet connection, so put her phone back in her pocket and the silver box on the floor.

"I don't know what it means and I don't know what's inside," Hugo said apologetically.

"So how come you didn't open it?"

"Well, Pascale, I was interrupted. By agents of the Enemy. I heard them coming down the tunnel from the King Alfred's Head pub, so I closed the box and put it back, covering the inscription with dust from the floor. I turned to face them and I was confident that I'd be able to deal with them and then return to my exploration. I was wrong..."

If ever a cat could look sad, Iago was the very epitome of such a thing. His head was inclined to the floor, his eyes seemed set on the near distance and he was still. Completely still. Silence filled the chamber. It was as if they all knew that Hugo's story would end in his apparent destruction, and that this moment was near at hand.

Pascale felt a rising in her love and compassion for her friend, Hugo, embodied in this cat. If he'd been in human form she would have embraced him. Instead she leaned forward and, slightly hesitatingly, stroked Iago on his head. Iago looked up and began, ever so slightly to raise his head towards her hand as she continued to stroke him. Even Isobel joined in for a while. Iago eventually started purring.

"I was hit by something, a tremendous beam, that quite literally knocked the energy out of me. I turned to send a bolt of energy back but could only manage the weakest riposte I've ever delivered. I began to feel panic, fear even, as I scrambled towards the mill from where we've just come. I stumbled many times before making it to the Goods Inward office. I could hear my attackers still close behind me but I dared not turn to look in case it slowed me down.

I ran through the yard towards the mill stream and turned right towards the little nature reserve where I thought I could catch my breath. Instead I was feeling weaker and weaker, I felt like Achilles must have felt when he was shot by an arrow in the ankle."

The self-aggrandising comparison between Hugo and Achilles was not lost on the women, but both elected to remain silent.

"I waited for a sign my pursuers were nearby, they weren't. I left in the direction of Priory Road and eventually made my way back to the marketplace, skirting around the church. It took me a couple of minutes to go down Grove Street and head towards the library. Somewhere I thought I'd be safe for a while. As I turned into Stirlings Road I saw them, three of them, gathered together near a black four by four in Waitrose's car park. I was in the open and if they looked my way I knew I was done for. I turned back towards Grove Street past the end of the old Wheatsheaf when I saw a black gate. I tried the handle and found it unlocked. I opened the gate and found myself in a small courtyard garden.

I knew I was fading quickly and that if I was to survive I needed to do something and fast. I saw a cat lying in the sun. It had seen me but paid little attention. That's when I had the idea of hiding inside the cat, taking over the cat's consciousness, or spirit if you like, came into my mind."

"How the hell did you do that?" Asked Isobel.

"I'm not really sure. Fear and adrenaline certainly played a part, but I simply imagined myself as the cat, projecting all my energy towards it. I heard the gate to the yard open and close and I knew I had very little time. With one last effort, I found myself in the cat, literally looking out of his eyes, hearing through his ears."

"What was that like?" asked Pascale with wonder and incredulity.

"It was absolutely revolting. Seriously, you do not want to do it. Everything was on sensory overload but the worst of it was the taste in my mouth."

"Seriously?" Isobel couldn't believe this man.

"Have you ever smelled a cat's breath? I can tell you the taste in its mouth is ten times worse!"

The absurdity of the situation combined with the tension Hugo had evoked was threatening to make the two women laugh. They deliberately avoided each other's gaze and Hugo continued.

"I looked back to my former body, which was now lying on the ground looking like an empty sock. It appeared as though it was alive as my pursuers caught up. There was a look of grim satisfaction on their faces as they reached down to check the pulse in the neck of my body. They exchanged a few words, picked my body up and then left."

"So how come I eventually found you, I mean Simon, in the Wheatsheaf?"

"I have no idea."

"This cannot be a good thing. You disappeared Hugo and then four years later Pascale finds your facsimile in an ex-pub in the same town you disappeared from. I mean was he, Simon, here all the time? Did he just suddenly appear more recently and why has he now disappeared?"

"Hang on Isobel. I wondered around the Wheatsheaf for a few weeks before I caught sight of my facsimile as you put it – "

"Can we please just call him Simon," implored Pascale.

"Caught sight of Simon then. The house was empty but not uncared for. As if it was waiting for someone to return. He certainly seemed surprised to see me and, as it turns out, he was delighted, as he thought I had been lost."

"So how come you didn't let me, us, know what had happened to you?" Pascale looked troubled as she asked Hugo to account for himself.

"I had lost so much energy, I had none of my former powers. To be honest I was terrified – I thought I might have to exist as a cat forever, or at least for as long as the cat was likely to live. Then slowly, very slowly, I began to feel some measure of my old abilities returning.

At first it was simply the ability to meditate deeply, then I could achieve a partial separation from Iago but I was frightened. What if I couldn't get back into his body, what would happen then? It seems ridiculous to me now...

Anyway, I decided that I should focus on regaining my energy and hope that a period of rest would make all the difference. In the meantime, I kept an eye on Simon – he had my body after all.

One day I felt well enough to try a full separation from Iago's body. To be honest I was bored too, nearly bored to death, and I was more than ready to take a chance on separation even if that meant I couldn't get back. I sat in the yard at the Wheatsheaf in the morning sun. I relaxed and soon enough felt myself peeling away from Iago's body. I felt elated! I didn't travel too far at this point, just a quick roam around the town. The sense of freedom was extraordinary.

I didn't want to be away for too long so after an hour or so I came back to the yard. And there, lying on ground was

159

Iago's body only he was dead. I was really beginning to panic. How could I still exist when the body I had been inhabiting was gone? Then it dawned on me. I'd used my powers before to bring someone back to life – "

"What!" Exclaimed Isobel. "You did what? You know that any kind of necromancy is explicitly forbidden on pain of *death*. What were you thinking?"

"I was a young boy at the time, so not very much as it happens."

Isobel and Pascale were stunned. Neither said anything. For Isobel it confirmed the worst elements of Hugo's character, a causal – dismissive even – relationship with the rules. Even as she thought this, her own misbehaviours surfaced before she quickly and efficiently supressed them. Pascale, on the other hand, was in awe that Hugo, as a child, could wield such incredible abilities.

"So, reanimating a dead cat really wasn't that hard. And here I am."

The sound of Pascale's phone chirping, to indicate the battery was low following the torch being on for so long, broke Hugo's silent narrative.

"I don't think we've got long before my phone gives out."

"Mine's in the car. Sorry. Let's take the box and go back to the car."

Isobel picked up the slender box and put it in her jacket pocket. It felt quite light and yet, she sensed its incredible power within. Keeping the box secret and safe suddenly seemed very important.

"I'll go first, I can see better than you and if the guard is around he won't care about the presence of a cat."

With that Iago disappeared quickly from view only to return again a minute or so later.

"He's in the Goods Inward office. We can't get out that way."

"Well how about the pub – the King Alfred's Head – I fancy a drink to be honest. It's only been about 14 years..."

"Good idea Isobel," Pascale agreed.

Hugo led the way along the tunnel that led, as it turned out, to a manhole cover in the pub's beer garden. The sight of two women, one of whom was holding a cat, clambering out into the daylight would have been worthy of note but being mid-afternoon on a weekday there was nobody there to see them.

Brushing themselves down and placing Iago on the ground, the two women headed inside to the bar.

"I'll wait here then shall I?" Hugo projected into their minds.

Neither turned around; Pascale did, however, give a thumbs up as they both disappeared inside.

Chapter 15

My deep meditations on my mental locked door were interrupted as I became aware of a presence in my room.

I pulled myself back into consciousness.

"Simon."

Sitting in her wheelchair at the foot of my bed was the woman in the wheelchair

I sat up and regarded her. I felt considerable antipathy towards this woman and didn't much care about showing it.

"I can understand why you might not like me Simon,"

I harrumphed.

"I know I've done some rather unpleasant things to you but it's nothing personal, I assure you. You see, in a way, I made you who you are. Conjured you up from almost nothing, and now here you are, sitting up in bed, acting with autonomy and, you might even mistakenly say, free will."

"What the fuck are you talking about? I mean really, what?"

"What's the earliest thing you can remember, Simon?"

"I can remember plenty, thanks"

"Then tell me. What is the earliest thing you can remember?"

I started hunting my memory but kept on coming up against that locked metaphorical door.

Sensing my failure, the woman in the chair went on.

"Ok, so how about your wedding day or something from being at school. Where did you go to school Simon?"

I knew the memories were all there but I kept on coming up blank.

"I shouldn't tease you really, Simon. The fact is that you won't remember – you can't remember – unless I let you."

"Then go ahead and let me then."

The woman looked momentarily triumphant, as if a long and detailed plan had finally come to the point of fruition.

"You know I just might. Or I would if it weren't for just one thing."

"Which is?"

"When we found your near lifeless body four years ago, we were very careful how we handled you Simon. Or should I say Hugo."

I felt stunned. The silent words of the re-animated Iago came rushing back into my mind like a bullet. My head began to ache once more.

"Starting to remember, are you? Well let me help you bring some more memories back to life. You wielded very considerable powers, Hugo, and were the most significant threat to our plans, along with your rather less impressive friends. But we made a discovery that helped even things up, even against your formidable abilities. As a result, we disarmed you. And when we found you, close to death, we scooped you up and nursed you back to life. We took weeks to interrogate you, using the most advanced and most unpleasant techniques, but we got nothing. Nothing at all. In the end we believed that you had either buried Hugo so deeply that he'd never return, or that somehow you had escaped your body on a more permanent basis. In either scenario, you, Hugo, was gone. "

That's what you think, I thought to myself. I still didn't largely understand what this woman was going on about, but somewhere deep inside me, I felt a rising feeling of nausea. Like motion sickness or the spinning head suffered after drinking way too much alcohol. I just wanted it to stop.

"So, we put a hypnotic lock on your mind Hugo. One that we think will keep you in there, locked away, for ever. If you are in there at all, that is. And if you're not, you're going to have a hell of a job getting back in. Though your recent display of imaginative powers suggests the raw materials, the elements that made you, you, Hugo, may still be capable of being activated. And that's a cause for concern..." She paused.

"From that point onwards it was simple enough to create a new persona for you. Dear Simon – just a bit dull, just another middle aged divorcee trying to make his way in the world with a minimum of pain. We had plenty of materials to work with, harvested from our early lucid dreaming clients. We could have made you anything at all, could have made you stand out from the crowd, but we were happy to play a longer game than that."

"What do you mean?"

"We didn't want to make it too easy for your friends to find you. We wanted to make them work, to invest time and effort that could have been spent on other matters. We had to make them really believe that the great Hugo Durand might have been found. You have been such an excellent distraction Hugo. You've quite literally made the rest of the plan possible, along with a few other fireworks we set off."

She looked at me, as if she was trying to see what was happening behind my eyes, trying to decide what to do next.

"I really think you've served your purpose, Hugo. I can't see what further use I have of you."

With that she turned her chair around 180 degrees and sped off towards the wall. The hidden door opened and then closed behind her.

*

For the next few hours I thought about everything that she had said. Was I really 'made up'? A confection of bits and pieces from other people's dreams and experiences? I felt like a psychological Frankenstein. I'd quite literally lost my persona. When I say lost, it was still around – in the body of a cat – but it didn't feel like *me* any longer. I fell into a slough of despondency. After a short, fitful snooze I determined to bring a different set of thought processes to my current predicament.

Being the product of bits and pieces of life experience is not so different form anyone else is it? Sure my persona was actually manufactured (apparently) but we are all the product of chance and luck – good or ill. Where we're born, who are our care givers, schools, friends and all of life's vagaries create the person who we become.

And none of it is in our control.

At best we can observe our own behaviours and work to modify these where we can. And even possession of those faculties is a matter of chance.

My thoughts continued. However I became who I am, I decided it just didn't matter. The only thing that mattered now was who I was going to be. Hypnotic lock or not, why should I let Hugo Durand back into my psyche? He chose to leave, I'm here now.

A matter of days ago (I'd lost count of how many) I was feeling a little bored hoping for something a little more interesting when Pascale's email announced its presence in my inbox. The experiences since, and how I react to them, are what I *choose* to define me from now on. And I am *fucked* if I'm going to stay here and wait for *that* woman to decide my fate.

The energy of my newly found anger was surprising and exhilarating. I thought,

'And fuck that bloody cat too, or Hugo or whoever he is. I do not *deserve* to be here. I have been *royally used* by all these *pricks*. And if any of them think I am helpless, and a dull, middle aged divorcee wasn't it? Well they can go screw themselves!'

I was in a proper rage. Giving expression to my anger only served to intensify it. The recollection of all of my suffering and pain of the last few days came rushing towards me, building and building like a giant wave. I felt alive to the ends of my fingers and the depths of my soul, and I was now filling full of rage, rage like I'd never felt before, until I could contain it no longer.

In a moment preceded by a profound silence, my rage literally exploded. Like a nuclear explosion I emitted a blinding light, followed by a shock wave radiating in all directions. The first thing I saw was the full height window bowing outwards to the point where I thought, even in that split second, that it would break. It didn't, not yet. But it did start to oscillate – large cracks start drawing crazy patters all over the thick glass until, with an ear-splitting boom it disintegrated. Luckily for me, the oscillation was outwards when the window finally gave way.

As the laminated glass fell to the ground, covering the garden with a shower of reflective pieces, I saw the hidden door had also given way and the bed was upturned leaning against the opposite wall.

I knew I had no time to think about what I should do next. I stepped carefully over what was left of the window in its frame and then ran into the garden beyond. The white walls of the garden were about two metres high, but with a good run up – fuelled by adrenaline and what remained of my rage – I easily vaulted over the wall at the farthest end of the neatly trimmed and carefully watered lawn.

I found myself in the street. I looked around and half ducked down. It was a most peculiar street – there were many large, walled houses most of which looked empty and those that were not, had expensive cars on their driveways from all different parts of Europe. The roads were clean and smooth but there were no pavements. Soulless, I thought.

Up ahead I could hear the noise of a busy road. I decided to follow the noise and hopefully camouflage myself amidst a throng of people. I turned a right hand corner – more walled gardens but a bit more street life and, joy of joys, a pavement – at least on one side. As I slowed to a brisk walk so as not to look too conspicuous, I saw that every property had a notice in Spanish saying that the place was alarmed and activation would elicit an immediate response. So I deduced, not unreasonably, I was in Spain.

Walking up an incline now I could see what was an urban motorway ahead of me. Further away and to my rear I heard shouts of men and the slamming of car doors. I realised I didn't have long and ran the rest of the way to the junction.

As I arrived I could see absolutely no means of walking alongside the road and no bridge or underpass to cross it. I was starting to panic. If I was recaptured I was pretty certain that would be the end of me. Shit! I turned round to see if I could go back the way I'd come. Two black SUVs were slowly cruising up the road, the occupants no doubt scanning the street and driveways to find me.

From my back I heard a vehicle sound its horn. I turned around. Facing me was the open doorway of a bus, the driver evidently asking me, in somewhat impatient terms, if I was actually going to get on. In an instant I was on the bus as the doors closed behind me. I tried to keep my balance as I made my way towards the rear of the bus to take a seat. I looked back along the road to see I had, by pure and unimaginable good luck, been standing by a bus stop. I started to feel a wave of relief wash over me. The worst I had to fear, at least for now, was being caught without a ticket.

As my adrenaline surge continued to abate and my pulse started to return to something like normal, I reflected on my predicament. The foundations of my world, my self-image and even my history had been shaken. No not shaken – they had been utterly destroyed. And here I was – I could either fall apart and wallow in a pit of misery (a seriously tempting option it has to be said), or I could do something else. The thing is, I was not really sure what that other thing might be.

I continued on the bus journey, not knowing where I was going or even when I was likely to arrive, I could see the obvious symbolism. I looked out of the window, I saw that we were taking an exit off the urban motorway towards Malaga. Pleased with my surmising that I was in Spain, I decided I would get off the bus once we'd arrived at somewhere busy enough to potentially hide me from the eyes of my captors. Soon enough the bus pulled up at Malaga's bus and coach station. Everyone left on the bus started to leave and, to my relief, there was no kind of ticket check to bring me to the attention of the authorities.

I scanned the bus station and headed in the direction of a waiting area. I took a seat and in front of me was a departures board for national coach services. Pondering the various destinations whilst trying to recall any actual memory of locations in Spain to which these names might correspond, I saw one that I recognised: Bilbao.

I remembered having visited the Guggenheim Museum in Bilbao. At least I think I did. This memory thing was going to take some getting used to, I realised.

In any event, I knew it was on the northern coast of Spain and, if I was going to try and get back to the UK – which seemed a reasonable option – arriving at Bilbao would certainly get me closer than staying in Malaga.

I looked at the departures board again: the next coach to Bilbao was due to leave at 2015hrs. I realised I had no idea what time it was. The departure board said 1234. I had seven hours 41 minutes to work out how I was going to get on that coach without a ticket or any money.

In the meantime, I thought it was probably wise not to loiter around a transport hub. If I was searching for someone who had escaped from me, then that would be the first place I'd look. I ventured out of the bus station and made my way across the Calle Mendivil and was confronted with a great grey slab of a building. I could only see the entry to a car park, Entrada 2, but decided to walk down the ramp anyway, taking me largely out of sight.

Eventually I made my way up a level and found myself in a vast shopping mall attached to the central railway station. A huge array of shops, restaurants, cinemas and even a casino. I didn't like these places but right now they offered me the best chance of remaining unseen whilst I considered what to do next.

It was going to be difficult to get home. I thought about hitchhiking but that was a sure way to be visible, possibly for hours, until I was picked up: a foreigner with no Spanish to speak of and no money or even passport. The absence of luggage might also raise suspicions. If I'd had my phone I could have called someone. Someone like Pascale, for instance. She'd tried to warn me on the morning I was abducted. I wished I'd reacted more quickly. I wished she was here now.

Then it struck me: maybe I could make contact with her on the hypnotic plane? Whether by travelling or simply calling her to mind. Either way it had to be worth a try.

I found a comfortable-ish place to sit on one of the mall's public seating areas and settled myself in. I started by working through all the muscle groups – from the crown of my head to my toes – relaxing them all as I went. I realised just how much tension I was carrying as it took me a good half hour to loosen my body up. Finally, when I was properly relaxed, I turned my attention to the same imagery Pascale had shared with me on that afternoon in Wantage. I found it hard to concentrate, being as I was in a public place, not to mention probably being hunted by people who thought I had served my purpose for them.

I kept trying and eventually I could feel my consciousness slipping into the imagined scenes created in my mind. As I went deeper and deeper, I felt more and more confident that I could do this. With Pascale, she'd asked me to imagine a place in great detail and by doing so I travelled there. The problem was, I had no idea where Pascale was. So instead, I just imagined her, in as much detail as I could remember. I felt a certain sense of embarrassment, alone as I was, when I realised I could paint a very vivid picture indeed from my memory, such was the impact she'd had on me.

As her image came to life in my mind's eye, I could feel myself peeling away from my physical form. I could see everyone with that faint shimmering effect I'd observed before. I turned round to see myself. To all intents and purposes, I looked asleep. I only hoped I'd be left along long enough for me to try and contact Pascale.

Chapter 16

Inside the King Alfred's Head, Pascale and Isobel were waiting at the bar. There was only one other customer in the pub, half hidden from view in a dark corner, nursing his drink. He was dressed in blue jeans and a blue bomber jacket and looked somewhat out of shape.

"Can I help you ladies?" asked the barman, having appeared like the shopkeeper from the children's series Mr Ben.

"Yes please. I'd like a diet coke and my friend will have the same," said Pascale. Isobel looked disappointed.

"With a shot of whisky in it please," Pascale added with a smile.

"What about Hugo?" Pascale enquired.

"I dunno, a saucer of milk?"

With that both women collapsed in raucous laughter, made only more so when the barman, having taken their request seriously, produced one from behind the bar.

Whether as a genuine act of generosity or merely that he wanted these women to leave him alone, he told them there would be no charge for the milk.

Barely containing themselves, they went back outside. They took a seat at the outside table upon which Iago was sitting. Pascale placed the milk down in front of him. Without saying a word, he started lapping it up. A quick glance at each other threatened to start them off again, so they both looked around, looked anywhere, other than at each other.

Their resolve was tested beyond breaking point when Iago lifted his head, milk all around his mouth, and Hugo said,

"Ah, that's better."

*

Patrick had made good progress and having peeled off the A34 at the Milton interchange was now heading along Charlton Road. Soon enough he rode past the BP petrol station, then Waitrose, and entered the market place. He parked up near the statue of King Alfred in the motorcycle bay, next to two other bikes.

"That's a classic bike, that is." A nearby biker asserted.

Patrick killed the engine, dismounted, removed his gloves and then pulled off his helmet.

"And he's a classic biker," His friend joined, in seeing Patrick's face for the first time.

Patrick raised an unseen eyebrow as he made his way to the western end of the marketplace, his hypnotic instincts telling him of the presence of fellow travellers.

As he got closer to a café called Marmalade and a bar called Blackbird, he was instead drawn to the pub next

173

door, The King Alfred's Head. He opened the door and went inside.

Chapter 17

I resumed visualising her and she started to appear in front of me. Only very vaguely at first: She was sitting down somewhere, somewhere outside. There was another woman there and also... also that bloody cat!

I also sensed the presence of some others, others on the hypnotic plane. There were four back-clad figures, much like the ones we'd seen at the Tate Modern, and they appeared to be standing guard over Pascale and her group. It made no sense to me and I wasn't sure what to do but I *was* really scared for her and before I knew it, that emotional energy had helped propel me to where she was.

As I arrived I recognised the King Alfred's head beer garden. What was she doing in Wantage? My arrival went unnoticed by the black clad figures, arriving as I did some distance away in Alfred Street.

Almost immediately, I saw someone I recognised – a short, out of shape man in a blue bomber jacket and jeans, my pursuer on the hypnotic plane that night in Wantage. He came out of the pub door towards Pascale, the other lady and the cat. They paid him no attention as he rapidly advanced towards their table. As he did so I saw him draw a long knife from the back of his jacket. Shit! I didn't know what to do. He was closing rapidly and in just a second or two he would be in striking range of Pascale, and then the other two.

The next few seconds were a confusing blur at first – an older man emerged from the pub and seemed to take in what was happening. As the blue bomber jacket man raised the knife behind his head, the cat launched itself towards Pascale who instinctively ducked just as the blade came slicing through the air towards the place where the back of her neck would have been. The knife removed the tip of one of the cat's ears, the cat yowling and hissing in pain as it landed neatly in the lap of the other woman. At the same time, the old man threw a glass that was in his hand – a heavy old fashioned beer glass. The glass the head of the would-be attacker. The blue bomber jacket man dropped to the ground unconscious, or worse, as the blade left his grip and fell beside him. The older man moved with incredible speed and balance and scooped up the knife before lifting the unconscious man's head by the hair and moving to slit his throat.

"No, Patrick!" yelled the other woman. "We need him alive."

The older man, Patrick I assumed, paused before removing the knife from the attacker's throat, dropping the man's head to the floor.

During the melee I had involuntarily shouted out a warning to Pascale, not that she would have heard me. The black clad figures did however and having heard me they turned to see me. If anything they looked a little pensive until, after exchanging a look between them, they came at me with great speed and ferocity.

I hadn't appreciated how much energetic force could be given out in the hypnotic plane until they started pummelling me. It hurt but rather than cowering, I started to get angry. This time I recognised the power of my anger almost instantly and I wondered if it would have the same impact as it did in the physical world.

As blows continued to rain down on me, each one only made me more and more rageful until at last it exploded and radiated from me in the same extraordinary blast form as it had done in the physical world before. All four figures were torn, quite literally, to pieces before they evaporated and disappeared before my rather astonished eyes. My rage quickly subsided and I turned my attention back to the four humans and one cat I was previously observing in the physical world.

*

The older man was the first to understand what was happening. They had all, blue bomber jacket man included, felt a massive disturbance on the hypnotic plane. Coming so quickly after the physical world attack, the others were understandably at a loss for a while to appreciate what was going on. It was as if an earthquake had hit their location and had left them literally reeling from its shock.

He manifested himself on the hypnotic plane with great speed, practically next to me, just in time to see the torn up remnants of the black clad figures disappearing. He turned to me and said,

"You must be Simon."

He had a calm yet powerful presence which at once put me at my ease.

"Yes I am," I replied.

"My name is Patrick. I am friend of Pascale's, and I think it's about time you and I had a chat."

"I think I'd like that," I said, taking comfort from his kindly gaze. "But I need to make my way here first, in the physical sense that is."

"Where is your bodily form now?"

"In a shopping centre in Malaga."

Of all the places I could have been, this seemed to be one of the least likely, at least judging by Patrick's look of surprise, tinged with just a tiny bit of amusement.

"Is it a nice shopping centre?"

"Not really."

"No, I imagine not. Would you like me to meet you there, in person?"

I surprised myself when I replied,

"No. Thank you. I think I need to make my own way back."

"I understand. And for what it's worth, I think you're probably right.

"Well then."

"Well then."

"See you when I get back."

"Yes," Patrick said, with what could have passed for a knowing look in his eyes.

Blue bomber jacket man was starting to come round, as Patrick reinhabited the body he had so briefly left.

"We need to get him out of here."

"I'll bring the car around." Pascale disappeared from view as she ran out of the pub garden and down Alfred Street.

Isobel was, to her surprise, comforting Iago. She'd found the small piece of his ear but doubted very much whether there was any such thing as a plastic veterinary surgeon. She carefully put the piece of ear in a handkerchief she had in her pocket and returned it there, for now at least.

Patrick meanwhile had his knee in the back of blue bomber jacket man, to keep him from getting up off the floor.

"I was too busy trying to sense where you were to notice the presence of this little fucker. I'm sorry Isobel. And I'm sorry for your little pussy cat too."

"Less of the little pussy cat, if you don't mind," Hugo projected into both of their minds.

Patrick immediately recognised Hugo's voice and rapidly looked around him for something that resembled Hugo.

"I'm here, "Hugo wearily said, raising a paw.

Patrick stood and stared while he tried to understand what the hell was going on.

"It's a long story. I'll tell you about it later. But we really need to move."

Isobel put Iago on the ground and helped Patrick lift up blue bomber jacket man, still groggy from the heavy blow to the back of his head. To any passer by he'd simply look rather worse for wear, being helped by his friends to get home.

As they made their way out of the pub garden, Pascale pulled up outside. Iago hopped into the front seat while Isobel and Patrick bookended their prisoner in the back.

"Where to?" asked Pascale.

"The Eagle and Child," said Patrick and in a moment, Isobel had floored the accelerator and the car sped off towards the market place and Oxford beyond, leaving no trace behind of the extraordinary events that had just unfolded.

Chapter 18

I focussed on returning to my body, and almost instantly I felt myself sinking back into my human form. I opened my eyes.

Everything was just as I had left it. People were milling about. Children running around and the occasional cry of a baby. Nothing seemed out of place and no-one I could see was taking any interest in me at all. A sense of relief came over me and for a moment I really felt like crying. If doing so wouldn't have brought with it the risk of unwelcome attention, I'd have done so.

"No time for that now," I said out loud as I pulled myself to me feet. Stretching and feeling remarkably refreshed, all things considered, I decided to go back outside, sit in the sun somewhere, and think of a plan. It seemed to me the key thing was to try and get some money.

When I got outside, the afternoon sun was making the whole place remarkably hot. So much for sitting in the sun. I skirted the vast station cum shopping mall staying in the shadow as much as I could. I wondered if there were any phone boxes or vending machines from which I might be able to prise some loose change. I was out of luck. Then, with a look recognisable in the countless millions around the world with nothing, but in search of something, I walked along with my eyes fixed to the floor. Hoping I might find something of value dropped by a hapless owner.

A car pulled slowly past me, and the driver got out. He hesitated before closing his door to hear the instructions from someone within. Someone whose voice I recognised instantly – the wheelchair woman! As the driver disappeared inside the shopping mall, I drew level with the driver's door. The windows in the rear of the car were blacked out. Although the voice was unmistakable, I couldn't see who else might be in the back with her. Deciding I had very little to lose, I opened the driver's door and jumped in. I glanced in the rear view mirror and there she was, my interrogator and tormentor, staring down at her laptop. There was no-one else in the car.

"Now get the fuck on with it and take me home. I had a shocking flight from London and now I need to clear up this mess that that bloody man has made. And book yourself a prostate check when we get back. If you can't drive for me for more than an hour without peeing, you're no use at all."

I decided to drive off before she had any reason to look up. I pulled into the traffic and looked for signs to Marbella. I reasoned that there was a chance she lived on the premises, or at east nearby, of the place of my recent incarceration. Driving in that direction would arouse less suspicion while I decided what to do.

As I drove off, I saw a sign for Cordoba on the A45. My geography was pretty shite but I knew Cordoba was inland and quite possibly north of where I was now. I turned swiftly and started making my way north out of the city. I looked again in the rearview mirror and was relieved to see her still looking down, the noise of her fingers tapping the keys on her laptop keyboard confirming her attention was where I wanted it to be.

We were soon driving on a much faster, sweeping motorway that cut through the mountains on either side. I decided to accelerate as the inklings of a plan started forming in my mind.

The acceleration drew the woman's attention away from her laptop momentarily and she looked up and out of the window.

"Where are we?"

"*We* are going for a little drive," I replied.

Looking at her in the rearview mirror as I delivered these words revealed more than a trace of anxiety, panic even, as she recognised my voice and began to piece together the jarring intelligence her brain had just received. It took only the briefest time before, composure regained, she retorted:

"Ah Simon, how nice. The two of us, alone, just like old times."

It was my turn to feel discomforted. What exactly did she mean? I didn't have to wait for long to find out.

"These days, I am known as Olivia Beaumont. I chose that name to represent the most English of names with just a hint of my real origins, my actual name from birth. I'm not sure if you do know who I am or not, but I suspect you don't. Not after the going over we gave you to create your current identity."

I remembered the vague familiarity of her voice the first time I heard it but, despite my efforts to get through the metaphorical door, I was unable to access anything more from the recesses of my mind which were still available to me.

The motorway started to descend as we passed out of the mountain range and towards a massive, flat plain beyond. There were nothing but olive groves ahead and either side of us for miles and miles. I decided to take the next exit and get off the motorway. In part to make us less easy to find and also to allow me to stop driving and fully engage with Ms Beaumont, or whoever she really was.

Soon enough we were bowling down a road barely wide enough for one vehicle let alone two, with olive trees either side of us. I pulled into a farmer's track that led off the road and into the trees. Despite the air conditioning in the car, it was hot and likely to be more so as I turned off the ignition. The shade of the trees would have to do for now, I thought.

"What do you want, Simon?"

Now that was a good question, I thought to myself. I sat in the driver's seat, looking ahead at the line of olive trees that disappeared into the distance. An endless repetition of tree upon tree as far as the eye could see. Conformity, uniformity rendering each tree effectively invisible amidst the whole.

"Who am I?"

"Ah, now that's an excellent question. And it's one which I've been grappling with as well. Who you are I mean, I know very well who I am..."

Olivia's words trailed off and I sensed the merest hint of sadness in her tone.

"When we found you, we soon discovered that the essential part of you was, well, missing. Your core had gone. Despite us probing around your mind for weeks on end, we found nothing of interest – no offence. Just a freshly cleaned mind like that of a baby. For a long time we tried to replicate that clean slate with human subjects we acquired, but we couldn't do it – can't do it – at least not yet."

God this woman was chilling! I could feel fear and anger rising in me, but I did my best to transform them, transmutate them if you will, into exquisite curiosity.

"Go on."

Before I do, what exactly are you planning to do with me?"

I had no idea. My strategic formulation had only extended to getting out of Spain and eventually home. The opportunity to steal the car and capture Olivia had presented itself in a moment in time. It felt like a gift, an opportunity. I decided the plan would unfold if I let it, especially without any interference from me. I was acting out of instinct, intuition. And so far, it had served me very well indeed.

"I've no idea, Olivia," I said as I pondered the question out loud.

"Perhaps we could run away together, start a new life far away from here."

I was beginning to enjoy myself.

"We could get a place in the country, a few goats and chickens, maybe some children, in time. Ah yes, I can see it now – a quiet life in the country, feeling the rhythm of the changing seasons year after year. Growing old together, watching each other age, sitting silently with a deep sense of knowing each other, souls entwined until death do us part."

My mockery felt cruel, even considering what this woman had made me endure. The merest flicker of guilt became a definite flame as I looked in the rearview mirror to see tears running down Olivia's face. She looked back at me and for the first time I saw beyond the carefully curated visage that she had showed me and those around her. There was vulnerability, sadness even. I wasn't sure what I'd done to elicit these feelings, what had triggered this response.

Olivia looked down to her lap. Closed her computer and tossed it to one side. I could see her examining her fingers, rubbing her finger nails, in the way some people do when their minds are in deep thought. I opened the driver's door and went round to the rear. I opened the rear door and sat down beside her. The heat of the day was incredible, even in the shade of the trees.

She barely glanced at me as I sat down beside her. Tears continued to fall, silently, from her eyes. I began to feel sceptical. Did she really feel so sad, and if so, why? It didn't take long for me to find out.

"Do you have any idea what you've just said?"

"What do you mean?"

Do you have any idea what you just *said*? She asked again.

I was struggling to understand the question, though I did detect a trace of anger now in her voice. Real, passionate anger born out of suffering.

Perhaps noting the look in my face at hearing this rising anger, she changed her tone and expression to something more friendly, kindly even.

"I just need to know – do you have any recollection at all of having said these words before? This is *really* important."

I noticed that Olivia had stopped using – over using – my name. Whereas before she had never missed an opportunity to call me Simon, now it was missing. My reflection was soon interrupted.

"Please. I need to know."

I took time to search my memories (what there were of them) and see if I could bring any association to what I had said. Nothing. I closed my eyes and tried to relax. Aware of Olivia's presence next to me and the risk that may pose, nevertheless I warmed to my task and felt myself falling deeper and deeper into my subconscious mind.

After a minute or two, I started to detect the memory of a smell. Feint at first but growing stronger. Then a taste – an odd, chemically taste – what was that? In my memory I was now chewing, definitely chewing. I know what this is! It's bubble gum, not only that but it's Bazooka bubble gum! I heard the laughter of a girl. I could see me and this girl were sitting down on some grass, in the sunshine, with a pile of penny sweets in front of us, including the Bazooka bubble gum. Looking up at her face I could see an enormous pink bubble extending from her lips growing bigger and bigger until at last it burst, creating a strange pink addition to her nose as the thin gum stuck to her face, flaccid now that the air had escaped.

She was laughing as she started to pull the thin sticky layer away from her face. She was radiating joy. I could feel myself beginning to smile as I recalled this childhood moment. Then it went black and in place of joy I felt an overwhelming sadness, grief even.

"What is it? What did you remember?"

"Bazooka bubble gum," I said, not wanting to reveal too much.

"Go on."

"That's it really," I lied.

"No, please. Try again."

Her voice had become soft and imploring. For my own curiosity, I closed my eyes again. I wanted to avoid the sense of sadness that was so overwhelming so I tried to return to the sunny day, sitting on the grass. Starting with the smell again, I found my way back quite quickly.

After the bubble gum had burst, we were both laughing, looking at each other. I reached out to take her hands in mine. I heard myself say,

"Let's stay together for always. We can live in the country and have lots of animals,"

"Can we have chickens?" The girl asked.

"Of course we can, we can have anything you want!"

"How about goats? I love goats."

"Yep. And maybe we can have children too – "

I could sese the embarrassment between me and this girl, but also the child-like love: pure and uncomplicated by the world that will arrive for every child, stealer of innocence and bringer of suffering...

I opened my eyes in astonishment.

"It's you."

I turned to look at Olivia. She looked guarded.

"And your name isn't Olivia is it?"

I'd never seen an expression on someone's face like the one I was seeing now. What was it? A mixture of horror, joy, terror, and relief. She looked down again at her hands placed on her lap. After a long silence she asked me,

"So, what is my name, Hugo?" She raised her head to look at me.

I didn't know why but her calling me Hugo made me catch my breath. I felt vertiginous and at the same time I could feel fragments of memories flying towards me like leaves on a windy autumn day. Impossible to catch as a whole, elusive, but for the first time I could remember, they were at least in sight.

Then one did land, was in my grasp, so I took it. I didn't understand the significance, but I knew it was the answer to her question.

"Your name is Claudine."

Chapter 19

As they approached the Seacourt Tower coming off the Cumnor bypass, the silence that filled the car started to be punctuated by groans from their prisoner.

They had been conscious during the journey that anything they said would be overheard. Even Hugo had kept his silence for fear that he would be overheard in the head that was now so painful for its owner.

"You're all fucked, you know that don't you?" the man said.

There was no need for a reply. Each of the ASH members, Hugo included, were trying to make sense of what had happened not just today but over the last week or so. It felt to most of them that events had been unfolding at such a pace that there had been no time to properly comprehend any meaning or to discern any pattern that might bring them closer to some kind of understanding of their current predicament. An understanding that did not prelude the prediction made by their prisoner.

Making good progress now along the Botley Road it was only a few minutes before Pascale had driven past the noodle bar and had pulled up in front of the Eagle and Child. Patrick opened his door and dragged their prisoner out of the car and, more or less, onto his feet. Isobel got out of the other side and quickly joined Patrick on the pavement as they man handled him inside. Pascale drove around the corner to park, Iago remaining seated in the front.

Both were aware that this was the first time they had been alone since Hugo's disappearance, creating an awkward atmosphere in the car with so many questions unspoken and answers unsaid.

Pascale turned to look at Iago, only to find him already staring at her. Hugo's voice invaded her mind.

"We need to get inside the pub. There'll be time for you and me to talk. It's just not now."

"I know." Pascale said out loud, breaking her gaze from Iago.

She got out of the car and opened Iago's door. Having locked the car, she set off back towards the Eagle and Child, with a cat in tow, following at her heel. She must look like a modern day witch, Pascale reflected, a thought that pleased her and brought a faint smile to her lips.

Isobel and Patrick had entered the pub and were now in the room Pascale had ushered Simon into previously at their first meeting. The fireplace, table, three chairs and second door facing the one that led from the bar were seemingly unchanged. The single bulb still hung from the pendant fitting in the ceiling, the bulb barely penetrating the gloom.

As Pascale, followed by Iago, opened the pub door, they were directed by the man behind the bar with a nod of his head towards the same back room.

"They're in there."

At the table, Patrick was seated opposite the man, now tied to his chair with his arms behind him. Patrick was leaning towards the man, staring intently, powerfully, into his eyes.

"You can't touch me old man. You don't have the power to enter my thoughts. Pathetic!" he virtually spat the words out at Patrick.

Iago jumped up onto the table. This caused the man to flinch ever so slightly. As if to recover his swagger he said

"Gonna get your cat onto me are you?"

"Hold his head, down onto the table," Hugo commanded to his collected comrades.

Without hesitation they grabbed the man's head and forced it down on to the table top. His head rested on his chin, his eyes scanning Patrick, with the first outward sign of fear in his eyes. But it was not Patrick of whom he should have been afraid.

Iago moved in from of the man's head and, sitting back on his haunches, placed a front paw on each of his temples.

"What are you *doing*?" the man half screamed, anticipating what was about to begin

Hugo, through the form of Iago, began violating the man's mind, searching for information. It was a technique that was outlawed except in the most extreme of circumstances. Not only for such a gross invasion of privacy – unexpressed thoughts and feelings could hardly be more private – but also for the risks that attended such a manoeuvre. More often than not, it was the hypnotic equivalent of a frontal lobotomy, depending on how robust the unfortunate recipient of this invasion was. Those weaker subjects were left conscious but mute. Unable to comprehend anything around them other than the simplest and most mundane events.

Simon's experience had not involved any searching as such, merely psychological support, distraction even, when Iago had placed his paws either side of his head. Hugo had been very careful not to damage what he regarded as *his* brain.

As Hugo set off inside the man's mind, keen to discover anything that might be of use, the others heard a commotion on the other side of the door that led to the pub.

Raised voices were soon accompanied by the sound of some kind of a struggle.

"I don't know what you're talking about!" broke through the muffled hubbub. It sounded like the barman's voice.

More loudly now he said, "You can see there's nobody here, worst luck. Bloody awful business running a pub these days, you've no idea"

"Shut up! What's through that door?"

"Just a private room. But there's nobody in there. If you want I can get the key and show you."

Isobel looked down at the lock. There was a single key on their side of the door. As quietly as she could she began turning the key, hoping it would move smoothly and most of all silently. Both to delay the people outside the door and to corroborate the barman's story.

"Let him up," said a voice outside the door. "Get your key and be quick."

Isobel looked down at Iago, channelling Hugo's theft of the man's mind.

"You need to hurry up," she hissed.

All the light in the man's eyes was beginning to fade. He appeared increasingly empty, vacant even.

"He's nearly there," Pascale raised a hand as if to prevent Isobel from interfering.

"Right then, now where did I put that key," came the barman's voice somewhat too loudly. If he did that again, they'll know he's trying to warn us, thought Patrick. At the same time they saw the doorhandle turn sharply and someone trying to force the door open.

"It is locked boss, and we're not getting through that door in a hurry. It's oak-"

"I don't give a fuck what kind of wood it is. You've got ten seconds before I make you wish you'd never been born, now find that key!"

"Ok, ok, I think I've found it," the barman hurriedly spoke.

"I've finished," Iago removed his paws from the man's temples.

Patrick had already opened the other door in the small room and was ushering the others through it.

"What about him?"

"We need to bring him along as well Pascale, at least for now. If they find him, our barman will be in big trouble."

"Ok Patrick, then give me a hand." They both struggled to get the man out of the chair and onto his feet.

"Right then, it's definitely one of these keys..." came a voice from just outside the door to the pub. The friends exchanged a worried glance and quickly made their way through the other door, closing it behind them.

"Wait!" explained Isobel. She opened the door and re-entered the room, carefully removing the key from the door lock and putting it in her pocket.

"Not this one," came the barman's voice.

"Ah, here it is!" The key turned as loudly as the barman could make it and two men burst into the room, followed by a woman, who was clearly in charge.

"I told you no-one was in here," said the barman triumphantly from the doorway. He was treading a very thin line, if he had only known it.

The woman scanned the room.

"What's through there?" she demanded, pointing at the other door.

"It's just a cupboard," the barman replied.

"You, open it."

One of the two men reached gingerly for the doorhandle, turning it to release the latch, and then with a flourish pulled back the door. In front of them was a shallow cupboard with perhaps half a dozen shelves with assorted tut - papers, beer mats sporting brands of long departed breweries, and odd glasses.

"Told you," said the injudicious barman.

"Get out of my way!" screamed the woman as she pushed past him and walked swiftly towards the front door of the pub, followed by her henchmen.

Waiting until they had left and turned out of sight of the pub windows, the barman let out an audible sigh. He returned to the small room and open cupboard door.

"They've gone," he said in a voice barely recognisable from the one he had been using up to this point. He reached underneath one of the shelves and found a catch. Soon the entire collection of shelves and tut were swinging outwards into the room, effectively another door.

On the other side of the cupboard, crammed together in a space barely big enough for half their number were two women, a cat, an older man and a man who looked for all intents and purposes to have lost his mind. They spilled back into the room, still on high alert.

"Follow me," the barman said as he led them back into the bar and towards the rear of the pub. We've got some rooms in the cellar that might be just what you need, he glanced at the comatose man.

Without protest, the friends followed and were led down some stairs accessed from behind the bar. At the foot of the stairs were three doors in front of them, and the cellar stocked with bottles and barrel behind them.

"These rooms were used by the Chancellor of the Exchequer during the English Civil War, so I reckon they'll be good enough for you," he winked at Pascale. Iago looked scornfully in his direction.

Each room was modestly furnished with items that could easily have come from the 17th century or earlier. Each had a bed, a chair or two and rugs on the stone floors. The middle room was slightly larger and had a fireplace.

"I can get that going for you if you like?"

"Yes please," Patrick replied. "I love a proper fire."

The barman passed Patrick a remote control.

"This button to turn it on or off, and the plus or minus buttons to make the flames bigger or smaller. Gas. You can't beat it."

Patrick was left with the remote control in his hand, somewhat crestfallen, as the barman made his way back up the stairs from the cellar.

"Afternoon ladies, now what can I get you?" They heard faintly as the barman continued his day.

*

After settling into their new environment and deciding who should get which room (Patrick was allowed the larger room in deference to both his status and his age), they all settled in front of the gas fire. Patrick on his bed, the two women on chairs and Iago on the rug in front of the fire, of course. The comatose man was laid out in the recovery position at the side of the room.

"I think it's time we all pooled what we know and try and make some sense of everything that's been going on."

"What about him Patrick?" asked Isobel, indicating the comatose man.

"Whilst I doubt he's ever coming back, it may be better to put him in the other room for now."

With that, Isobel and Pascale dragged him into the next room and left him lying on a rug on the floor, closing the door behind them.

Returning to their chairs, the three people, one cat and one disembodied spirit sat in silence looking at the gas flames originating from a quite convincing ceramic wood-effect log bed. The effect would have been soporific were it not for the adrenalizing events of the last many days.

For the next many hours, the friends updated each other with what they knew and what they had experienced. Pascale's search for Hugo, her discovery of Simon and his apparent aptitude for hypnotic travel, and his subsequent abduction.

Isobel's attacker in the Old College Library and the revelation that Hugo was now embodied in a cat.

Patrick's story of his pursuers and his escape by steam train had them all in stitches. The description of the pursuers in Isobel's house, the woman in a wheelchair and her election as the new Chair of the Council of Elders soon put an end to their laughter.

Hugo shared with them his seeking sanctuary in the body of Iago following the ferocious attack he had endured in Wantage, as well as his subsequent adventures and tracking down of Simon to Spain where he had witnesses how he had suffered at the hands of the same Olivia Beaumont.

Finally Patrick revealed that it was Simon, on the hypnotic plane, who had come to their rescue in the beer garden of the King Alfred's Head, and who was now making his way back from Spain under using his own resourcefulness and endeavours.

"Do you think he can make it?" Pascale sounded doubtful.

"Definitely not," Hugo practically snorted.

"I'm not so sure," Patrick replied. "I think he has more than enough talent and strength to do so. The question is simply whether he will find those things, that dwell within him, in time."

"He reminds me of someone I know," Isobel looked intently at Patrick. "And I think he did pretty well. In the end."

Patrick knew exactly what to what Isobel was referring. His early life had been successful, if somewhat unspectacular, but it was events in his midlife that defined Patrick, or rather which Patrick used to define himself, to become who he was always meant to be.

"May be so. But that's not a story to be told tonight, Isobel."

"Perhaps not, Patrick, but I find the parallels very striking. Despite having had Hugo ripped from his body, Simon is developing from *something* left behind. It seems to me, if that's the case, then you can't have projected all of your being into this cat Hugo..."

"I don't know how to explain it. But sometimes I do feel like I am a little incomplete. I had thought that it was my physical form that left me feeling like this, but I'm not sure that's right. And anyway, he's nothing like me."

Pascale who had said little all evening interjected.

"He is," she said flatly. "He's more like you than you might care to imagine."

Pascale was the only one to have spent any time in the physical world with Simon, a fact that hadn't escaped the others' attention.

"He's not like you are now, or how you were over the last few years because he's *nicer*. He's kinder and he's funnier. And I'm sorry Hugo, but he hasn't got your ego. He's just a better human being than you were."

The room fell silent.

The fire flickered.

Iago rose to his feet and stretched. The sound of Hugo's voice in everyone's heads notable for its absence. He walked to the door and managed to open it a crack with his paw and walk out of the room.

"That was harsh," said Isobel.

"I thought you didn't like him?"

"I don't Pascale but fuck me that was a hearty kick to the bollocks of someone who's lost almost everything, including his girlfriend, apparently. "

"I am *not* his girlfriend," she hissed.

From somewhere Hugo's voice entered their heads simultaneously.

"He's gone. The man we captured has disappeared!"

As the friends regained their focus, they rushed to the next door room. Iago was there and the comatose man was not.

"Where has he gone Hugo?" Asked Patrick.

"I don't know. He's not upstairs either, and our barman is dead – stabbed through the heart with a knife. I think I should get outside and look for him –"

"No Hugo. First you need to share what you found out about him, then we go after him." Patrick's authority was not in question.

"Alright, but let's do this the fast way."

Patrick nodded. The friend returned to the middle room and sat in a circle on the rugs on the floor. The humans held hands, and the human-cat interface was accomplished by gently holding a paw, Isobel on one side and Patrick on the other.

"Are you ready?" Hugo asked.

They all nodded.

"Right, then let's begin."

Images, light, sounds and smells came flashing through their minds in an almost overwhelming torrent. The whole process took a little less than a minute but left them all reeling.

"Jesus Christ!" Exclaimed Patrick, in an unusual emotional outburst.

Pascale and Isobel looked shell-shocked, staring straight ahead.

"I don't think you were expecting that, were you," Hugo's disembodied voice underscoring the obvious.

Chapter 20

The heat of the sun was making the oppressive atmosphere in the car almost unbearable, despite the shade of the olive trees. I turned the car's ignition on so I could lower the windows. A breeze instantly passed through the car, carrying the distinctive smell of what must have been a nearby olive processing plant – sweet and green, even appetising. I looked up the track ahead of the car. The land rose to a point when it disappeared from view. Olive trees for as far as the eye could see. Judging by their size, most would have been here for more than a hundred years, some several hundred. Young trees in the history of olive cultivation in Analucia over thousands of years.

I was lost in my thoughts, trying to catch hold of my own short history, but again and again I was coming up against that damn door. I took comfort from my surroundings, lost as I was in a sea of olives – sight and smell. Perhaps it didn't actually matter all that much, that I couldn't remember. The present moment was blissful. A welcome calm in what had been a complete emotional, physical and spiritual storm.

"I can't believe you remembered."

Claudine spoke quietly and without emotion. I was not sure at first if she was even speaking to me, to herself, or to no-one at all.

My attention came back into the car and my passenger.

"What else can you remember Hugo?"

I wasn't sure I liked being called Hugo, but a part of me lit up, like an electric circuit, when she used that name.

"Nothing. Just..." I contemplated telling her about the white door in my mind's eye that prevented my access to what I presumed were the memories beyond. Then I remembered.

"We've had this conversation already, haven't we?

"Yes, Hugo, we have."

"And you've put a hypnotic lock on my memories."

"I thought so, but you seem to be circumventing that lock. I've no idea how you've got around it, even a tiny bit. The person who applied the lock to you was extremely confident that you'd never be able to break it."

I was seized by annoyance, anger even, that I had been so completely violated and then had my memories confiscated, put beyond my reach. I could feel the same build up of energy that allowed me to escape my captivity early on in the day. I could see Claudine sensed something dangerous was developing by the look of fear in her eyes. Oddly, that look of vulnerability worked like a switch on my emotions and my anger rapidly subsided.

As my emotions subsided, a thought, an important thought, began to be revealed to me. Slowly at first, and somewhat out of my grasp, this thought came forward. It was something that Claudine had said about the hypnotic lock, 'I've no idea how you got round it..' she said. Perhaps that was all I needed to do. I didn't need a key for the white door, I just needed to step around it.

My thought was interrupted by the sound of a tractor approaching from behind. It was a small, blue tractor with a similar sized trailer behind it on which various tools and implements were loaded in simple crates made of wood. I'd have to move the car to allow the tractor to pass. But before I could do so, the tractor's engine had been shut off and a woman of about my age came up to the open car window.

"¿Está todo bien? ¿Se ha averiado su coche? Este calor puede provocar daños terribles en la maquinaria moderna."

I understood very little of what she said, but I hoped my reply would suffice.

"Sí, todo está bien, gracias."

The woman looked into the back of the car, regarding Claudine with some curiosity. Whatever conclusions she reached, it seemed to be enough. She climbed back onto her tractor and started the engine. I manoeuvred the large car to one side of the dusty track to allow the tractor and trailer to pass.

"Give me your phone."

"What?"

"Give me your phone – now."

Claudine passed me her phone and I waited util the trailer had drawn up alongside the car before tossing it into one of the wooden crates. If Claudine's phone was being tracked, there would be a false trail, at least for now.

"Time for us to get moving," I said as I fired up the engine and began reversing along the track which led back to the road. A huge cloud of dust billowed behind us, immediately obscuring the view of the olive grove and the tractor. I reversed onto the road and the cloud of dust caught up with us, momentarily obscuring the road ahead.

"Where are we going, Hugo?"

"My name's *not* Hugo. It's Simon."

I was surprised to hear these words coming out of my mouth at first. But they had come from a very deep place. In that moment I had decided, though not consciously, to accept my identity as it is now, today. The sense of liberation from an unknown past, from memories that were, for now at least, inaccessible to me, was immense.

"You may have created Simon, or you think you did, but that's who I am now, and I am real! However you pieced me together, like a modern day Frankenstein's monster, I'm not in your control anymore, I am *me*!"

I shouted the final word and, once again, felt that energy rise inside me. I felt more in control this time, my anger energising me, sustaining me as my real renaissance began. It was an extraordinary feeling – set free from any and all expectations, memories or obligations. I was free, completely free, to do whatever the hell I wanted.

And right now, I wanted to go to Wantage.

Chapter 21

"How could this have happened?" Isobel exclaimed.

Sensing it was more of an accusation then a question, Pascale glanced nervously at Patrick, who was looking at a spot on the floor perhaps a metre away. Impassive and hard to read.

"We've been completed out manoeuvred," she continued, "and what the hell are we supposed to do now,"

Patrick was about to speak.

"Do *not* interrupt me, Patrick. I am so angry right now. I've never held the Council of Elders in much esteem, obviously, but to allow themselves to be so manipulated and to have sold out to *them!* Fucking Hell!"

Patrick looked ashen faced. Pascale looked like she was about to say something, and then caught a look from Isobel and thought better of it. And Iago simply sat and looked straight ahead, in that way cats do sometimes, either indicating complete focus or mental vacancy.

Hugo's disembodied voice interrupted the various private thoughts each of the friends were having.

"I really don't think we should stay here. It's only a matter of time before they come back, and I really don't want to bring any more attention to this place then its already had."

"Is there another place we can use, nearby I mean?" Asked Patrick.

Pascale chipped in, "Why don't we go to the Wheatsheaf? Simon's not there and I know the code for his key safe."

Looking from one to the other of her companions, there were no voiced objections, so she took the initiative.

"I'll bring the car round. Be outside in two minutes."

Pascale left, climbed the stairs to the main bar and disappeared from sight.

"Christ," Patrick said first words since Hugo, via Iago, had shared the intelligence he'd taken from their former captive.

"I honestly had no idea. I mean I realised something was up when I went to RSA House, and that Beaumont woman was obviously bad news, but I had no inkling that she worked for those tech bastards. With her in charge of the Elders, they'll have access to everything, our entire history. This is the biggest threat to ASH since the early days in France and French Fucking revolution." Patrick practically spat out the last three words and was in full, venomous flow.

Isobel, on the other hand, had regained her composure and was issuing instructions to her compatriots.

"Upstairs, now. Hugo, take a look in the bar and make sure we're still alone. If I don't hear anything I'll assume we are. Let us know when Pascale arrives. In the meantime I need a word with Patrick. Alone."

Iago bounced effortlessly up the stairs and out of sight.

"Patrick, when I was summoned to appear in front of the Council of Elders, you told me you knew something and that you would tell me what was happening."

"Yes, I did."

"So how come all of this was a surprise to you?"

"I'm glad you think so, but it wasn't.

Isobel looked confused, just for a moment. Then she understood.

"You don't trust Hugo, do you?"

"No. I don't. He always had a bit of an ego, but then he was always the most talented hypnotist most of us had ever encountered. His apparent transportation from human to cat has rarely been seen in the western world, although other cultures can, and do, make such changes as a matter of course. But for Hugo, it must be almost intolerable."

Isobel snorted, suppressing a laugh.

"Sorry, but it still makes me smile that he's reduced to such awful circumstances."

Patrick looked stern, and was about to say something until his serious façade began to crumble. Both old friends looked at each other and then burst out laughing.

"Seriously, though," said Isobel barely regaining her composure, "do you think Hugo could betray us?"

"I'm not sure. I only know that if he were given the right incentive, he would be capable of almost anything. And what do you think he wants, above all else?"

"He wants his body back."

"She's here," Hugo's voice interrupted.

Isobel and Patrick made their way upstairs and joined Iago as they left the pub and clambered into the wating car. The doors shut, and that familiar silence filled the car.

"Right then," said Isobel, "to the Wheatsheaf."

Chapter 22

As the dust cleared outside the car, the long, straight road made its way almost to the horizon, flanked either side by countless olive trees. I put the car in drive and pressed my foot to the floor. The Mercedes growled and set of at an alarming pace. I glanced in the rearview mirror and was pleased to see a look of alarm cross Claudine's face, however briefly.

"Well then, *Simon*, where are we going?"

"Wantage."

"Oh, I see."

Silence.

"And how are you proposing to get us there?"

"Other than driving towards Santander, I've no fucking idea. But I can tell you this, one way or another I'll either take us there or I'll blow the fuck out of you, me and this fabulous car."

Hearing myself was decidedly odd – I was not one to express my anger as a rule, although recent events might suggest otherwise. In fact, I felt good. Knowing I had the power to let my anger loose, to really let it go, and to use that energy in such a destructive way thrilled me. Who knew I had such a dark side to my personality? Not me, but there it was. And I liked it.

Claudine looked thoughtful, and indeed she was. Nothing less than an extraordinary tactician, she was turning over various permutations, combinations of events, possibilities and probabilities, in her mind. After a moment or two, she appeared to settle on a plan.

"Simon, I can get you to Wantage."

I was immediately suspicious. Nothing this woman had ever done had ever worked out well for me. Still, as a human hand grenade, I always had the option to blow it all up again if I didn't like what was happening.

"Go on."

"I have access to a private jet,"

"Of course you do-"

"I have access to a private jet that's in an airfield not too far from here. You've no idea how useful it's been in the last few days."

"What do you mean?"

"It doesn't matter. Take the next right. Then head towards Villamartin. When we get closer, you'll see signs for the aerodrome."

I decided to plug the location into the onboard satnav. As always, it seemed to me, the car's satnav interface was fiddly. I had to take my eyes off the road in order to press the right areas of the touch screen. Not only that, but I was struggling with the spelling. For a couple of seconds, engrossed in the satnav, the car drifted to the side of the road, running on loose dust and stones. My attention quickly returned to the road and I recovered the car's course.

"Sorry about that," I said a little sheepishly. I heard no reply, so I glanced in the rearview mirror. Claudine was sitting staring straight ahead and trembling. All colour had drained from her face. She seemed to be breathing heavily and rapidly. I may not be Sherlock Homes but I worked out (eventually) that she was having a panic attack.

"You ok?"

Claudine didn't respond. She appeared to be focussing on managing her breathing, making it slow down, with very deliberate in and out breaths. A layby was approaching so I decided to pull in. Having done so, I turned off the ignition and swung around in my seat to face her.

By this time, Claudine had regained some of her composure and was definitely trembling less, though still trembling. After another minute or so, she turned to face me.

"You won't remember this, Simon, but I have a thing about travelling by car."

She paused, scanning my face for the merest flicker of recollection. She saw none, so continued.

"When I was a little girl, my parents were killed in a crash on the motorway in England."

Pause.

"I'm sorry to hear that," I said, even now obeying social convention. I made a mental note to say less in future, preferably nothing at all.

"And so was I."

I didn't understand what she had just said and, without thinking, said,

"So were you what?"

It was Claudine's turn to experience confusion as she untangled the words I had just directed at her.

"Killed."

It still took me a moment to comprehend what she had just told me. I replayed the recent conversation in my head – her parents had been killed in a car crash on the motorway and so had she. It made no sense.

"That makes no sense." I said out loud.

"Indeed it doesn't."

Claudine now looked, well, cross. Cross was an understatement, in fact she looked like she was on the verge of fury.

"You saved my life. You came and you found me and you saved my bloody life."

I had no recollection of this, of course, and before I could stop myself, social niceties intervened once again.

"Glad I could be of some help," I said weakly.

"You really are a prick. You don't get it, do you?"

I really didn't get it, so I decided honesty was probably the way to go.

"No, I don't," and then added, "Sorry." Something I almost instantly regretted.

"Sorry? Fucking sorry? You left me as a paraplegic orphan, while you went back to your comparatively idyllic existence. An 11 year old girl, alone, disabled. You should have left me, Simon, you should have left me in the mortuary. My whole life I've struggled, for the first ten years I didn't want to live. Do you know what it's like to live in a care home Simon?"

I shook my head.

"It's like hell! A pretty girl, paralysed from the chest down, at the mercy of anyone and everyone? There were predatory paedophiles everywhere in the 1970s and they all knew how to get close to children, especially vulnerable children. Become a priest, a youth worker, a teacher, a scoutmaster, a social worker – you name it and they were there. And *you* did that to me."

Her last words were practically spat out at me. I was feeling aggrieved. I didn't do those things, at least not me as I am now. It was that bloody Hugo. I heard myself punching back.

"Now just hang on – *I* didn't do any of those things to you, *I* didn't save your life, so you can stop venting spleen at me or I'll fucking well kick you out of the car here and now."

Claudine looked surprised.

"I hate Hugo. I've hated him since he brought me back, and I will never forgive him. Why do you think I spent so long trying to find him?"

It was a rhetorical question, I said nothing.

"Not because of those tech boy arseholes, no. I couldn't give a flying fuck for what they want. Controlling dreams means nothing to me, even penetrating ASH – which was pathetically simple by the way – I couldn't give a shit. Everything is in service to destroying Hugo. And I so nearly had him, but somehow he left his body and all I got was you."

I knew what ASH was but I didn't know what Claudine meant by 'penetrating ASH', other than it couldn't be good news for Pascale, or that old man. I did know where Hugo went though, and I briefly considered telling her, until good sense prevailed.

"Well, here we are. You want Hugo and I want to go home. So let's get on with it."

I started the car and continued our journey towards the aerodrome at Villamartin.

After no more than 30 minutes, I saw a sign for the aerodrome and turned down a narrow, dusty road.

"Take the next left or you'll end up on the runway."

Hardly reassuring as to our onward journey, I did as she said and found myself driving up to the front of Hotel La Antigua Estación. Its bright, white walls with ochre highlights looked impressive in the late afternoon sun.

"I'm assuming you don't have a passport on you," Claudine stated with more than a little irony, "Given your unusual means of arrival in Spain."

"I'm assuming you don't either, Claudine, given your unusual means of arrival at this aerodrome," I countered.

"Then it looks as though we're in the same predicament."

"One for which I imagine you already have a solution."

"You may be right, but it all depends on who is at the customs and immigration post today, if anyone."

"Well why don't we go and see."

And with that, I drove around past the hotel and along a dusty track with what looked like an aircraft hangar to our right. Taking the next right, I drove the impressive black Mercedes onto a large forecourt in front of the hanger and adjacent to the runway. This all felt very James Bond. In a moment, a young man came scurrying towards the car from an open, person sized, door in the hangar. He went straight to Claudine's rear window, her arrival clearly being a familiar event, and waited for her to open the window.

Claudine pressed the button to do so and her demeanour become one of charm tinged with efficiency.

"Buenos tardes, Mateo, good to see you."

"Buenos tardes, senora. How may I be of service?"

"Can you please prepare the Cirrus for a flight to England, the Cotswold Airport please?"

"Of course madam."

And with that, he was scurrying back towards the hangar as Claudine closed her window.

"Are you seriously telling me there's an airport in the Cotswolds," I asked. I couldn't quite reconcile the idea of the Cotswolds and an airport.

"Yes, south west of Cirencester as it happens. Don't tell me you've never flown your private jet from there before."

I was getting tired of her endless, dripping sarcasm.

We sat in silence for the 20 minutes or so it took for Mateo to do whatever he had to, to prepare the jet. Eventually a large, aeroplane sized door opened and a diminutive aircraft appeared from the shadows, pulled by a small tractor.

"Is that it?" I asked with incredulity and some amusement.

Clearly stung by my mirth, Claudine quickly put me in my place.

"How big a jet do you think would be capable of taking off and landing from a short runway? Do tell me, Simon, I'm all ears."

I said nothing, but watched as Mateo parked the jet and got down from the tractor. He disconnected the jet from it's coupling and drove back towards the hangar.

"Follow the tractor and park in the hangar."

I was getting irritated by her orders now but decided not to show it. Instead I did as she asked. As we entered the hangar I had to pause for my eyes to adjust to the relative gloom. Looking around, there were three other aircraft, all with propellers, neatly lined up. All of them were emblazoned with "Skydive Emotions", presumably a local firm or club. It's name neatly summed up my emotional journey of the last few days. I parked the Mercedes and turned off the engine.

"Now what?"

"Now you'll carry me to the aircraft."

I sighed. "Yes ma'am."

Claudine was surprisingly light as I reached into the back of the car to lift her up. Holding her closely to me, for reasons of balance, I felt decidedly strange being in such close physical proximity to someone who had apparently been a close childhood friend and more latterly a mortal enemy. My overriding emotion was one of affection. I quickly shook this off and walked across the forecourt towards the jet. Ascending the steps that Mateo had put in place, while he hovered around us, not sure if he should be helping or not, was harder work but we were soon ducking our heads as we entered the cabin.

"Which seat do you want?"

"The pilots seat you idiot."

I was really close to saying something, but with Mateo now lingering at the top of the steps, now was not the time.

"Of course madam."

I looked at the closed door to the flight deck in front of me and before I had a chance to ask, Mateo's role in following us up the steps was made manifest as he opened the door and prepared the pilot's seat for its incumbent. After he had vacated the compact flight deck, I carried Claudine towards the pilot's seat and unceremoniously dumped her in it.

"Ooops," I said in an effort to ensure she knew it was no accident.

"Mateo?"

"Yes madam," he replied as he leaned in through the door.

"There's no customs or immigration officer here today?"

"No madam. He was here when you arrived but I suggested he take a break. You understand."

"I do indeed and I'll make sure your service is duly recognised. If he asks where I've gone, tell him I've flown to Madrid for a few days – just an internal flight so no need to complete any logs, is that ok?"

"Of course madam. Have a good flight."

Claudine smiled at Mateo and then swung back round in her seat and scanned the controls and instruments in front of her.

"Go and sit down in the cabin."

I hesitated.

"No. I'll sit up here with you,"

Claudine shrugged as I struggled to attach the multipoint seat belt I was confronted with. In the meantime she started the engines and did loads of other things with which I had no familiarity whatsoever. We started to taxi onto the runway and turned right, continuing until we reached the end. We then turned 180 degrees and faced the seemingly endless tarmac in front of us. Within seconds we were hurtling down the runway, gathering speed.

"It's not really long enough, the runway, so I'll leave it until the last possible moment to rotate."

"Rotate!" I exclaimed, imagining some kind of roll. The end of the runway was getting closer and closer.

"Like this, dummy."

Whereupon Claudine pulled back the control column and just in time we ascended rapidly. I looked across at Claudine to see her smiling broadly.

"You've no idea how liberating flying is for me."

Ignoring her last comment I asked,

"How long is the flight to Cotswold Airport?"

"About three hours."

"Fine," I said.

I was beginning to feel very sleepy. Much as I didn't want to nod off, I decided now was probably the best time to get some sleep. What with Claudine being otherwise occupied. I hoped I'd hear any radio communication, and spying a spare headset, I put it on.

"Fancy a stint as my co-pilot, do you?"

Claudine's voice came through loud and clear on my headphones.

"Something like that," I replied.

In a little over four minutes, I was sound asleep.

Chapter 23

As Pascale drove towards Wantage, her mind was filled with the information Hugo had shared with them. How could ASH have been so corrupted and what was going to happen to them? And what was happening to Simon? As this thought crossed her mind she felt the slightest butterflies-feeling in her stomach. She interrogated the feeling, wondering if this was for Simon or for Hugo. She wasn't sure, which in itself, suggested there was more to her affection for Simon than his physical form. That night in the Wheatsheaf could have gone in a completely different direction, and a part of her wished it had.

Isobel was contemplating the potential betrayal by Hugo, turning the possibility over and over in her head. She'd never warmed to him and she was trying to make sure that her feelings towards Hugo were not interfering with her analysis and judgment. Patrick might be right, but then again... There may be others who would betray ASH, *had* been others over the centuries, and if it was Hugo, what if he was not working alone?

Patrick was silent. He was sitting bolt upright with his eyes closed, but he was not sleeping. He was replaying recent events, over and over, in his mind. Seeing if the subconscious processes of his remarkable mind had yet done their work in creating a coherent view of cause, effect and probable outcome of what he now knew. Not yet. Instead he continued to ponder Hugo, and his potential capacity for betraying the ones he had been closest to, including Pascale. He wasn't sure, but it was certainly a possibility. That still didn't explain how Olivia Beaumont got on to the Council of Elders, let alone as its président. And what on earth did the Federation of Digital Entrepreneurs want with ASH?

And all the while, Hugo sat there as Iago. Implacable and, for once, in silence, without any invasion of the others' thoughts.

He used to quite enjoy travelling in Pascale's car, at least when he was in human form. But since his change of body, car travel had become nauseating and uncomfortable, and something to be avoided. The revelations he had extracted from the now dead man, had shaken him deeply. Of course he had had plenty of time to contemplate the near fatal attack he had suffered, and what betrayal may have led to that happening. And no-one would have anticipated his escape into the form of the cat, in which his consciousness now resided. But he had never been able to pinpoint an individual as the traitor. Despite this, his thoughts kept returning to Pascale. He knew he had treated her poorly, and for a long time, but would she, could she, have betrayed him with such devastating effect?

"We're here," Pascale announced as she drove into the Waitrose car park and selected a parking space nearest to the Wheatsheaf.

222

"I suggest we all pass to the hypnotic plane and make sure the building is empty and safe. For now, at least. Apart from you, Hugo. For obvious reasons."

The others murmured their agreement and all became motionless in the car. Iago had to be asked to be let out of the car, an indignity he did not enjoy.

To a passerby, it would have looked as though someone was playing some kind of elaborate practical joke – everyone staring straight ahead, motionless, waiting for the unsuspecting victim to walk by, as a cat made its way from the car towards the back gate of the Wheatsheaf.

On the hypnotic plane, however, they were assembled and began fanning out across the road that led to the front door of the one-time pub. Iago silently jumped onto the rear wall that enclosed the back yard. He scanned the area circumscribed by the wall and saw nothing to alarm him. He jumped down from the wall and jumped up to the windowsill which gave him a view of the hallway. Nothing. Isobel and Patrick projected themselves upstairs while Pascale entered the downstairs, soon joined by Iago (who entered through the cat flap) in the drawing room.

"Looks like it's all clear."

"Yes," Hugo's voice replied inside her head.

She looked at Iago and tried to imagine what it must be like for Hugo, trapped as he was inside the cat's body. Although she'd taken some pleasure, amusement even, from his predicament, it was clear to her that he must have suffered greatly. And continued to suffer, existing in that form.

"How do you manage to cope with this?"

"It's not easy. To begin with, although it was hard, I thought it wouldn't be for long. And that made it easier to bear."

"But it's been four years now," Pascale reflected, sadly.

"It certainly has. And my body is occupied by someone else. I just don't know, even if I could reinstate myself in the body, whether it's the right thing to do. I mean what would happen to... what's his name?" Hugo was testing Pascale.

"Simon." She said, seeing through him immediately.

"To Simon." There was a lengthy pause. "You care for him, don't you?"

Pascale was taken aback both by the question and by Hugo's insight. She must have betrayed her feelings with her expression.

"It's ok. In a way I'm flattered. It's still my physical form you're interested in."

"I don't know whether I *am* interested in him, Hugo. I don't know whether it's your body or Simon's personality that attracts me to him."

"Perhaps it's both."

Pascale was rocked by this and deeply irritated. Hugo had struck a deep nerve, which suggested to her there was some truth, a lot of truth, in what he had just said.

"Maybe you're right," she barely whispered.

"That's not really why I wanted to speak to you."

Pascale looked a little crestfallen.

"What else is there?"

"I didn't share everything that I learned from the man in the Eagle and Child."

Pascale felt a sense of dread creeping up on her.

"We were betrayed by Patrick." Hugo let these words sink in before he added, "He conspired with Antoine to remove Rebecca from the Council of Elders and to appoint an outsider as the président."

"I don't believe you."

"It's true, Pascale. I'm not lying and the man I took this information from certainly couldn't have lied. The Enemy are cock-a-hoop that they've turned the most powerful member of ASH into their ally. They think it's only a matter of time before the whole organisation is destroyed, taken over by the new président and her shadowy friends."

"This is a lot to take in Hugo," Pascale looked anxiously around her, half expecting Patrick to come into their presence.

"I know."

"Who is the new président exactly, and who are her shadowy friends as you put it."

"She's called Olivia Beaumont and she works for the Federation of Digital Entrepreneurs, or FoDE for short."

"I've heard of them. Aren't they all those twatty boys who made millions, billions even, from tech inventions?"

"The very same. And they're not to be underestimated."

"And what do they want from us?"

"The same as anyone who covets the secret knowledge and skills of our world – they want to control the hypnotic plane. To take it over for their own ends. Imagine the value

225

of our secrets! If they were available to the highest bidder, what state actor wouldn't be prepared to pay out vast amounts of cash and power to secure them? For all the reasons that Puységur took such pains to protect the knowledge held by ASH, we can't let this happen."

"Well they've made a bloody good start by getting Olivia Beaumont installed as président!" Pascale was frightened, but used her anger to make her fear, her anxiety, more manageable. "And how could Patrick sell us out? He's always been like a father, to all of us."

"I know. He and I fought side by side in the last conflict and when I learned of his betrayal, I couldn't accept it, couldn't believe it was true."

"We need to bring ourselves in from the car. And I need to think about this some more."

"I know you do. Just... be careful Pascale, and don't talk to Isobel about this."

Just as he was finishing his sentence, Pascale disappeared as she returned to her physical form. The other two were already back in the car. Pascale had the sense she had interrupted their conversation.

"Ah, there you are," Isobel said. "We were wondering where you'd got to."

"I'm here now. Why don't we go inside?"

Chapter 24

It was getting dark as we flew up the west coast of France. The shore remained in sight which was a comfort to me. I'm not usually a nervous flier, but Claudine was flying the jet at a very low altitude, it seemed to me, and the chances of crashing seemed unreasonably high. Not that I was in anyway an expert, I kept reminding myself. Although I had had fallen asleep soon after take-off, once I had opened my eyes, pure adrenaline was keeping me awake now.

"Where are we going to land?"

Claudine looked across at me.

"You're awake then. Seeing as you ask, Cotswold Airport."

I nearly burst out laughing.

"The Cotswolds really has an airport?"

"Where did you think we were going to land, Heathrow? That would take some explaining, now wouldn't it? No flight plan, passports, clearance from Spain to depart."

"Yeah ok, so how come we can avoid all those things at the Cotswold Airport then?" I asked, with some attitude.

Claudine rolled her eyes before replying.

"Because they close at 5pm, and we won't be there until nearer 7pm."

"What do you mean they close?"

"I mean, their opening hours are 9am to 5pm Tuesday to Saturday."

"And how will we land if it's closed?" I was starting to get even more anxious.

"On the runway of course. My god you really aren't all that bright, are you?"

I was stung by Claudine's last insult and decided to stop my lines of questioning, despite having plenty more to go down. Instead I sank a bit lower in my seat and watched as the French coast soon gave way to the sea, indicating we were over the English Chanel. Even at the ludicrously low altitude we were flying at, the sheer number of craft using these shipping lanes was astonishing.

In a few minutes we passed over the very edge of England and turned to my right, presumably towards the airport. I thought I could make out the Cornish coast, as we made our way north east, further in land.

"When we approach the airport, we're going to be coming in very low and very fast to keep off the radar. When we land we'll taxi towards some parking spaces owned by a flying club. If you see anyone, say nothing. Look in my bag for some keys, they've got a plane as a key ring."

I did as Claudine asked and found a car remote fob for a BMW and a high security key for some kind of door lock or padlock I imagined.

"I've got them."

"When we taxi up to a small hangar, I want you to get out, open the hangar doors and drive the car out. I'll taxi the plane inside and then you can come and get me out."

"Ok," I said. This all sounded ridiculously easy.

"Then I want you to take me to the Bear Hotel. I take it you know where that is?"

"I'll take you wherever I want, Claudine. I've got rather an explosive temper, remember?"

"I do remember, Simon," she said using my actual name. "But I think you deserve to know a bit more about who you are and why you're in the predicament you're in. And the Bear Hotel is the only place that that's going to happen."

I knew the Bear well, of course. The only hotel of any scale in Wantage and it was directly on the marketplace. Legend has it that Paul Weller stayed there once. Quite why he would want to stay in Wantage had never been made clear in the retelling of this story but, being before social media had made all things credible and incredible to someone, I imagined the story was true.

"Ok, the Bear Hotel it is."

With that, Claudine dropped the nose of the aircraft, picking up speed in the process, and banked sharply to the east. The sun had set behind us some ten minutes earlier and what little light remained didn't seem anywhere nearly enough to land by.

"I assume the landing lights won't be on?"

"Correct," Claudine said with some relish as she flew the plane even lower and even faster.

Up ahead I could make out a small town to our right and cars on what looked to be a fairly busy road to our left.

"That's Tetbury," said Claudine, as if reading my thoughts.

"The runway is not far now."

She throttled back the aircraft and the noise in the cabin dropped. For a moment I thought we were going to land on the road – we crossed it at what seemed to be a very low altitude – but instead, as the fields below got closer and closer, I heard what I imagined was the undercarriage moving into place. We passed over some barns with neatly stacked, plastic wrapped sileage adjacent to them. I stopped myself from asking Claudine exactly when we were going to land, deciding to let her put her full attention to the task in hand. I realised we would be landing imminently when I saw two hangers to our left and the vague outline of the runway coming into view.

She flared the aircraft and landed with some skill on the rear wheels before gently nudging the nose down as we lost speed. Braking sharply I felt my body weight being taken by the seatbelt across my chest and lap. Improbably for Cotswold Airport, there were large commercial passenger jets parked up on our left in front of some more hangers.

"Do you want to see something weird?"

I hesitated.

"Go on then."

We taxied to the end of the runway before turning left. As we did so I saw the outline of maybe half a dozen jets, each in differing stages of dismemberment. Engines missing, one or more wings removed. It was a strange and sad sight.

"This is where old aircraft come to die, to be taken apart, components re-used or melted down for scrap."

Claudine said this with some pleasure. I sat still, uncomfortable.

Heading back in the direction from whence we had come, Claudine turned the aircraft to the right and pulled up close to a hanger.

"Off you pop," she said.

I did as I was asked, working out how to open the door and let down the steps. As I crossed the hanger I took out the keys I had previously taken from her bag and looked for the right key for the padlocked hanger door. In a few moments the door was open and I was driving out a rather plush BMW 7 series. I considered just driving away. To be honest I was getting pretty sick of Claudine but her promise of more information persuaded me to go along with her requests for a little longer.

Once the aircraft was safely in the hanger, I helped Claudine into the car. The front passenger seat this time. Then, having re-secured the hanger door, we drove away and joined the A433 towards Cirencester. In a little less than 15 minutes we'd navigated this ancient town and were on the A417 heading towards Wantage. My own estimate was that we'd be there in about 50 minutes.

"Did you book us some rooms then, in the Bear?" I felt like needling Claudine and this seemed to fit my inclination in that moment.

"You took my phone, remember?"

I did remember and hoped that whatever attempts had been made to find Claudine had resulted in her would-be rescuers drawing a blank in some remote olive farm in Andalucia. The reality was somewhat less helpful.

Claudine's goons had tracked the phone down, sure enough, in a matter of a few hours. The farmer who drove the tractor and trailer had been spoken with and descriptions of the two people in the car provided. The farmer's description of Olivia (as they knew her) was not hard to recognise and they soon made sense of the description of me. Especially with my very English-accented Spanish. They'd arrived at the aeropuerto less than an hour after we had departed and poor Mateo had been unable to resist their entreaties for information, despite loyally (so he thought) feigning ignorance of any recent departures.

The would-be rescuers were on their way to Seville airport within minutes, booking a commercial flight landing in Gatwick late the same night.

We were close to Wantage now. The pretty towns of Lechlade and Fairford on the old A417 gave way to Faringdon, some 10 miles short of our destination. As we briefly drove on the A420, before turning off onto the A417 once again, I began to let my mind wander.

What exactly was Claudine going to tell me and, whatever she said, how likely was this to be the truth? I wasn't at all sure that I would be able to discern lie from actuality and I saw the considerable potential Claudine had for

232

manipulating me. I had no external points of reference against which to judge whatever she told me. Any normal person can triangulate statements against things they already know to be true. But if my existence had been conjured up by Claudine and injected into my mind, then what on earth could I do to test whatever she was telling me? The only means of doing so, to my thinking anyway, was to get past the door that had blocked my recollections when I'd try to access them before. If only I could find the damn key!

In a few minutes we were pulling into the marketplace in Wantage, conveniently able to park a few metres away from the Bear Hotel.

"I'll just go and check they've got some rooms for us."

I made my way across the road that circumnavigates the central car parking spaces and across the cobbles towards the hotel. As I entered, the bar to my left was half full, as always. Regulars and hotel guests co-existing uncomfortably, favourite chairs being sat in by the unwitting, and unfriendly looks exchanged. Experience had told me that by 10pm the antipathy would be well on the way to changing, alchemically, into long lost friendship and promises to meet again the following night. The power of alcohol. Either that or a proper punch up and a visit to A&E.

The receptionist looked up as I approached, leaving his mobile phone face up the desk behind which he sat.

"Can I help?"

"Yes. I'd like two rooms for tonight please."

"*Two* rooms?" Accompanied by a sucking of teeth.

I decided that silence was the best response.

"Well," he said, looking like he was about to deliver both bad and good news at the same time. I was not wrong.

"The good news is, we're not totally booked up for tonight. The bad news is that we've only got one room. Although it is a banger, to be fair." He winked, left me at a complete loss to know what on earth he meant.

"Double or twin?" I asked, already knowing the answer.

"Double sir," the receptionist replied with the slightest impression of a smile playing out across his lips.

"I'll take it."

"It is quite expensive, I'm afraid. £120 including breakfast."

"That's fine, I'll take it."

"Well, if you're sure..." The receptionist doing his bed-selling job left me far from sure, but I could see no other option other than going to my home, and that was not going to happen.

"You can pay tomorrow morning. It's on the ground floor and it's a disabled room, I'm afraid. All this bloody political correctness means we have to accommodate everyone, if you know what I mean."

"I'll just go and get my friend. She's a paraplegic – that means she can't walk, if you know what I mean."

I turned on my heel after briefly glancing at the receptionist, now looking rather pale and unsure whether I'd made or joke, or he'd made a major faux pas.

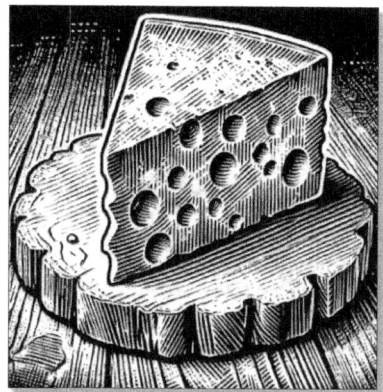

Chapter 25

Inside the Wheatsheaf, Isobel had lit a fire in the drawing room from the logs she found in a basket to one side of the chimney breast. The four of them were seated. Two in armchairs (Pascale and Isobel) and two on the sofa (Patrick and Iago). All of them were staring into the flames, looking for something. Perhaps inspiration, truth, a sense of what was happening and how it might resolve. All of them were dog tired and in need of a decent night's rest.

As the logs slowly burned down to a bright red glow, their heat intensifying, one by one they fell asleep. First Iago, then Pascale, and finally Isobel. Only Patrick remained awake, his mind still waiting for an answer to what was happening and what must be done.

His thoughts kept on returning to the last meeting of the Council of Elders and the election of Olivia Beaumont to président. The clear irritation in response to his questioning process and the protestations that he had in fact agreed were beginning to trouble him more and more.

At the time, he'd thought this was merely an affection, a ploy designed to cast doubt on his views and to minimise his opposition. Antoine was many things, but an accomplished actor he was not. The more Patrick reflected on Antoine's reactions the more he came to think that they were genuine. And then there was Janice. In all the years he had known her, she had never made any kind of error in organising the meetings of the Elders, and yet she thought he had given his apologies for the meeting.

Involuntarily, Patrick reached up to stroke his temple, the one he had so spectacularly smashed against the door frame in Aberystwyth. Could he really have done some damage to his brain? Were his memories starting to go, was this the beginning of some kind of dementia. He had felt more tired of late but nothing that would have led him to think that he was losing his grip.

Whilst he wasn't so arrogant that he would rule it out completely, Patrick decided to put this particular explanation to one side, at least for now. Could someone be impersonating him? It seemed so improbable as to be ridiculous. In any case, how could anybody without the requisite skills access the hypnotic plane, let alone take on his appearance?

The only person who had the skill to do anything like this was sitting next to him. If Hugo could take the form of a cat and reanimate it, who knows what else he could be capable of. But even so, he had known Hugo since... His thought trailed off.

"Patrick," Hugo spoke to Patrick's mind. He replied in kind.

"Yes, Hugo?"

"I need to tell you something."

Silence hung between them, both primed and ready for whatever was coming next.

"When I took the information from that man in the Eagle and Child, he told me things that I didn't share with the others."

"Go on."

"He told me that you betrayed us. That you sold us out to FoDE and that woman, Olivia Beaumont."

"And did you believe him?"

"Yes, I did."

"Oh."

Hugo was relieved to have told Patrick what he knew, what he believed. Patrick was satisfied that he now had a chance to challenge Hugo.

"Well, my friend, I have my doubts about you."

"Go on," Hugo answered in slight mockery of Patrick's earlier reply.

"What would you be prepared to do to get your original body back?"

Hugo said nothing. He knew the answer and he knew that Patrick knew the answer. A motive for betrayal was very clear and very present.

"So perhaps you can understand why I have my doubts about you, Hugo."

"Of course I can. But why would that man believe what he did about you betraying us?"

"I've only got your word to take on that, haven't I Hugo? No-one else got inside his head, now did they?"

Unusually for Hugo, he had jumped the gun. Of course Patrick was right but he knew what was in the man's head.

"Here's another perspective for you: even if he did believe that I had betrayed you and the others, it doesn't mean he was correct, does it?"

"No."

Silence.

Both knew where their line of arguments were heading, it was inevitable. If cats were capable of shuddering then Iago would have done so on behalf of his reluctant tenant. Patrick felt his pulse rise and adrenaline start to flood his system until he consciously brought them back to something like normal.

"Who should do it?" Asked Hugo.

"We can't ask the same person to work on both of us."

"Ok, then I'll take Pascale, you can have Isobel."

"Out of the question. Her misplaced loyalty to you would make it impossible. You have Isobel and I'll have Pascale."

"Very well."

The fire was dying down, only a few embers were left. Patrick stood up and put more logs on the fire. This woke up both women, as he knew it would.

Turning his back to the fire he addressed both women directly.

"Hugo and I have been having a little chat. He thinks I have betrayed ASH and I think he might have done so. We need to resolve this quickly and decisively –"

"No, Patrick!" Isobel interrupted the old man. Pascale gently placed an arm across her as an entreaty for her not to interrupt.

"Quickly and decisively. And we all know there is only one way to do that."

In the early days of ASH, Puységur has battled continuously with spies and infiltrators. Interrogating suspects took much time and considerable effort, and even then the results were never clear. Instead, and much to Puységur's distaste, a simple, effective and incredibly brutal means of summary interrogation and punishment was discovered from ancient Saxon Palimpsests from more than a 1,000 years earlier. The practice was known as Corsned or the Morsel of Excreation, another word for curse.

Originally, a small piece of bread and cheese was consecrated with a form of exorcism. If the person receiving the Morsel was able to eat it, all well and good. If it created choking or convulsions then they were guilty of the crimes of which they were accused.

In ASH's version, the subject was placed under hypnosis and told that if they were guilty of lying, then after having drunk or eaten whatever object their accusers determined, they would die. The results were spectacular if brutal.

Although all ASH members knew of the Morsel of Excreation, its practice had been outlawed, if only relatively recently, in the 1920s. It was one of a number of forbidden practices for which the penalty for defying the ban was severe, ranging from an amnesiac hypnotic lock all the way to death.

"I agree with Patrick."

Pascale and Isobel looked at the man and the cat before them, both finding it hard to believe what was being said.

"It's really very simple," Hugo continued, "I *know* Patrick betrayed us, and he *thinks* I may have done. Until we resolve this, we can't possibly deal with the circumstances we now find ourselves in. Which are, may I remind you, a direct threat to ASH's continued existence and therefore the existence of the Hypnotic Plane."

"We are not the only guardians of the Plane Hugo," Patrick said by way of a rebuke. Before Hugo could reply he added, "But I say again. This is the only way to resolve this quickly and... accurately."

"You know the consequences if either of you are caught in a lie, don't you? You're not some idiotic pubescent public schoolboys playing the biscuit game, whose consequences may be disgusting but, as far as I know, never fatal."

Pascale unwisely asked, "What's the biscuit game?"

"Look it up!" The other three rejoined in unison. A slightly uncomfortable pause ensued, Pascale wondering what on earth they had meant.

Isobel was the first to break the silence.

"Fuck it, let's just get on with this. I hope you both know what you're doing."

"You need to do this as well Pascale."

"Patrick, I'm really not sure – "

"I want you to perform the ritual with me as your subject, Isobel you take Hugo."

"Fine with me," said Isobel.

Patrick fixed Pascale with his legendary look and soon enough she acquiesced. Without saying anything else those in human form cleared a space around the sofa, moving it to the centre of the room. Once this was completed, they stopped and looked at each other.

"Right then," said Isobel.

"Right then," said Pascale with rather less conviction.

"Right then," Patrick practically growled.

"I'll go first," Hugo's voice declared as Iago hopped up onto the sofa.

Isobel wasted no time in settling down in front of Iago, her back to the fireplace.

"Hugo," she said out loud, "Hugo we are about to perform a sacred and potentially deadly ritual. It is important that you understand that the combined hypnotic powers of those present will cause your immediate death if anything you say is untrue. Do you accept the terms of this ordeal?

Without hesitation Hugo responded that he did.

"Then we will begin."

Isobel, using the ancient ways of ASH, proceeded to place Hugo in a deep, deep, state of relaxation and then, finally, hypnosis. The others in the room could easily sense when this had happened from their many years as hypnotisers and from being hypnotised – even when the subject was a cat. His consciousness was that of Hugo, and it was this they sensed.

Hugo, you will soon be brought to consciousness whereupon you will be asked to eat the Morsel of Excreation. If you have been lying about Patrick then eating the Morsel will cause your immediate death. This hypnotic edict is irrevocable and is eternally embedded in your hypnotic mind.

"I now turn to those ASH members here present and invoke the power of the Corsned. Each of you shall pour your full and deadly hypnotic curse onto the Morsel of Excreation."

Pascale looked at the other two.

"We have got a Morsel of Excreation, haven't we?"

"Oops," Isobel remarked, before reaching into her pocket. "I've got a wine gum?"

"For fuck's sake," Patrick sighed, "do cat's eat wine gums?"

"Probably not..."

With that Isobel disappeared into the kitchen at the other end of the house. She soon returned with a piece of cheese. A bit dry and a bit mouldy but probably still appetising to cats.

Each of them placed a hand over the cheese before Pascale said,

"By all the values we hold dear, our scared oath to ASH and the glory of the Hypnotic Plane, we each place an excreation in this Morsel, bound together in deadly effect, for any deceiver who takes it."

Visible lines of energy left each hand and focussed on the cheese, leaving a vague aura of illumination around it.

Pascale continued," Hugo, I command that you return to consciousness now and face the consequences of your choice – be you truthful or a deceiver."

Hugo's consciousness awoke his cat-form which stretched and arched it's back before looking at the three humans standing around him. Hugo's voice was heard clearly.

"Right, so what have I got to eat then? I'm feeling a little peckish actually."

Pascale placed the old cheese in front of him. Iago bent down and sniffed the cheese. He recoiled slightly before Hugo's voice entered their minds once again.

"Nice – mouldy cheese. Couldn't you find anything else?"

Isobel was about to volunteer that she did indeed have an alternative, but a look from Patrick persuaded her that now may not be the time.

Bending down again, Iago nudged the cheese with his nose and then licked at it, before tilting his head to one side and chewing what was before him. It took a little more than 30 seconds until he had eaten it. The humans stared at him intently, looking for any ill effects. After a few minutes it became clear to all of them that nothing was going to happen. Relief around the room was palpable for whatever their differences, none wished death upon Hugo or his feline form.

The relief at their friend's survival started to turn to the inevitable meaning that arose from it. Hugo had been telling the truth. Slowly, one by one, each turned their head to look at Patrick. Feelings of shock, sadness, anger, disbelief were present in all of them, even Hugo.

"Well then," Patrick said.

"Well then," Hugo's voice replied.

Chapter 26

Helping Claudine into her powered wheelchair, helpfully already stowed in the boot of the large BMW, was somewhat inelegant. My own lack of dexterity brought me and Claudine face to face rather too closely on a few occasions. This three dimensional game of wheelchair twister finally came to an end when I clumsily dumped Claudine into her seat. Whatever irritation she must have felt was dulled by the sheer fatigue we were both now feeling.

The cobbles of the hotel forecourt continued beyond the reception area right up to the door of our so called disabled room. I opened the door and Claudine went inside.

We were soon settled in, having not yet grasped the thorny issue of where we would sleep, and after ordering some food to be brought to the room, we sat regarding each other. Claudine on her chair, me on the bed.

"Aren't you curious as to why I wanted to come to Wantage?"

There was a softness that I'd never heard in her voice before. I immediately put it down to tiredness.

"Now you come to mention it, it does seem a little... unlikely."

"It does, doesn't it!"

Claudine broke into a chuckle. Something else I'd never heard before. She was clearly more relaxed than I'd seen previously, something that left me feeling distinctly uncomfortable. Claudine paused, as if deciding whether to tell me something.

"Have you ever heard of King Alfred?"

I snorted with derision.

"I'll take that as a yes. Well our AI came up with some fascinating information about the old cake burner. It turns out a scholar in Oxford had been to the Vatican Library and had uncovered some rather intriguing records. It turns out Alfred was able to travel on the Hypnotic Plane. Not only that but he used his abilities to spy on the Vikings, hence his many successes in battle, at least once he learned how to travel. But of most interest was a reference to a weapon. If you know your history, you'll have heard of it. It's known as the Alfred Jewel."

It was my turn to scoff.

"What, the Alfred Jewel in the Ashmolean Museum? That's a pointer to help people read – the English translation of the Bible probably. Aren't you taking the old 'the pen is mightier than the sword' a bit too literally?"

"Do you remember what is inscribed on the Jewel?"

246

"Something about Alfred giving an instruction?"

"Close, but no. For centuries, scholars have translated the inscription, Aelfred Mec Heht Gewyrcan –as 'Alfred ordered me to be made'. They were wrong. The word Gewycrcan comes from a Batavian verb, Gawirkijan, meaning to work. I can see why they got I wrong, but the real translation is 'Alfred orders me to work' meaning Alfred activates the special properties the Jewel has."

"Thanks for the history lesson, but so what?"

"Ah dear Simon, you're missing the point – literally. The records hinted that the Jewel, in Alfred's hand enabled him to focus extraordinary amounts of hypnotic power through the Jewel and to direct that at whatever or whoever he wished."

"Like a light sabre!" I exclaimed excitedly, immediately feeling embarrassed. Claudine sighed but went on.

"Yes, if you must. There was something about the gold and rock crystal that allowed him to focus the energy into something quite extraordinary."

I contemplated what she had just told me and tried to see how that related to me and my current situation. I failed.

"Go on," I said, hoping things would get clearer.

"It wasn't something that could only be used as a destructive force. He could use it to open the Hypnotic Plane to anyone and by doing so, he was able to move his soldiers from place to place. Either their hypnotic projections or the real, physical forms. That's how he was able to defeat the Vikings and become the greatest monarch of them all."

I contemplated what Claudine had just told me. Then the penny dropped.

"You've got it, haven't you? The Alfred Jewel?"

"Yes."

"So what's to stop you doing whatever it is you want to? Finding Hugo, for example?"

"We did find Hugo and one of our very best agents tried using the Jewel against him."

"What happened?" I asked with trepidation, expecting the story I had been told in Spain by Hugo as Iago to be confirmed.

"We had some success. After all you're here in Hugo's body. But where is Hugo, that's the question."

"He's probably dead," I lied.

"Oh no he's not. I can still sense him. He's alive somewhere, in someone, but I don't know where or in whom, not yet."

"Why don't you just use the Jewel?"

"An intelligent question, at last. It seems that using the Jewel has some, well, disadvantages. Learning to use it is hard enough but anyone who has tried to use it in earnest more than a few times, has ended up losing their mind."

"What do you mean?"

"Just that. They psychologically disintegrate, go insane if you will."

"How many have tried this?"

"Enough for us to know it is a very costly instrument to use."

I couldn't help feeling relieved that Claudine didn't have access to the Jewel's powers herself, the thought of it made me shiver.

"You said you were going to tell me more about my background?"

"I did, didn't I?" Claudine replied.

"You also told me you'd put a hypnotic lock on my mind."

"I did say that."

"And that I'd started to get around it"

"Also true."

"Why would you help me?"

"Now we're getting to the heart of things, aren't we? For one reason and one reason only Simon, to take my revenge on Hugo. If I let you into the history of your mind, to fully integrate what you know and what you can't currently remember, then you can fully occupy that little head of yours. I'm hoping that will mean Hugo will be obliterated for ever, with no prospect at all of coming back to his body."

"You really hate him that much?"

"Well yes. And I'm just a little bit curious to see if you can take being confronted with the truth of your previous existence as Hugo, and the loss of your present identity. Does your ego have sufficient strength I wonder? For all intents and purposes you are only four years old, albeit an adult for all that time."

For the first time, I stopped to consider what exactly I might find behind that locked door in my mind. So much of our mental process is invisible to us at the best of times, but I'd been created, a personality imposed on me, to suit the whims and desires of others. As time went on, especially after the explosion in Spain, I'd felt more and more estranged from the implanted personality I'd apparently been given. Not to say I wasn't feeling more confident, I was, I just had no idea of what had led me here, what informed the way I was behaving every day.

This was definitely a red pill versus blue pill moment. Just like Neo in the Matrix, I knew what I wanted to do, whatever the consequences.

"Fine. So tell me."

"You are an impetuous little bunny! It's not a matter of me telling you, Simon. It's just a matter of releasing the hypnotic lock, and guess who's got the key?"

"I'm tired of you patronising me. Give me the key or fuck off. Even better, I'll fuck off and leave you to the delights of room service."

Claudine regarded me with what appeared to be a mixture of curiosity and amusement. She paused.

"Come here Simon. Please."

I moved off the bed and stood by the side of her chair.

"Bend over so I can whisper something in your ear that'll release the hypnotic lock."

I did as she asked.

"Seven-seven-zero-eight-one-two."

"That's it."

I was confused. And also embarrassed to ask her how to use these numbers, so I said nothing more. A knock came on the door.

"At last, I'm starving," Claudine said as she manoeuvred her chair towards the only desk in the room. "Get that, will you?"

I sighed and opened the door to let whatever culinary delights the Bear could muster, be brought into the room. In front of me were two men dressed in black. Before I had a chance to speak, let alone move, I was jabbed with a cattle prod or taser like weapon. I felt a surging pain throughout my whole body followed by going completely rigid before I felt myself collapsing onto the floor. Before I even hit the ground, all went dark.

*

From far in the distance I heard the sound of knocking. Then again.

"Hello? Hello? It's room service."

"We've got your dinners here, can you open the door?"

Somehow the voice of the hotel staff member penetrated my consciousness. They knocked on the door once again as I just about managed to get to my feet.

"Come in," I managed in a hoarse whisper.

"Oh, I've woken you up, I am sorry."

A kindly-faced woman of about my own age pushed a trolley into the room, upon which were two plates under metal domes, presumably concealing the meals we'd ordered.

"Where would you like them?"

"Sorry?"

"The plates, where would you like me to put them?"

Given there was only one desk in the room it seemed a redundant question. In the bathroom, I was tempted to reply, but instead simply indicated the desk that was last occupied by Claudine. I looked around the room. She and her chair were gone.

"Did you see my friend?, the one in the wheelchair?"

"I did, yes. She was leaving with two other gentlemen, towards the square. They got into a big car parked in the market place I believe."

I felt my pockets for the car keys and of course they were gone.

"Ok thanks."

"Will there be anything else?" The kindly-faced lady asked.

"No, thank you."

Looking a little peeved, she pushed the trolley out of the room and closed the door behind her. I gingerly lifted the domes that covered the two plates, expecting something awful to be lurking underneath. Instead, the food looked very good. I wasted no time and greedily got stuck into both dishes. One a Thai green curry and the other some kind of cassoulet. Both were delicious and, hungry as I was, I polished off both in a matter of minutes.

My immediate need for sustenance having been met, my aching body made its presence felt along with pressing fatigue. I barely had the energy to check the door was locked before I returned to the bed, asleep in seconds, fully clothed and on top of the covers.

Chapter 27

"Let's get this over with," said Patrick in an entirely matter of fact manner as he virtually pushed Iago off the sofa and lay down in his place. His brusqueness perhaps masking an element of fear – an unusual emotion for Patrick, outside of actual conflict.

Isobel, looking concerned said "Are you entirely sure about this Patrick?"

Before he could reply, Hugo's voice joined in, "Patrick, you don't have to do this. We can work things out together."

Patrick looked around at his compatriots at first steely eyed and then with what seemed to be affection – love even – before he replied.

"And what good would that do any of us? Your suspicions would remain and I would resent that, knowing I have only spoken the truth."

Isobel, Patrick and Iago turned to look at Pascale, the one who would carry out this ritual with Patrick. She shifted uneasily on her feet, looking anywhere but at Patrick until, having clearly made up her mind, she said,

"No. I can't do this. I won't do this." She left the room and shortly afterwards the others heard the sound of the front door closing.

"Well then, Isobel, it will have to be you," Patrick said as he gave Isobel a kindly smile.

"But what if you are a deceiver, Patrick? What then?"

"Then I will die." He replied plainly and with no emotion.

Patrick entered the mind of Isobel and quickly spoke, "Isobel, I had to do this to draw out Hugo. And now we know he is not the betrayer. If I have really lost my mind, and I am guilty of betraying ASH, then it's better that I do die. So, please, let's get this over with. One way or another."

Out loud, Patrick made a request.

"I really don't fancy that mouldy cheese – which may kill me either way – so how about one of your wine gums Isobel?"

He winked at her as she reached into her pocket. Retrieving her packet of wine gums with tears in her eyes.

Isobel performed the ritual as she done before. She and Iago place a hand and paw on a wine gum and they imbued it with the energy of the excreation. She brought Patrick back to consciousness and, like some kind of truth-telling communion, administered the Excreation Morsel.

"Patrick, I command that you return to consciousness now and face the consequences of your choice – be you truthful or a deceiver."

Patrick came round quickly and, with one last look around the room, held out his hand. Pascale placed the wine gum on his hand. Patrick fixed his gaze on Isobel, who stared with love and hope back at him. Without looking down at the Morsel of Excreation, Patrick brought his hand to his mouth. He chewed and quickly swallowed, eyes still locked on Isobel. After a few seconds the expression on Patrick's face began to change. Isobel tried to control her growing alarm. His face contorted and he started to look like he was going to wretch. Isobel couldn't believe her eyes. She knew there was a risk, but Patrick had been insistent, demanding even. Patrick started to cough.

"Oh my god, Patrick, I am so sorry!"

Patrick fell to the floor, on all fours as he continued to wretch and cough. Isobel knelt down next to him, her arm around his shoulders. Even Iago sat close to Patrick, offering what physical comfort he could.

Patrick turned to face Isobel, he looked pale and drawn. He whispered something.

"What's that Patrick, I can't hear you"

She drew closer to him, inclining her ear towards his mouth. Patrick finally drew in enough breath and spoke clearly into her ear.

Chapter 28

Pascale had closed the door to the Wheatsheaf behind her, after she left the room with the others, and turned right onto Grove Street and walked in the direction of the marketplace. She couldn't believe how stupid men could be. Or rather, how stupid males could be. Given that one male was a human and the other male was in the form of a cat.

There had always been tension between Patrick and Hugo but those around them had managed this more or less effectively over the years. But this! This was too much *and* it meant the focus of the group was looking inwards instead of outwards, all due to the pride and ego of those two idiots.

Although she hardly relished the idea of potentially killing an old friend and senior member of ASH, the reason why she refused to perform the ritual was because of its stupidity, and not for lack of stomach on her part. Plenty had perished at her hands over the years and for them she felt nothing. They had died as an enemy and where there was no other choice. But these two had choices, they just refused to acknowledge them.

As Pascale walked along Grove Street she was suddenly struck by the absence of people around her. The houses on either side looked pretty and even the tyre depot had its place in the town environment. But there was no-one around.

She reached the end of Grove Street as it meets Mill Street and joins the marketplace. She paused, her instincts interceding with her thoughts. Looking carefully around the corner she saw two men dressed in black and a woman in a powered wheelchair making their way from the Bear Hotel towards the parking spaces in the centre of the marketplace. Without showing herself, she saw them climb into a large black car, stowing the wheelchair in the boot, and driving at speed out of the square along Wallingford Street and hence to who knows where.

After waiting for a minute or two to see if there were any other potential threats or things that peaked her instincts, she let her curiosity take over. She walked across the square and made her way towards the Bear Hotel. She wanted to know who they were and why they were here. And whether they were coming back.

Finding the reception desk, she rang the bell.

"What can I do for you miss?"

"It's Ms." Pascale replied

"It's what?" The receptionist looked confused.

"It doesn't matter. A friend of mine is staying with you, a lady in a wheelchair. Can you tell me which room she's in?"

"Ah well, the thing is you see, you might be out of luck there."

The receptionist practically licked his lips, being the custodian of information that this beautiful woman in front of him required.

Pascale simply fixed him with a look that made him feel more and more uncomfortable and, unfathomably, warmer and warmer to the point where the receptionist tried to loosen the collar on his shirt. He decided the best thing to do was to tell her whatever he could, and hope that she would go away. He said, rapidly:

"She left a few minutes ago with a couple of her friends. But the man she came with is still in his room, I think, enjoying a bit of room service."

The receptionist managed to resist the temptation to wink at Pascal, who continued to look at him adding to his growing discomfort.

"He's in room 104, in case you wanted to go and see him," the receptionist said, almost pleadingly, and completely defeated by this strange woman.

Taking full advantage, Pascale slid the guest register across the desk towards her and looked for the registration details for room 104. Her finger travelled down the page until, for the very last and most recent entry, she found the room she was looking for. She tried not to show any emotion. It can't be! She thought. But of course, her ruminating continued, only he would use his real name to sign into a hotel.

Saying nothing, Pascal turned on her heels, following the signs for rooms 100 to 110. The receptionist breathed a sigh of relief with her departure and the sense that his body temperature was starting to cool down.

She paused as she approached the room. Could it really be him or was this some kind of elaborate deception. She returned to the reception desk. The receptionist visibly shrank as she approached.

"This man in the room, what does he look like?"

"I-I-I..." the receptionist was struggling to speak.

In the interests of saving time, so Pascale told herself, she decided to extract the information from the receptionist's head directly. She reached over to him and placed a hand on each temple.

"Stay still," she said, looking around her to make sure she was not being watched. "After this, you're going to sleep very peacefully for a long time."

The man barely nodded, struck with fear while Pascale went to work. He passed out as she quickly and as carefully as she could, delved into his recent memories. Soon enough, Pascale was satisfied and gently pushed the unconscious man back into his chair.

"Night, night."

Pascale returned to the door that belonged to room 104. For some reason she felt a little anxious, almost reluctant to knock on the door. She knew better than to dismiss her feelings as they almost always had something useful to tell her. She paused for a moment.

"Simon?" She spoke closely to the door, hoping her voice would carry through it.

"Who is it?" I asked.

"It's me, Pascale."

Hearing her voice, I flung the door open and launched myself towards Pascale, holding her with a powerful embrace. She guided me, still held in my arms, back into the room and kicked the door closed behind her.

"I am so glad to see you," I said as I extended my arms to see Pascale properly.

"I'm glad to see you too, Simon."

Pascale felt more emotion than she had expected in those words, which surprised her, but not as much as what happened next.

"I've had such a shit time, it's been like hell, and now you're here in front of me, and I'm nearly home, and..."

I stopped speaking to make way for what started as a sigh and grew into a moan and eventually a full on wail. When I caught my breath, I sobbed. Full body sobbing accompanied by floods of tears falling down my face. I couldn't speak, all I needed to do right at this moment was to release all the tension, fear, sheer terror that had been my life for the last god knows how long.

It was Pascale's turn to hold me, and she did so with tenderness and love. Part of me, despite my uncontrollable crying, felt huge emotion welling up feeling her so close to me. As my sobbing began to ease up, I felt wetness on my shoulder.

Pascale pulled away and tried to dry her eyes without me seeing her face. She gave up on the attempt as she was still crying. She looked at me through her tears.

"I am so sorry, Simon. I never meant for you to suffer in any way, and god knows what they must have done to you. I –"

"Hush, Pascale." I took both of her hands in mine. "I'll tell you, all in good time, but you mustn't blame yourself. At some point, it was inevitable that they would take me. They knew I was there all along, after all."

Pascale's face was a picture of consternation, not knowing what to make of what she had just heard and seen.

"There's more to you than meets the eye, Simon," she said, mustering a smile. "Who are you, really?" She said in an almost rhetorical way.

"Ah, well now, that's an interesting question to ask. The last few days has opened my eyes in so many ways and has allowed me to find parts of myself that I didn't know existed before."

"What do you mean?"

"Well, I know that this body I'm in belongs or belonged to someone else and I know *he* is now in the body of a cat. I was also told that my personality was made up, it's a fiction, implanted into Hugo's body. So I'm a kind of no-one, a squatter apparently."

Pascale moved as if to interrupt me, so I quickly continued.

"But the thing is, my beautiful Pascale, I don't feel like a fictional character, and during the last few days I've begun to feel very much like *me*."

"Oh," was all that Pascale had to say. He called her 'my beautiful Pascale' and that was strange enough. She wondered if remnants of Hugo were still in him. She also noticed that she had rather liked being described in this way.

261

"So what now?" Simon asked.

Pascale's thoughts immediately landed on an image of her and Simon in bed, making love passionately. Instead she shrugged and said,

"I don't know."

"I do," Simon replied with great presence and self-assurance.

Oh my god, thought Pascale, I really want this.

"I need your help to solve a puzzle."

This was really not what she had in mind and it took all her energy to try to not look disappointed.

"And if you can help me solve this puzzle, you can unlock what's been hidden from me."

Simon went on to explain the hypnotic lock, the door he saw when under self-hypnosis, and his inability to find a key to that lock. He also told her what Claudine has said to him, 7-7-0-8-1-2. He looked at Pascale expectantly, as if she would know what to do, know the answer to his puzzle.

Pascale looked back at Simon, inwardly astonished at how much he had grown and in so short a time, and yet still so unworldly.

"It's a combination lock."

"What?"

"The hypnotic lock, it's a combination lock."

"Seriously? It's as simple as that?"

"Of course. Hypnotic locks need to have a key but it can't be a real key as you've been discovering. Instead, the person who put the lock on you told you that if a certain number was spoken to you, then your memories would be unlocked. It's a way that hypnotic locks can be shared between people. Useful if the person administering the lock dies, wouldn't you say?"

"I suppose I would," I replied, my brain busily trying to catch up with the new information Pascale had imparted.

"But why can't I access my memories now then?"

"Silly boy! You have to be deep in hypnosis *and* be ready to have the hypnotic lock removed."

"Well go on then. Hypnotise me"

"Really?"

"Well why not?"

"For starters, what happens if you don't like what you find out once the lock is released?"

I honestly hadn't stopped for a moment to think about this. The possible consequences ran through my mind like lightening. I sat down on the bed, feeling defeated. Sensing my disappointment, Pascale sat next to me and put her arm around me.

"Hey, look at me."

I did as she asked.

"It's your choice, Simon. You don't even have to decide now. Not today, not next week, not even next year, but whenever you want, whenever you're ready."

I waited to see what my feelings told me. I didn't need to wait long before I knew what had to be done.

"Pascale, if I wait, I may never have the courage to look into my past, to see who I am, where I'm from and perhaps even why I am the way I am. How many people have the chance of unlocking their memories, of looking back in time like this?"

"Yes, you're right. But you may not like what you find, Simon. Have you thought of that?"

"Not until you mentioned it. But it doesn't change who I am now, today, and if there are awful things in my past, isn't it better that I face them, bring them into my consciousness, and deal with them?"

"You are an extraordinary and brave man Simon."

"I'm really not Pascale. I don't have any choice, it's who I am."

Pascale looked at me, searching my eyes and face for something.

"I believe you," she said, "and who you are is exactly what I want, what I *need*, right now."

Before I had a chance to ask Pascale what she meant, she gently held my face with both of her hands and brought her lips to mine. I closed my eyes, not really believing what was happening. My brain was trying to push a thousand questions towards my conscious mind but, for once, I pushed them away and surrendered to the feelings I felt surging through me, through us. I opened my eyes briefly to see Pascale looking at me as we kissed. She drew slightly away as we gazed at each other. Her eyes told me of her power, her vulnerability and most of all of her passion in this moment. I drew her towards me, and we fell backwards onto the bed.

Chapter 29

"I hate the yellow ones."

"What?" Isobel drew away from Patrick, confused.

"The yellow ones – they're disgusting!" An impish glint shone briefly in Patrick's eyes, when Isobel finally understood.

"Patrick, you absolute cunt!"

By this time Patrick was laughing so much that he was struggling to catch his breath, tears running down both cheeks.

"I hope you suffocate," Hugo projected the words into his friends' minds.

"You have to admit it was a bit funny," Patrick was regaining his composure and sat upright on the sofa.

"I thought you were dying, you twat! I'm almost sorry that you didn't."

"Almost? But not quite?" Patick looked with great affection at Isobel.

Isobel moved towards Patrick as though she was going to embrace him but checked herself.

"I haven't decided yet," she said, somewhat haughtily.

"Well while you two sort out your spat over Patrick's incredibly funny joke, we're still no further forward."

Turning his attention to Hugo, Patrick replied, "Oh quite the contrary my dear Hugo. We are considerable further forward in that neither you nor I have betrayed ASH. "

"There is that."

"And so, please will you accept my apology Hugo?"

Patrick bowed in contrition as he faced Iago's form to apologise. Hugo paused for what seemed an unnecessarily long time before he replied.

"I do Patrick. And for the fact that I believed what I found in that man's mind, I also apologise.

Iago inclined his head towards Patrick and lowered his gaze, mirroring Patrick's bow.

"All very touching, I'm sure, but don't ever, *ever,* ask me to anything like that again."

Silence.

"Do I make myself clear?"

"Yes Isobel."

"Yes Isobel."

"Good. Then I suggest we each try and find somewhere to sleep and reconvene in the morning."

"Where did Pascale go?" Hugo asked.

They three of them looked at each other until Patrick spoke out.

"She was clearly upset, but she's very accomplished and resourceful. She'll come back when she's ready and in the meantime, I suggest we leave her alone. In other words, let's not go looking for her just yet."

"Agreed."

"Agreed"

Iago went to sit in front of the fire on the rug and Isobel and Patrick both made their way up the wooden stairs to the long landing above the ground floor. Having each found a bedroom, with bedding already on the beds, it took little time for them to settle down and fall asleep.

Downstairs, Iago stared into the dying embers of the fire, almost trance-like. In the four years since Hugo had inhabited Iago's form he had had plenty of time to reflect on events. How Simon reappeared in his body after being taken away by The Enemy. The months and years he tailed Simon and his dull, dull life until Pascale had reappeared, having hunted him down. He guessed The Enemy had let Simon go in order to find members of ASH and even himself, Hugo. But he hadn't thought they would take Simon away again. Somewhere along the line they must have have lost track of Simon and what he was thinking. Perhaps they thought ASH would never find him. What was clear, was that for the plan to work, ASH had to have no inkling that the Enemy had placed Simon there, ready to be found.

And what of Pascale? He was excited to see her, but for him, time had moved on. He had never treated her well. A constant on-off state of affairs, almost entirely at his instigation. Now was not a time to woo her back, but neither did he feel like pushing her away. Still too selfish to put her first.

A log shifted as the fire continued to burn down, bringing Hugo's attention momentarily back to the room. He sensed something was about to shift between him and Pascale, but he couldn't divine what that was.

He resolved that there was nothing he could do, so returned his attention to the fire and, rhythmically opening and closing his cat eyes, slowly fell asleep.

Chapter 30

Lying in the darkness of the room, Pascale's warm body interlaced with mine, I felt reborn. Not in a macho or cocky way – although I had just spent half the night making love to the most fantastically, gorgeous woman – but in a way that made me feel fully human again. No, that's not right. Fully a *man* again. How interesting, I thought, that for me to feel fully a man, I had to connect deeply with a woman.

Pascale stirred slightly, as if alive to the shifting tides of my mind. I didn't want her to wake. I wanted to stay here, like this, with her, for as long as I could, hungry as I was for intimacy and comfort. There's an admission I'd never have made previously, or at least as far back as my limited mind would allow. Talking of which...

I needed to take the plunge: bring the memories that had been denied to me back into my consciousness. And I needed Pascale's help to do this. Our night together may have confused things somewhat, but equally I wasn't sure if being so close would actually help. That was, of course, an assumption on my part – the bit about being close. Perhaps I was a passing distraction for Pascale or perhaps she was simply projecting the old Hugo onto my physical form. The more I thought about it, the gloomier I became. A kind of inverse relationship to the early morning sunlight finding its way into the room.

"You look sad."

Pascale, I realised, was staring at me, wearing a look of concern. She reached out her hand and stroked my face. I turned to face her, my heart leaping for joy for this sign of affection and expression of concern.

"I was just thinking about you."

"Oh..."

"No, no, I mean I was thinking about you and me and," I stopped, realising I was digging a big hole for myself. I composed myself, took a deep breath and said,

"This means a lot to me, being here with you. And I don't want it to end."

Pascale gently placed her index finger on my lips, as if to say 'shh'. Then turning her body to face mine she reached up and brought my head down towards hers and kissed me deeply. If this was intended to stop me speaking or thinking, or both, it was working.

*

I came round to the sound of knocking on the bedroom door. I hadn't even managed to get out of the bed before the door opened, then closed again with a well-rehearsed 'sorry, I'll come back later'.

I sank back onto the bed and stared at the ceiling. Pascale was gone from the bed, but I could hear the shower in the en suite so assumed she was in there. So much had happened to me over the course of what, a week? Much of it deeply unpleasant, some of it (being totally honest) rather exciting, and now this bit. The best bit. The bit with Pascale, here and now. I resolved to enjoy the moment as much as I could, for as long as it lasted.

"Breakfast?" Pascale asked me as she emerged from the bathroom, naked, towelling her hair.

God she was beautiful! I started to feel turned on – again, amazingly – a look she must have recognised.

"Not now, I need to eat."

She came over and gave me a consoling kiss on the forehead, then continued with preparing herself for the day ahead, whatever was left of it.

By the time I had finished my shower, she was fully dressed and wore the countenance of the Pascale I had known before our coming together: still very striking but somehow carrying a burden at the same time. Before I had a chance to ask if she was ok, she spoke.

"Simon, if you want to release the hypnotic lock then I suggest we do it together with the help of some of my friends."

I was thrown rather. Of course Pascale would have friends, but it was simply not something I had considered up to this point. I even felt a pang of jealousy.

"Um, ok."

"I say friends, but they're more than that,"

The jealousy rose within me.

271

"They're also ASH members, and very skilled practitioners. So what I'm trying to say is I think they can help when we take off the hypnotic lock. It's also possible that you'll recognise them, once the lock is released."

"So they're people the cat-man knew before he left my – our – body?"

"Yes," Pascale was smiling "the cat-man knew them."

I wondered if the other man, would be there too – the one I'd briefly spoken with on the hypnotic plane in the beer garden of the Fred's Head. I was about to mention him but, instinctively, I decided to say nothing at least for now. Instead I shrugged my acceptance and finished getting dressed. Both of us now wearing the clothes we had arrived in. As we headed back towards reception and the exit, I remembered something.

"Shit!"

"What is it," Pascale looked concerned.

"I've just realised, I don't have any money on me."

I looked at Pascale, sheepishly.

"Ok," she replied evenly.

As we approached the reception desk to announce our departure, I overheard a woman, perhaps the manager, speaking into the phone.

"He's never fallen asleep before. It took two of us to wake him up and all he could say was something about having his mind read, it made absolutely no sense at all."

The receptionist looked up as Pascale dropped the room keys onto the desk and placed some cash in front of the woman at the desk. Her keen eyes counted the cash without touching it, confirming it was the right amount, and then mouthed a silent 'thank you' as we continued our way out of the hotel and into the fresh morning air of the market place.

"Where's good for breakfast? You're a local, after all."

"Well that remains to be seen, doesn't it?"

I reached for her hand – a bold move but one which I was prepared to explain as for guiding her to the other end of the market place. She drew her hand back at first, as if I had taken her by surprise, but then softened and let her hand rest in mine, slowly wrapping her fingers around my hand. I closed my eyes as I felt a rush of oxytocin wash through my body. I opened my eyes and looked ahead, gesturing with the other hand.

"There's a decent bakery over there that also serves more traditional fare, if that sound ok?"

Pascale nodded and we walked, hand in hand, towards Newbury Street, then Wallingford Street, past Waitrose and the late night convenience store until we arrived at the bakery.

Pascale opened the door for me and I walked ahead of her inside, smiling to myself and feeling another rush of oxytocin.

*

After breakfast, we'd both eaten heartily after our recent exertions, Pascale looked at me across the cup of black coffee she was cradling in both hands. It was not an unaffectionate look but neither was it one of unbridled love, that I might have hoped for. On reflection, I was happy she was looking at me at all. Ooooph! Another hormone rush. I decided to show some initiative, try to focus on something other than the one thing, or person, that was occupying almost all of my mind.

"So, shall we go?"

"Go where?"

"To wherever your friends are?

"Oh. It won't take long to get there."

"Ok, let's go."

"We need to pay first."

"Ah."

I felt embarrassed again and it showed.

"Oh Simon, I'm teasing you!"

Pascale laughed and she shone, and I felt weak all over. Utter bliss.

Paying with cash (again, I noticed) Pascale led the way out of the bakery cum café onto Wallingford Street.

"So where too?" I asked.

"To your place."

"What?"

"They're waiting at your place."

Momentarily I felt anger rise within me, but I didn't engage with it. Of all the places I'd like my memories to be unlocked, home – my home – seemed like the best place I could be.

Pascale was hesitating, I realised, waiting for me to take the lead in our short walk down Little Lane, across Waitrose's car park (messy as usual) and briefly along Stirlings Road until we reached my front door. Without thinking, I reached into my pocket for keys and of course found none. I was about to unlock the key safe when Pascale reached out to touch my arm (oooph!) to tell me not to bother. Instead she took the key that appeared in her hand and unlocked the door.

Stepping inside the vestibule I could briefly hear the voice of a man and a woman. They stopped and I got the distinct impression they were listening. As Pascale closed the front door behind me, I opened the inner door. As I did so, the door to the drawing room opened and a friendly face filled the opening.

"Hello," she said, with a broad smile.

I stood looking at her.

"Well don't just stand there. Come in, come in."

A week ago, being welcomed into my own house by a woman I didn't know would have freaked me out, but not anymore. I felt Pascale's hand on my shoulder – a gesture both of reassurance and also to guide me into the room. I stood, just inside the door. The smiling woman was there, as was the man dressed in black – he looked at me with kindness but also with intensity. And sat at one end of the sofa was Iago.

"Hello again," the familiar voice of Hugo sounded inside my mind.

I nodded. I then turned to the man who introduced himself as Patrick. He looked at me warmly and knowingly, acknowledging our earlier meeting in the beer garden. Finally, I turned to the only one I'd not met before. She turned to me and offered her hand.

"I'm Isobel, pleased to meet you."

"Likewise," I replied, unsure of what else to say.

"Sit down Simon."

Pascale guided me to the opposite end of the sofa from Iago and sat herself in the middle. Isobel and Patrick looked expectantly at her. Shifting slightly in her seat she spoke.

"Before we talk about Simon, what happened here? When I left you two were squaring up like a pair of pubescent schoolboys."

Patrick looked ever so slightly uncomfortable, Iago looked inscrutable, as a cat always does. Isobel explained.

"We completed the ritual for both of them and, as you can see, neither of them was lying. Which means – "

"- Which means," broke in Hugo, "neither of us has betrayed ASH."

"It also gives us a line of investigation," Patrick joined in, for once speaking in sync with Hugo.

"What do you mean?" Pascale looked inquisitive.

"The man whose memory Hugo interrogated couldn't have deceived us, so we need to understand exactly how I was set up as a traitor."

"You mean this was done deliberately?" Pascale's voice had changed to one of utter seriousness and concern.

"I do. And that's not all. When I visited John Adam Street and attended the Council of Elders, there were some things that made no sense at the time but which are now starting to create a picture.

"Such as," Isobel chimed in.

"Janice was surprised to see me as I had, apparently, given my apologies for the meeting. I put it down, in my irritation, to an administrative error. Something entirely unfamiliar to me in my dealings with Janice in nearly 30 years."

"Janice doesn't make mistakes..." Pascale said in little more than a whisper, as though to herself.

"Indeed she does not. But I let myself think it anyway. And then, in the meeting, I had thought Antoine's annoyance was entirely confected when he claimed I had already agreed to the changes to the constitutional process for selecting our new Président. Clearly, it was not."

Patrick looked grave and a little dejected.

"Patrick," Isobel said soothingly, "we've been over this already today. You can't blame yourself for this."

"Au contraire old friend. I missed two very obvious signs that something was amiss. And haven't I aways said to you, that it's the noting of the small details that give us the insights, the warnings and the intuition upon which we have to rely for our own survival and success?"

The room was silent. I took that silence as agreement with what Patrick had just said.

"And then there's the matter of the man whose mind I read. He believed Patick was a traitor. So what made him think that? What did he see or hear?"

The room returned to silence. No-one offered any answer to Hugo's mind-voice.

"They can control dreams, maybe that's it."

Even before I'd finished my sentence, I was feeling a little intimidated. As the three humans and one cat turned to face me, I could feel myself reddening.

"What do you mean they can control dreams, Simon?" Patrick asked kindly though I could hear a note of 'what the fuck' in his voice.

Isobel looked astonished as did Pascale. Iago continued to look inscrutable.

"It was just something that Olivia Beaumont told me – and that's not her real name by the way." I was starting to enjoy myself.

"Go on," Simon.

"They've learnt how to control dreams and can create lucid dreaming for anyone who wants it. Or doesn't in my case."

I remembered the awful insects in the place in Spain, and inwardly shuddered.

"And you think they could have used this dream-control to plant false memories in Janice, Antoine and others?"

"I don't know, but it's possible, I guess. They did it to me."

Isobel could sit down no longer and leapt to her feet.

"Christ almighty! This is appalling! Imagine the power it gives them."

"I am imagining," said Pascale grimly.

"So, that may explain some of the incongruities that we've come across," Patrick turned to me and narrowed his eyes, "you said Olivia Beaumont wasn't her real name, Simon. I can't help feeling that may be significant."

Oh shit! I regretted telling everyone this, especially Hugo. And now I had to say something. Lying really wasn't my forte, so I decided to tell them what I knew. I doubted it would land well, and I was right, only not in the way I'd thought.

"Her real name is Claudine." I paused for any reaction. Nothing.

"Oh," Patrick said, looking rather underwhelmed. He turned his gaze to the others in the room. Blank faces (among the humans), Iago looked round to meet Patrick's gaze.

"Ah..." Hugo's voice sounded simultaneously in everyone's heads.

Isobel, hawk like, stared at Iago.

"Is there something you'd like to tell us, Hugo?"

"Well, yes, there is."

Hugo went on to tell everyone the story, more or less as Claudine had told it to me. Even in his disembodied voice I could hear the emotional impact this still held for Hugo. The others in the room could hear it too, for each of them appeared visibly moved by the story which Hugo was concluding.

"...So after she came out of hospital, she refused to speak to me ever again. I felt so awful. I was only 11 eleven years old and I thought I had done a wonderful thing, to bring my friend back from the dead. I never thought for an instant that she would be so, so angry and ungrateful."

"But why is she infiltrating ASH?" Pascale asked.

"I don't know," Hugo replied.

"I do." I said flatly. "Because she told me."

"Go on," Patrick said in a voice laced with dread and expectation.

"Because she wants to destroy *you*, Hugo. She said she doesn't give a damn about the Federation of Digital Entrepreneurs, or FoDE, she just wants to destroy you. She was behind the attack on you and she's mightily pissed off that she neither killed you nor found you. And that's the reason I came back in our body,"

"My body."

"Not now Hugo," urged Pascale.

"I was the distraction."

"The what?" Isobel exclaimed.

"The distraction, the feint." They knew ASH would be looking for Hugo, just like they were. So they left me for ASH to dedicate resources to finding me, a distraction, while they got on with other things – like infiltrating ASH I suppose."

"And the attack on you, Isobel, and the other attacks I was told about at the Council of Elders," Patrick joined in.

"I saw it all and I followed Simon on the hypnotic plane to Spain, somewhere between Malaga and Marbella. I kept him company for as long as my weakened powers would allow."

"Yes, you did, Hugo. And for that I am very grateful. I wasn't quite so keen on the dream torture, but that's a story for another day. Suffice to say, Claudine knows you're not inside this body, Hugo, and that I am."

I was warming to my task.

"I managed to escape."

I chose to omit the circumstances by which I found my freedom, wisely as it turned out.

"And then by luck or something else, I managed to find my way back, with a little help from Claudine. Not that she had any choice."

"Was that who I saw, driving away in the black car last night?"

"Probably, Pascale. Before she disappeared, one of her goons smacked me in the face and laid me out cold. Again."

"Wait a minute, this doesn't make sense." Isobel brought the conversation to a standstill.

"If they'd already taken you, knew that Hugo wasn't in this body, why did they take recapture you?"

"I don't know for sure, but Olivia – Claudine – said something shortly before I escaped. She said she was concerned about my hypnotic powers, my abilities despite the absence of Hugo and the hypnotic lock they'd placed on me."

Hugo's interest was piqued.

"They put a hypnotic lock on you?"

"We'll come back to that, go on Simon," Patrick interjected.

"I think they had me under observation, so when me and Pascale went travelling, they started to wonder if Hugo was back in his body or if I'd developed some of the same skills..."

"I doubt it," Hugo said haughtily.

"We saw the men dressed in black in the Tate Modern! And that's why they came back for you. Oh Simon, I'm so sorry."

Pascale's sadness for having caused me so much pain and suffering was written all over her face, once again.

"That's not all," I began to feel a little sheepish now.

"That same night, when I went travelling on my own for a while,"

Patrick's eyebrows involuntarily moved and inch or two towards his hairline.

"I was spotted by a woman and a man, they were on the hypnotic plane as well. He was short, overweight and she was tall and rather intimidating. Anyway, I managed to evade them and that's when I came back to my bedroom in the Wheatsheaf. You remember don't you Pascale?"

Pascale visibly blushed. Isobel snorted, suppressing a laugh. I sat there feeling confused while Hugo remained silent and Patrick looked curious and it was Patrick broke the silence.

"What's clear to me, is that we've been thoroughly played. Out thought, out manoeuvred and now, as we sit here, we've no idea what their next move will be."

Right on cue, the front door bell rang loudly followed with a determined banging on the door.

"Simon, the door."

"Sorry Patrick, but when I open doors, I seem to get smacked in the face. You open it."

Patrick looked annoyed, but said nothing, though he clearly intended to show his annoyance.

"Fine," I said, before leaving the room, opening the door to the entry vestibule and then looking through the spyhole in the door.

Standing at the foot of the steps was a small, impeccably dressed woman of around 60 years of age. She may have been a good deal older, or younger, but her rather old fashioned clothes, cut beautifully to fit her slim body, made putting an age to her somewhat tricky. She had a small, wheeled suitcase in one hand. I sighed to myself and muttered before I opened the door.

"Good morning," she said, smiling with more efficiency than warmth.

"Hello," I replied before adding, "You're not going to punch me in the face are you?"

The woman in front of me looked momentarily non-plussed but rapidly regained her composure.

"No, I don't think so. May I come in?"

It was my turn to look non-plussed, if not outright confused.

283

"Oh, I'm sorry. I should explain. I'm here to see Patrick."

Not really knowing how to answer her, I simply opened the door more widely and stepped out of her way.

"First door on the left," I said, as I closed the front door and followed her inside.

Chapter 31

She'd been far from happy for rather a long time. Unusual -no - *irregular* goings on had become all too frequent. Standards were being eroded and (in her way of thinking) the integrity of the whole organisation was therefore at risk. There was a limit to what she was prepared to tolerate. Her whole life had been dedicated to the service of ASH and its ideals, and she was not prepared for either be compromised.

She'd started out just making a note of who was coming in and out of the building. In effect, this was a copy of the visitors log she kept in its neat leather binder on the desk she had sat behind for so many years. Later, she'd started logging the phone calls – in and out – through which she manually connected ASH to the outside world. Eschewing, as they did, any level of technology that could be avoided through simple, human endeavour.

Through her quiet observations, the ever reliable and wholly unremarkable Janice had built up a fascinating picture of the comings and goings at ASH HQ. No-one thought it the slightest bit odd when she started to visit the Registry, in which all the important records – historical and modern – were kept. There was no way she could have copied all of them, even using the Minox sub miniature model B film camera she brought in to work every day, carefully secreted about her person. Instead, she applied her own formidable judgment and began secretly photographing those documents that she thought would be useful. Useful to whom, and when, wasn't clear to her when she started her meticulous work. But when it became apparent that Olivia Beaumont would be taking the role of Président of the Council of Elders, she knew it was time to intensify her efforts.

She began to spend more and more time in the Registry, extending her working day to do so. She explained her change in routine by saying she was researching the history of ASH as she was thinking about writing a book, only for members eyes of course, taking account of the earliest records up to the present day. Most ASH members were delighted at the prospect of appearing in print and were only too happy to help. Janice had learned long ago that to hold a mirror up for people to stare into, was as a good a means as any of avoiding their gaze.

Once Olivia Beaumont was on the scene, however, things got a little trickier. Surveillance cameras began to be installed, just for everyone's safety you understand, as well as smartcard access controls to all of ASH's rooms in Fellowship House at the RSA. Janice knew it wouldn't be long before her 'research' was questioned and her exact movements logged, monitored and then, who knows what?

She intensified her photographing of what she thought were key documents and before long she had a substantial collection of sub miniature film cassettes, each processed by her at her flat just off Marylebone High Street. The black and white slides all carefully catalogued. She was very proud of the system she used to make sense of what amounted to several thousand individual documents.

Her double life – photograph taking by day and processing and cataloguing by night – had remained a secret for long enough. She had a good instinct and hers was telling her it was time to quit.

Most days she was happy to walk home. 30 to 40 minutes was the usual time it took her to cover a little over a mile and a half between work and home. But today, she had decided it would be her last day at ASH. Though she had told no-one. Preferring both an absence of fuss and denying an opportunity for anyone with suspicions to act against her.

So today, she wanted to be a little less easy to follow. She walked along John Adam Street towards Bedford Street and caught a 139 bus towards Oxford Street. Hopping off at John Lewis, she walked into the store, went up the escalators to the top and then, when she could see no obvious follower, she took the back staircase and exited onto Cavendish Square. Heading quickly towards Wigmore Street, she glanced around her. Still no-one.

Crossing Wigmore Street she walked up the western side of Wimpole Street. 'Nearly home', she thought to herself with some relief. The weeks spent spying on her former employer were beginning to take their toll. A fact that her increased consumption of Johnnie Walker Black

Label bore witness to. A modest indulgence had become somewhat medicinal. Janice resolved to reduce her consumption to her customary levels – after tonight. Tonight was a time of, if not celebration, then satisfaction combined with relief.

Turning the key in the large black-painted front door of number 76 Wimpole Street, the adrenaline began to drain away. Five flights of stairs completed the process and another set of keys was produced to open the front door to her top floor flat. She knew it was somewhat old fashioned, but it was well appointed and it suited her very well. Opening the door and going inside, she caught a smell of something unusual. In that brief moment she couldn't place it and then, like a whisper, it was gone. Without skipping a beat, Janice turned to her left and walked down the long corridor, past her bedroom, to the tiny kitchen. She reached up to a high shelf and brought Mr Walker, as she liked to address him, onto the work top. From beyond the end of the corridor, her drawing room, she heard a click. She paused, bent over in the act of retrieving a glass from a cupboard.

The drawing room had a beautiful, if somewhat dated, parquet floor. Age and innumerable social engagements in the century or more since its installation, had caused some of the parquet tiles to break free of the bitumen that previously held them securely to the underfloor. The familiar sound of a loose tile being walked on was unmistakable to Janice.

Nonetheless, she cracked open the seal of this latest bottle and poured herself a generous, very generous, measure into the heavy glass she held in her left hand. Tempted though she was to take a large gulp, she did not. She knew she would need all her wits about her in the next few minutes.

She returned to the long corridor and forced herself not to act timidly or slowly as she walked into the drawing room. As she crossed the floor of the large, sunlit room, she saw the figure of a woman in her peripheral vision.

The woman spoke.

"Still drinking Johnnie Walker, Janice, after all these years. Well, well."

Without turning to look at the woman, Janice spoke.

"Rebecca, what a pleasant surprise."

Janice's grip on the heavy glass in her hand tightened, the only outward sign of her increasing anxiety. She continued across the room to her favourite chair, by the window. From this vantage point she could see all the way down Wimpole Street to the junction.

Janice turned to face her intruder who sat, expressionless, in a leather club chair. The years had not exactly been kind to this woman, but her clothes and appearance in general served her well, she thought.

"So what brings a member of the Council of Elders – sorry, ex-member of the Council of Elders – to my home. Uninvited?"

"Aren't you going to offer me a drink, Janice?"

"No, I don't think so."

Janice wasn't in the mood for pleasantries. Although it was pretty obvious, she needed to understand what Rebecca knew and why she was here. Both questions had very obvious answers but as a further source of intelligence, the information could be important.

"That's not very nice. But neither is spying on your employer, is it darling?"

"I'm not spying, I'm researching for a book I intend to write on the history of ASH -."

"Cut the crap, Janice. We've had suspicions about you for a while and your off-pat book story isn't going to cut the mustard any longer, I'm afraid."

"Rebecca, I'm shocked. Why would an ex-Council member take such an awful view of me? I've been nothing but faithful to ASH these last 40 years."

Janice couldn't help but poke Rebecca with her status. Few people had been removed from the Council, and hers was a testament to her own idiocy and malice as well as Patrick's considerable authority. Being provoked for the second time, Rebecca couldn't help herself.

"A reinstated Council member, Janice."

She scanned Janice's face for any reaction. There was none.

"It's your 'friend', Patrick who will find that he's been removed from the Council. Once we can find him, of course."

There it is! Janice tried to remain as neutral as possible, but was delighted Rebecca had let such vital information slip, despite its shocking implications. She decided to push on.

"Why on earth would Patrick be removed?"

"You can't be serious? He's clearly losing his mind – or his memory at least. Olivia was very thoughtful when she decided to end his appointment, even suggesting he be given Honorary Council member status to sooth his not insignificant ego."

Another gem thought Janice. She waited to see what else Rebecca would reveal, resisting any urge to fill what might become an awkward silence.

"Bringing me back to replace him was a great honour. Especially as Olivia told me that my reinstatement had been specifically requested by one of the FoDE members."

Janice had learned of their involvement in ASH – or rather their attempted colonisation of ASH – but she decided to feign ignorance.

"Well, many congratulations Rebecca. But I don't understand, who is FoDE? I don't believe I know him?"

Rebecca snorted.

"He's not a person," she said, practically spitting out the P.

"It's the Federation of Digital Entrepreneurs, you idiot. And now they've joined ASH, our future will be all the better and all the more powerful. I wouldn't expect anyone of your status to understand the immense power joining our world with the modern, tech world will bring. ASH will march proudly into the future, embracing all that it previously eschewed. And that includes old relics like Patrick, Isobel and, of course, you."

Janice was stung but was also shrewd enough not to retaliate. At least not yet. She made another play for information. Looking down at her lap, nervously fingering the glass of her untouched whiskey and looking for all the world as contrite and humiliated, she murmured.

"Does this mean my services are no longer required?"

She slowly brought her gaze up to look at Rebecca, even managing to bring tears to her eyes. Rebecca, like all bullies, was delighted at her apparent domination of Janice, and tears were the icing on the cake. She couldn't resist going in for the kill.

"You really aren't that bright, are you?"

Rebecca leaned forward, as if speaking to a child.

"Losing your job is the least of your problems. Any moment, a small team will be here to escort you to our new reception centre where you can join all the other dimwits and traitors that ASH has been indulging for so many years. I can't tell you how refreshing it is to have a new broom sweep out all the bloated, inefficient and unproductive detritus that ASH has accumulated over the years."

Janice took Rebecca at face value and assuming she only had a very short time to make her escape. Showing nervousness was not going to be difficult.

"Where will they take me, to this reception centre?" She asked weakly.

"It's in a charming spot in Herefordshire. It'll make a nice break for a city-dweller such as yourself. "

Bingo, thought Janice as she decided she now had to put her escape plan into action.

"Perhaps I should go and pack a case?"

"Perhaps you should. But only a small one. There won't be much room for personal possessions where you're going."

A triumphant, thin smile showed itself across Rebecca's lips. Janice detested this woman and she was almost looking forward to killing her.

Janice got up out of the chair and, head bowed, made her way slowly to her bedroom. She opened the door and paused on the threshold, scanning the room. It didn't look like anything had been disturbed, which suggested Rebecca either had little time, or little wit, to explore the flat before she had come home. She reached under the bed and retrieved her escape bag. Lifting it onto the bed she opened it. Inside were a few changes of clothes, passport and some cash in various currencies. She went to the wardrobe and retrieved the sub-miniature slides and her own paper records, placing them carefully inside the case. Finally, she reached into the wardrobe for her long overcoat.

She pulled the coat on, buttoning it close around her neck and down to below her knees, closed her case, extended its handle and wheeled it out of her room back towards the drawing room. She paused to hear the tail end of Rebecca on her phone.

"... like a lamb! We'll have no trouble from *her*. Yes of course I'm sure... Well stand them down then, I'm more than capable of handling some silly old relic. I'll see you back at John Adam Street."

"I'm ready," Janice announced meekly.

"Good girl," purred Rebecca, domination complete in her own mind.

Rebecca got to her feet and walked across the room towards the hallway and the front door to the flat. She walked past Janice and put her hand on the door lock. Aware that Janice hadn't moved she turned to look over her shoulder. She gasped, little knowing that she had already taken her last breath. A flash of metal caught the evening sun and Rebecca saw a cut throat razor travel fast past her face under her chin, as Janice grabbed her hair to pull her head back, opening up her throat. She cut fast and deep, severing both carotid arteries and making a deep incision in Rebecca's windpipe. Blood was everywhere, literally creating fountains either side of Rebecca's shocked, and rapidly whitening, face. Janice drew Rebacca to the floor trying to avoid the growing puddle of blood and to position her dying body away from the door and her suitcase. She was surprisingly easy to drag into the drawing room, the blood acting as a lubricant between floor and victim. As Rebecca was rapidly bleeding out, gurgling of air and blood coming from the open wound at her windpipe, Janice reached into Rebecca's coat and took her mobile phone which was largely uncontaminated.

"Goodbye Rebecca."

Janice returned to her bedroom and removed the long coat. She showered in her en suite bathroom and left her bloodied clothes on the floor where she had let them fall. Something she would never normally have done.

She got dressed into her clean clothes and stepped into her shoes. She selected another coat from wardrobe which she carefully folded and put over her arm. She inspected the suitcase for blood splatter. It was there, but not so visible as to cause her any difficulties in the outside world, she hoped.

Carefully stepping around blood by the front door, she cast a final glance at Rebecca, now motionless and surrounded by a still, bloody mirror. An image of Millais' painting of Ophelia lying dead in the water briefly passed through her mind before she rejected the comparison. There was nothing innocent about Rebecca, no sense of being a victim of circumstance.

Making her way downstairs to the building's front door, gave Janice time to compose herself and to mentally catalogue the information she had gained from the overconfident Rebecca. Dear god! She knew they were up to no good, but a detention centre was deeply troubling. She knew who she needed to contact, without delay,

Stepping outside the front door, she approached the edge of the pavement and looked around briefly. She could see no-one that caused her any concern.

She raised her arm as a black cab turned into Wimpole Street from Welbeck Way. The cab pulled in beside her and the passenger side window retreated as the driver leaned towards her.

"Where to love?"

"Paddington Station please."

"Hop in."

Janice got in the back of the cab with her suitcase and was pressed back into her seat as the driver accelerated towards the Marylebone Road, leaving her old life behind.

Chapter 32

"Janice!"

Isobel practically shrieked as Janice entered the drawing room in which Isobel, Patrick, Pascale and a cat were all sat looking expectantly towards the door.

Isobel sprang out of her seat and gave Janice a warm, powerful, embrace. Pascale stood, out of respect for this living institution of ASH, and gave her a greeting to which Janice smiled and nodded. Patrick, once Isobel's embrace had been released, stood in front of Janice and the two of them regarded each other for what felt like some time.

"So, you came,"

"Yes, I did, Patrick."

"In which case, I'm guessing the worst has happened, whatever that might be?"

"I'm afraid so..."

Janice's voice tailed off and she looked down at her shoes, feeling a sense of deep sadness that had hitherto been masked by the sheer speed of events over the last few hours.

Regaining her composure, she looked up and spotting Iago, she said,

"And this must be you, Hugo?"

"How did you know?" Hugo replied silently.

"Oh, I know a lot of things. Many of which will come as terrible news when I share them with you all."

Janice turned around to look at me.

"And you are Simon."

This was definitely a statement.

"I am," I replied.

Janice walked over to me and gave me such a tender hug, it almost bought me to tears. Pulling my head down to the same height as hers, she whispered in my ear.

"I'm so sorry, my dear. You've had to endure a terrible time. And yet, here you are…"

Releasing me from her embrace, she turned back to the room and addressed them as a whole.

"A cup of tea wouldn't go amiss. In case anyone was going to put the kettle on."

I laughed inwardly at the effect this had on all three other humans present, as they shuffled about not quite sure how to respond, looking one to the other. I put them out of their discomfort.

297

"How do you take it, Janice?"

"Strong, milk, no sugar and a slug of whiskey please."

Taking my instructions, I went to the kitchen and put on the kettle.

As I waited for the kettle to boil, I looked around my kitchen. It was comforting to be back in my home, alone in this part of the house. There's always something both familiar and unfamiliar when you return home after being away for a while. You see things in a slightly different way, at least until you settle back into your old habits and ruts. Contemplating my surroundings, I had the distinct feeling that I'd not be seeing this room again, or at least not for some time.

"You're looking sad, Simon. Again."

Awoken form my thoughts, I saw Pascale standing in the kitchen doorway. Oooph! She walked over to me and wrapped her arms around me. Oooph, ooph! My heart was full as I took her in my arms. I pulled away slightly so I could look at her. I gently stroked one side of her head and stared into her eyes. I took a breath to begin speaking. Pascale cocked her head to one side and raised her eyebrows. Her injunction for silence was clear.

The kettle clicked off as the water began to boil and we both set about filling a tray with mugs, filling the teapot with loose tea and hot water and retrieving some milk from the fridge. A deep sniff suggested that while it might be out of date, it had not yet soured. I lifted the tray and set off towards the drawing room.

"Aren't you forgetting something?"

"Am I?" I replied.

"Oui"

I thought for a second.

"She was serious, about the whiskey?"

Pascale nodded.

"Cupboard next to the cooker, second shelf down, I think there's some there."

As we returned to the others, the low coffee table was covered in documents, and a small projector had been set up, which was now throwing a surprisingly bright square of light against the wall opposite. I put the tray down on the hearth and invited everyone to help themselves. I couldn't keep my eyes off Janice to see if she really was going to take her tea with Whiskey. She didn't disappoint as she poured a substantial measure into her half full mug of tea. She took a large gulp and then looked directly at me. I felt colour rising in my cheeks, caught out as I was, and I glanced down at the table. When I brought my gaze back up, Janice was ready to meet my eyes. I'm sure I saw the quickest and most subtle wink in her left eye before she spoke to the assembled people and cat.

"Please forgive me, but I only got to finish my notes on the train on my way here. What I'm about to show you is only a selection of documents that I've been carefully photographing and cataloguing over several months. Most recently, information came into my possession that made sense of some of the other documents I'd found. Patrick, could you operate the projector please?"

Patrick did as he was told, loading and changing slides at Janice's command. Over the next 20 minutes Janice shared her remarkable discoveries. Her analysis and subsequent hypotheses were exceptional. And deeply alarming.

As Janice came to the end of her briefing, the room was completely silent, but for the cooling fan of the projector. Even that came to a stop a minute or two after Patrick turned it off, the silence somehow adding to the sense of shock.

I hadn't understood all of the references in Janice's presentation, but that didn't prevent me from being the first to speak.

"It's like the Nazi's have been resurrected."

"So, let me get this straight," all eyes turned to Isobel.

"The tech bros have successfully infiltrated ASH, taking over leadership of the Council of Elders, and have already created a detention centre in Herefordshire – wherever that is – which, as we speak, is being populated by anyone who doesn't fit in with their view of what ASH should be, or what views our members should hold. From what Janice has uncovered – outstanding work, by the way – their aim is to take control of ASH and exploit the abilities we have fought for, for so long, and for which generations have sacrificed so much, to promote their own hegemonic and commercial aims

Isobel finished, and all eyes turned to Janice.

"That's about it, yes."

Hugo provided further unnecessary, if succinct, commentary.

"So, we're fucked basically."

Again, the group turned to look at Janice, if only for a scrap of hope.

"Royally fucked." She replied.

Chapter 33

Some 92 miles away, at a former outdoor education and outward-bound centre, a growing number of unfavoured ASH members were beginning to arrive. As is common with such places, the accommodation could best be described as primitive. Shared dormitories, toilets and shower blocks were all designed to establish an esprit de corps in the past, but now served only to undermine the spirits of those whose misfortune brought them here.

More than two years ago, FoDE representatives had bought the buildings and land from the local council. The cover story was that they were hoping to restore the centre to its former glory – indeed better – for the use of underprivileged children from a variety of inner cities.

Instead, a range of subtle but effective security measures had been installed: cameras, remote locking doors, high fences that on close inspection appeared to emit a low hum. And then there were the guards.

Herefordshire has been home to 22 SAS Regiment since 1960. A ready supply of ex-soldiers all looking for well-paid deployments in various 'security' roles around the world has been in evidence for more than 60 years. FoDE already had a well established recruitment operation, ensuring the very best ex-regiment personnel were set to work as close protection operatives for their best and brightest (and richest) members. One rung down, ex-paras were now employed as guards at this new establishment, being paid more than enough to ensure their complicity in working at what everyone suspected was an unlawful detention centre. Suspected but really didn't give a fuck about.

A new, but still non-descript minibus was making its way along the ridge towards the centre. Three guards sat in the front, two in the back between six new ASH rejects. One of them, a woman of indeterminate age, wore a vacant look. She appeared to be almost staring inside of herself. As the van drew up to the new gates, the driver spoke with a sentry and the gate was opened. The minibus drove around the corner of the building and came to a halt with a slight skid on the newly laid gravel. A nearby guard banged loudly on the side of the minibus.

"Grab your stuff and get out. Then follow me!"

Ahead of them were four long, low, buildings that looked more like poultry houses than the dormitories which in fact they were.

"Stand there and get in line." Shouted another guard.

The drill was familiar by now – as no doubt it was intended to be – as the six detainees were once again searched, roughly. There was no purpose for these repeated searches (this was their fourth since being detained) other than to demonstrate control of those in whose custody they remained.

The six were now shepherded into one of the long, low buildings which, as the guard told them, would be their home until the powers that be decided what to do with them. It seemed unlikely that there was no plan, thought the woman of indeterminate age, dismissing the possibility in an instant.

After they had been shown to their bunks, the guards left them with the promise of an evening meal at 6pm. Looking at her watch, she noted the time – 3.37pm.

"I wonder what's going to happen to us?" Asked a young woman of 30 years, give or take.

None of the other women replied, increasing the young woman's sense of fear and isolation. Her head dropped and her hands started fidgeting, picking at the already bloody cuticle around the fingers of her right hand.

The woman of indeterminate age lay down on her bunk - a top bunk – and stared briefly at the ceiling. She closed her eyes, but not to sleep. She decided she needed to get out for a while, on the Hypnotic Plane at least. Her skills were considerable, and it only took moments for her to enter a deep state of hypnosis. She soon projected out of her body, looking around the dormitory it had assumed that shimmering quality that was so familiar to her and her many travels. Not wishing to hang around, she was nevertheless at a loss as to where she wanted to go. Home had only ever been determined by other people, not places. Her father and her son were the only two that she had ever really felt at home with. Her father was long dead, and her son had not been in contact for some four years and she had been unable to reach him hypnotically during that time. Something that grieved her deeply, although she could sense that he was still alive, somewhere. She decided to ty again.

Visualising him was easy enough, but the connection she would normally have expected was, as had been the case for four years, very weak. Somehow dispersed. Every time she tried to see him, she was distracted by the image of animal, a cat. Something of which she could make no sense whatsoever.

"Get in line – now!"

Her trance was disturbed by yet another guard. As the women lined up, he continued.

"Now then, we want to make sure that you're all fit and healthy while you're enjoying your stay with us,"

The flicker of a smirk passed across his lips as he said this.

"So we need to give you your vitamins, don't we?"

An orderly, next to the guard, was carrying a large bottle of red, white and blue capsules. Nobody in the room believed they were vitamins, but the lie was intended to avoid any kind of challenge or dissent.

As the orderly went down the line, a single capsule was put in the mouths of each of the women. After swallowing it, with a small cone of water to ease its passage, the guard took each woman's jaw in his large hand and forced the mouth open for an inspection to make sure the pull had been swallowed.

The woman of indeterminate age was last in the line.

"I don't need any water," she said, refusing to take the small paper cone.

"Hardcore, are we?" Taunted the guard.

The woman took the capsule and swallowed it, voluntarily opening her mouth for inspection.

"Who's a good girl then?" said the guard tapping her on the cheek.

"That's it. Fuck off. You're free until 6pm."

As soon as they left the room, the woman went to the long bank of toilet cubicles, trying not to rush. Once inside, she put two fingers down her throat and in near silence managed to retch up the capsule. She examined it in the palm of her hand. It was, thank god, intact. She had no idea what it was for but vitamins it was not. She put the tablet in the pocket of her jeans and returned to her bunk.

Some of the other women had begun to talk, quietly. Full of questions that no-one could answer. The other women gave her some room, sensing something about her that deserved respect. Instead of talking, the woman of indeterminate age decided to watch and wait. The more intelligence she could gather, the greater the chance of her being able to escape, she thought.

*

After the evening meal, the women in the dorm were joined by other, fresh detainees. Feeling a sense of camaraderie, the afternoon's intake began to talk with their new co-detainees. All had similar stories to tell: being 'invited' to leave various workplaces, homes, restaurants, gyms or wherever they happened to be. Their captors had extraordinary knowledge of where they were, and the removal of each woman was done with appalling efficiency. Courteous but with an underlying threat that could not be ignored.

Many of the women already knew each other, but not all.

The woman of indeterminate age was unknown to any of them, and for good reason. She had all but disappeared many years ago, finding the company of anyone, especially ASH members, deeply uncomfortable. She was, as the saying goes, a very private person, and an introvert to boot. The prospect of sharing a space with others was especially uncomfortable for her. Sleep was an obvious escape, so she closed her eyes and disappeared into her dreams.

*

In the morning, after breakfast, the women were escorted into a large classroom. Two banks of chairs, all facing a large screen flanked by two men and a woman who were dressed in smart business attire.

"Take a seat please ladies," an older man instructed. He continued.

"You are about to see a short film that will explain why you are here, and what is being asked of you. If you are unwilling to accept the task that will be set out, you will be free to leave immediately, no hard feelings."

A murmur went around the room like a Mexican wave.

"Quiet please, all will be explained," the man indicated to someone at the back of the room as the lights dimmed and the screen was lit up by a projector somewhere behind them.

The film was an apex-product of the sentimental, saccharin- drenched American advertising industry. Incredibly high production values and extensive use of AI and CGI. After taking the viewers through idealised bucolic scenes, the familiar faces of the three principal Tech Bros gently faded in.

"Hello my friends."

"Hello."

"Welcome."

If the effect was supposed to be warm it failed. In that room in an outdoor education centre on the English-Welsh border, it was nothing less than chilling and sinister. A few of the women looked around to see if their discomfort was shared by the others. Most stared straight ahead, determined to tell themselves this was all fine and that the events of the previous 24 hours were just some cultural misunderstandings. The film went on.

"For many years, we have been working tirelessly to alleviate human suffering. And today, we stand on the brink of a miraculous breakthrough. Which is why we need your help," one of the Tech Bros intoned.

"That's right," another continued, "what we are talking about is greater than the internet."

All three of the Tech Bros nodded on screen, looking serious, and doing their best to look benevolent, almost holy.

"Let me say that again – greater than the internet."

More serious nodding.

"Greater, and yet, perhaps not so different," said the third, trying his best to be enigmatic, but instead coming across as unnervingly weird.

"We have signed a deal with ASH – your own beloved organisation – to help fund and develop changes to the Hypnotic Plane that will benefit *all* mankind."

A lengthy pause followed, designed, no doubt, to encourage the ASH members who would watch this film to reflect on their selfishness for keeping the Hypnotic Plane out of the hands of megalomaniacs like those now appearing before them.

The first Tech Bros continued.

"Yes, we want to build on the traditions of ASH – born as it was out of the French Revolution – with our entrepreneurship that was born out of the information age revolution."

"We share a common heritage in so many ways. We look forward to welcoming you on the next stage of this incredible journey," the second declared as all three reached for their most authentic, perfectly white, corporate smiles.

The film cross faded back to its opening scenes and then displayed its closing message.

NOW YOU MUST DECIDE.

YOU WILL BE GIVEN A CONTRACT TO SIGN AND A SMALL PAYMENT TO REFLECT OUR HAPPINESS AT WELCOMING YOU INTO ASH 2.0.

IF YOU DO NOT WISH TO SIGN, YOU MUST LEAVE.

YOU WILL BE ESCORTED TO HEREFORD RAILWAY STATION WHERE YOU WILL BE GIVEN A COMPLIMENTARY TICKET HOME.

YOU WILL NO LONGER BE A MEMBER OF ASH AND FURTHER TRAVEL ON THE HYPNOTIC PLANE WILL BE IMPOSSIBLE.

The women read the notice on the screen, and a gasp went round the room as they reached its final pronouncement.

"That's outrageous!" One woman stood up and shouted.

"Sit down!" Retorted the man who had introduced the film. His tone was full of menace. Reluctantly, she did as she was asked.

The more junior personnel then began handing out the contracts for the women to sign. A few did so, but most either declined to take the contract, or quickly read it and then put it on the floor. The signed contracts were gathered up.

"Last chance ladies," the senior guard proclaimed as he scanned the faces in front of him. No-one moved.

"Right then, you, you and you," he pointed to the ones who had acquiesced, "follow me. The rest of you, leave the contracts on your chairs and follow my colleagues back to your minibus."

In silence, the women did as they were told. Apart from the woman of indeterminate age, who picked up someone else's contract and quickly folded it and put it under her clothes.

Soon, they were outside in the light of a fresh morning. It had been raining overnight, she thought, as she smelled the air. She followed the others onto the minibus. The driver closed the door and drove towards the heavily guarded entrance gate. Rather than letting the minibus through, the vehicle stopped, opened its doors and another guard came on board and took a seat at the front of the bus, next to the woman of indeterminate age. An opportunity, she thought.

"So how come you ended up working for these idiots?"

It was a bold move, but she had known men like this before and knew that a more nuanced approach would be even less likely to elicit a response. He said nothing, but she saw the corners of his mouth straighten as he suppressed a grin. She pressed on, on a different tack.

"You were obviously a professional soldier once. What happened – you got scared?" Nothing. "Oh, I see, you've been told not to talk to us and you're being a good little soldier and doing what you've been told."

"You have no idea," he whispered while staring straight ahead.

"Enlighten me, then."

He turned to face her.

"Alright, I will. Whatever you and the other witches get up to, when you go into a trance, that's over. Finished. No more."

"How so?" she asked. He said nothing.

"Ah, did mummy tell you to keep schtum?"

The guard's head whipped round to face her once again. She'd clearly hit a nerve.

"What do you think was in the little pill you swallowed last night?"

"I don't know."

"No, you don't." The guard turned to face the front again and said nothing for the rest of the journey.

The woman of indeterminate age, with her hands in her lap, felt for the outline of the capsule she had put into her pocket. She was glad she trusted her instincts the night before.

Much as she despised ASH, for so many reasons, she had always felt somewhat reassured by the role it had been carrying out for more than 200 years. And anyway, she let them be and they, on the whole, ignored her. Some individuals within ASH were ok, but since her son's disappearance four years ago, she had removed herself from all contact. But times had changed, and she knew that when they do, you need to adapt, and quickly. She resolved to get in touch with an old friend as soon as she got home.

Chapter 34

"So, we're going to have to fight them, then?" Pascale broke the silence.

"And how will we do that, Pascale, with people being rounded up and stuck in this detention centre in Hertfordshire?"

"Herefordshire," corrected Janice.

Pascale hesitated, wanting to say something back to Hugo that would present an alternative view, but she could find nothing to say. The sense of foreboding in the room grew, as each of the friends took on board the awful scale of the disaster that had so swiftly unfolded.

Time passed.

Patrick, who was deep in thought, wore a vacant look. His mind sifting and sorting, turning over decades of knowledge and experience, searching and searching for something that might bring even a scrap of hope to the present.

Patrick raised his head, as if someone had called his name and he was trying to identify who it was. His mind had half-remembered something, a fragment, an echo, which he was now trying to mentally grasp. Almost panicked, in case it should elude him, his expression suddenly changed to one of expectation, even hope.

"You've thought of something, Patrick, haven't you?" I said. Patrick turned to look at me with a searching gaze.

"I believe I may have," he said.

"I know what it is," I said, as the penny dropped.

"Do you? Then why not share your insight with this esteemed company."

Patrick was teasing me but also challenging me to have the courage of my convictions. I decided it was my intuition that led me to know what Patrick was thinking.

"You're going to ask the First Nation travellers on the Hypnotic Plane to help us."

Patrick looked surprised. He fixed me with his dark eyes and broke into a smile.

"You're full of surprises, Simon," he said.

Eager to please him, I went on.

"Pascale told me about them when we first met, and that you'd reached an understanding with them concerning your, ASH's, presence on the Plane.

"Indeed we did. The Treaty of Chenonceau, no less. Signed in the incredible chateau of the same name The treaty was created by Madame Louise Dupin, a most remarkable woman, just before her death in 1799."

Isobel became more animated.

"She was amazing," she said, "A feminist before feminism was truly recognised. Do you know, she was arguing that the sexes were entirely equal back in the 1700s?"

"Why haven't I heard of her before?" Pascale asked.

"I don't know darling, let me think..."

Isobel was taking the piss and Pascale knew it.

"Bitch."

"That's me!"

Both women broke into a laugh, lifting the mood in the room. Even Janice smiled broadly, before Hugo brought everyone back to the task in hand.

"So, how are we going to contact them?"

Janice spoke up, hesitatingly at first.

"Well, the usual way is to instruct one of ASH's envoys. Though that may be a bit of a challenge at the moment, given the fact that most ASH members have either been rounded up or are on their way to being so."

"Who are the envoys?" Pascale enquired.

"That's part of the problem. There's only two."

Janice, possibly for the first time in her life, looked decidedly sheepish. She continued.

"One is – was – Rebecca."

Patrick studied her, with a quizzical look on his face.

"Was, Janice?"

"Mmmm. I cut both of her carotid arteries with a razor blade."

I simply couldn't equate what I had just heard with the kindly (or so I thought) woman in front of me. Looking around the room, a similar reaction was painted on the faces of my compatriots – even Iago.

"You cut her throat?" I sounded incredulous.

"Well yes, but it was the carotid arteries I was trying to sever. If it's only the windpipe, it's not certain they will die, you see?"

"And is she dead?" Pascale asked.

"Oh yes dear. Very much so. She was arranging to have me rounded up, and I couldn't possibly allow that to happen. I needed to get here and tell you about what's been going on."

"So, who's the other one?" Hugo intoned. "You haven't killed them as well, have you?

I had the sense that Hugo knew the answer to the question before he asked it. I wasn't wrong.

Janice turned to face him.

"No dear, I haven't. It's your mother."

*

"The problem with dear old Mumsy, is that she's got no time for me and even less for ASH."

"That's not fair, Hugo!"

"Fuck off Patrick. You know very well that ever since I used my skills to bring back Claudine, she's practically disowned me."

Even projected into his compatriots' heads, Hugo's voice was heavy with the grief of rejection from his Mum.

316

"Believe it or not, she always cared for you. But she found it hard, no, impossible, to forgive what you did."

"I was a child!"

"Yes, and you were extraordinary talent, gifted beyond anyone's knowledge or imagination. And your mother never forgave *herself* for not seeing what would happen, to stop you somehow."

"So, she punishes me for that?"

"She punished herself."

"Bullshit!"

Pascale reached out to Iago and picked him up, holding him on her lap. It was a tender thing to do, but Iago was having none of it. He jumped off her lap and disappeared out of the room. Pascale watched him leave, helpless to comfort her old friend and lover.

Isobel came and sat next to Pascale, wrapping her arm around Pascale's shoulders. I felt jealous, and as Pascale's eyes met mine I was worried that it showed. She looked guilty, or ashamed. And here was I, in someone else's body, apparently. No sense of who I was, not really, beyond the story given to me by Claudine.

"I'll talk to him."

Patrick looked like he wanted to say something to me but changed his mind. Only Janice offered me any advice.

"Be gentle with him."

*

I wasn't sure which way Hugo would go but if Iago was still calling at least some of the shots, then he'd be outside in the courtyard garden. I went outside through the open door and up the steps. Sure enough, Iago was sat on a cushion, looking into the distance, the sun reflecting off his fur.

"Hello," I offered a greeting.

Hugo said nothing and continued to stare straight ahead.

"It sounds like you've had a rough time."

Silence.

"It must have been very hard for you, growing up, and then this –"

"Do you think?" Hugo shot back

"And do you know what's hardest of all?"

"I think I can guess."

"Enlighten me."

"Seeing me in your body while you're trapped in the body of my old cat."

"Bingo! Only you left one bit out, haven't you?"

"I'm having sex with your former girlfriend."

"Well I didn't know that, but thanks for enlightening me. I was going to say you've also, somehow, got hold of some hypnotic abilities..."

We both were digesting what we had said.

"You're actually having sex with Pascale, in a relationship with her?"

I didn't quite know how to answer. Ordinarily, I might have told him to mind his own business but being in his body having sex with his ex-girlfriend, it felt like it really was his business. Yes, was the best I could come up with. We sat in silence once more.

"Look, I think she likes the fact that it's your – our – body, of course. But she also finds me gentler than you. More affectionate.

"Why did you come out after me, Simon?"

I really wasn't sure. I wanted to say, 'I want to get to know you better'. As lame as that sounded, I also knew it to be true. I told myself that he was, after all, in the body of my old cat and that somehow gave me a proprietorial interest in him, but the truth was I was in *his* body and he really did have a proprietorial interest in me.

Then it struck me. The reason why I'd come outside.

"However different we might appear to be, Hugo, we are inextricably linked. Like twins."

"Twins that don't like each other."

"Yes, even so, if you want to put it that way. Tell me, Hugo, what don't you like about me?"

"Really? You want me to answer?"

"Yes, I do."

Hugo paused before erupting with a list of qualities he despised.

"You are:

Weak

Over-sensitive

Lacking ambition

Indecisive

Emotional

Un-manly

And

Just too kind!"

I took a while to digest these reasons for Hugo's antipathy. I decided they were more to do with him than me, but even I couldn't help firing back a list of my own.

"Well here's my starter for ten:

Arrogant

Conceited

Insensitive

Cold

Egotistical

And...

You're deeply hurt. Just like me."

I hadn't expected to come out with the last observation but as the words left my mouth I knew them to be true. From Hugo's silence, I wondered if he thought so too.

"And that's why I don't like you." Hugo said plainly.

"Because I'm hurt?"

"Because I see myself in you and I can't stand it. I can't bear it, it's too painful. All the qualities that make me vulnerable, all the reasons I've been hurt – again and again - when people leave me."

"Like Claudine, your mother, Pascale..?"

"Yes. If I deny all those qualities, I can be ok, not be hurt. And then you come along, vulnerability personified. How the fuck did it come to this?"

A good question, I thought. And given my memories were apparently implanted and false, it was impossible for me to know *how* we'd got here.

"Hugo, I don't know how we got here. But I can find out."

"I have no idea what you're talking about."

"The hypnotic lock."

"Oh yes. The hypnotic lock," was all Hugo could manage.

"You're scared, aren't you," I intuited.

Hugo paused before answering that he was.

"Me too. But I think I want to unlock it now. Find out who I really am. It might help."

"And it might not."

"True. But that won't change reality. I either face it, or I don't."

Chapter 35

I am sitting upright in the leather chair in which I had my first experience of the Hypnotic Plane, with Pascale by my side. I feel comforted by her presence.

In a gentle voice, she enquired,

"Are you sure you want to do this, Simon? To do it now?"

"Nope, but I think we should do it anyway."

Truth be told, I felt terrified. I heard Hugo's voice in my head. It had a sotto voce tone, so I guessed he was talking only to me.

"I underestimated you, Simon."

I was far from sure he had, but I said a mental 'thank you', not knowing if he would hear me.

Pascale took my hand and gently stroked my head.

"Are you ready, Simon?"

I took a deep breath and let out a sigh.

"Let's get on with it."

Pascale released my hand and I placed it gently in my lap alongside the other one. I started breathing deeply as she instructed, followed by a full body scan and progressive physical relaxation. The awareness of my body parts merged into one, each limb or digit indistinguishable from the other. Listening to her voice I felt myself drifting away, leaving my body behind. I began to visualise the door, the door that blocked my connection to my history, my previous life, and the entirety of the person who I was.

Approaching the door, this time I noticed it didn't have a keyhole at all. It was blank. I began to feel anxious until Pascale's voice, reaching through the infinite gap between consciousness and my current state, encouraged me to imagine the door with a combination lock on it, a keypad.

Sure enough, as soon as I shifted my imagination, a keypad appeared. Beneath it were small letters. As I approached the door, the letters came into focus.

Stop, Simon! Once you've gone through this door you can never come back.

As I read this warning, it changed.

You really don't want to know what's beyond this door.

And again.

Only madness and suffering lie beyond the threshold.

Where the hell was this coming from? I had no sense of it coming from within *me*. Was it a final part of the hypnotic lock? Either way, I was starting to lose my nerve.

I heard Pascale's voice, once again, offering calm reassurance, suggesting I enter the code on the keypad and push the door open. I looked at the door and I just couldn't do it. I was paralysed with fear. I heard another voice, it was Hugo's.

"Hey Simon, you can do this. I trust you."

I was finding all kinds of reasons not to enter the code, to delay, to put it off to another time in future, wait for nighttime, wait until I was alone.

Stop.

I did my best to empty my mind of these urgent injunctions, and I approached the door. I reached out my index finger of my left hand and pressed the first digit, which showed on the digital display.

7

I went to press it again, only it had moved to where the nine had been.

"Fucker", I thought as I pressed my finger on the displaced key.

7 7

This time, the key had gone blank. I tried to remember where the zero had been and pressed hard.

7 7 0

The labels on the keys returned. With relief, I went to press eight. Nothing happened. It didn't even move. I pressed harder. Still nothing. I tried to move it in all directions with no success. I stopped trying and emptied my mind once more. I reached out with the middle finger of my right hand – my eighth digit – I felt the key click and saw the number appear on the display

7 7 0 8

Two more keys to go, I thought. I pressed them quickly in turn.

7 7 0 8 1

7 7 0 8 1 2.

Nothing.

Then I heard a click, and the door opened a few millimetres as the lock was released. I was at peak stress now. All I had to do was to move through the door, and I'd know who I was and where I'd come from. To know myself. That was what was so terrifying – to come face to face with all of me. All the parts that were either hidden from me or which I'd decided to conceal, from the world and from myself. I made a choice and instantly felt calm, almost serene.

I pushed open the door and walked through into a brightly lit room. This wasn't how I'd imagined it to be, but of course it was exactly as my imagination intended it to be, I simply played no conscious part in its creation.

The room was vast, its white walls, ceiling and floor defying any attempt to define its exact size. About 20 metres away were two brown leather armchairs – the same as the ones in my drawing room. One was facing me, the other facing away. I saw the back of someone's head. Someone familiar.

"Take a seat dear."

Janice gestured towards the empty chair. I sat down.

"Well now, I'm sure you've got lots of questions for me, but first, if you don't mind, there's someone I'd like you to meet. Is that alright dear?"

How the hell had Janice appeared in my hypnotic world? My mind was racing. Then I heard Pascale's voice, as though from a great distance away.

"It's ok, Simon. I'm here. All you have to do is accept what you see and hear, don't question it, just accept..."

"That's good advice," Janice added, "Now, are you ready to meet this someone?"

"I suppose," I said with no certainty whatsoever.

"Alright then. Here she comes."

From way away, I saw a figure walking towards us. It was hard to make out any details but as they got closer and closer, I thought perhaps it was a woman. Hard to age her, but definitely a woman. She came round the back of Janice's chair and sat down in the same instant as a third chair appeared, the same as the others. The two women exchanged smiles, then turned to look at me.

"Hello," said the stranger.

"Hello," I replied.

She paused as she regarded me. She looked thoughtful and then, as if interrupting a thought, she said,

"My name is Marine. I'm an old friend of Janice. And I'm also your mother."

Weird, I thought.

"Well, hi, mum," I said, feeling no emotion whatsoever.

Janice joined in.

"She's also Hugo's mother."

Holy shit, he's my brother, I thought. Reading my thoughts, Marine went on.

"You're not siblings, Simon. You are Hugo. And he is you."

This was all getting way too trippy.

"He's not. And I'm not." Was all I could find to say.The women said nothing, just looked at me with a kind of curious beneficence.

Time passed and I said nothing. After some minutes, I could feel a sense of dread. The sense of Marine's words, having taken root somewhere deep in my gut, which were now growing and growing, forcing their way into my consciousness despite my best efforts to keep them at bay. My resistance was slowly being eroded by my acceptance, my acceptance of what I knew to be the truth. Had always known. I sighed and then looked back towards the women.

"So what happened to me?"

Janice and Marine exchanged glances, and Janice answered.

"On the day when the Enemy attacked you, you should really have died. They attacked you with an ancient weapon – of a type that ASH believed had been lost over countless millennia – but you survived."

"How?"

"Under enormous stress, your personality split. The ego has a tremendous will to survive, and that's what made its way into your cat, Iago. The rest of you, stayed where

327

it was and would have died but for the actions of one Olivia Beaumont."

"Claudine, you mean?"

"Yes, Claudine. We know all about her."

"But how did she save me, she doesn't seem the saving type, quite honestly. I know she was desperate to get to Hugo, but if I *was* Hugo, why save me?"

"She only knew that Hugo's body had somehow survived, that part of him, perhaps all of him, had escaped. She wanted to use this as bait. What she didn't know – still doesn't know – is that by giving you false memories and locking the rest away from you, she saved you, she allowed you to cope. Without the memories she gave you, your psyche would have perished and your ego, in Iago, would have perished too."

"So are you saying that if I, in this body, had died then Hugo in Iago's body would have died as well?"

"That's it dear."

"And is that still the case, now, today?"

"Yes it is." Janice said smiling.

"So, now I know I'm not Simon and that I am Hugo, and that my ego is in the body of my cat, what's to stop my psyche and me from dying?"

Janice looked to Marine for an answer.

"That's the extraordinary thing. Your psyche has had a chance to repair itself. Everything you've been through has played a part in the regrowth of the person inside you – your true self if you like. Being cut free from the enormous ego that Hugo still possesses, has given the

Self a chance to recover and occupy the space that was once unavailable."

I understood immediately what Marine was saying – at least on an intuitive level.

"I hadn't expected the unlocking of my mind to bring me to a conversation with you two. How come?"

Janice replied.

"I think you know the answer to that, dear."

Almost immediately I said,

"My mind decided this was the best way for me to understand who I am, who I was."

Both women smiled at me.

"So what about my history?"

"It's yours and you can access it anytime you like," Janice replied.

I thought for a moment. How can I possibly see my own history? In an instant, I found myself in a small cinema. It was dark and welcoming. Either side of me were Marine and Janice, both eating popcorn and looking for all the world like a pair of kids, excited to see a long-anticipated movie. I drew a breath and turned to Janice to ask her what the hell was happening. She placed a finger across her lips to shush me and pointed forward to the large screen in front of us, which had come alive, illuminated from behind us by a powerful projector.

The opening credits were like those of a 1930s film – rousing music and a list of characters. The titles eventually gave way to the interior of a hospital, a maternity delivery room. There on the bed was Marine, evidently in the midst of labour. Janice leaned forward to look at Marine, who beamed back. The film cut to Marine holding the baby. She looked adoringly down at the infant and then up, with love in her eyes to someone standing over her, in silhouette. Presumably the father, though his face could not be seen, his voice was instantly recognisable to me.

The film went on and I lost all sense of time. It was not edited highlights, it was *everything*. Literally every moment in my life was played out on the screen. Going to school, meeting Claudine, going on holiday. The only obvious absence was my father.

Teenage traumas and young heartbreak, it was all there. I saw Pascale from years ago and my heart leapt. Of course it did. I felt a strange empathy for the boy, youth and then man I saw who looked like me, exactly like me. As he fought bravely in conflicts with the Enemy and bore the grief of fallen friends and comrades, tears fell into my lap

Finally, the film came up to the near-present. The last four years played out and I now understood it. I understood everything. My place in the universe, my purpose.

In my hypnotic state, I closed my eyes. I wanted to return to the physical world now. I felt like I had been gone for hours, and I was eager to return. To be reborn as a complete man, a man with a history.

*

I slowly became aware of my body. Just as whole to begin with, and then, limb by limb, I could start to distinguish the individual parts. Through my closed eyes I could sense sunlight coming into the room. I could

330

smell Pascale's perfume. Before I had opened my eyes, I felt the warmth of her lips on mine. She whispered in my ear,

"Welcome back my love."

I opened my eyes and saw the same familiar, cracked, ceiling above me and a large gold chandelier in the (more or less) centre. I took in a deep breath and stretched. I looked around the room.

It was as though I was sitting with my oldest and closest friends, which of course I was. I hadn't seen it before, couldn't have done so. Sensing my rebirth, my full occupation of my Self, one by one they came and hugged me, offered encouraging words or simply welcomed me back. Everyone except Hugo, sat in the body of my old cat.

"I could do with some time alone with Hugo," I said, in a voice I didn't recognise but which was both authoritative and kind.

The others looked slightly surprised at first and then looked as if they understood. Which was interesting as I wasn't quite sure what I had to say to him. They left the room, in any case. I waited until I heard the front door close behind them, then I turned to face Iago.

We sat in quietly for many minutes, softly regarding each other. We had no need for words yet – either spoken or conveyed mentally. Time passed until I broke the silence.

"I want to thank you, Hugo, for keeping me safe."

"I had a degree of self-interest, you know. This wasn't altruism."

"I'm not sure I agree with you."

"Think what you like."

"I know you're hurting and I know you're terrified of getting close to anyone. "

Hugo snorted before replying.

"Oh do you?"

"I know how it felt to have an absent father, a distracted mother, a best friend who died. And then, after doing something extraordinary, to be effectively exiled by your own family. I know how much you loved Pascale and how it hurt you so much that you couldn't maintain a relationship with her."

Hugo was silent.

"And I know that so many of the things you did, the way you reacted to even a hint of emotional danger, was all meant to keep me safe."

Still Hugo said nothing.

"I want you to know that it's ok now. I'm safe. And I can deal with life as it comes. And you can stop fighting now. Let it go Hugo."

When Hugo replied, I'd never heard him speak with such a small, vulnerable voice.

"I can't..."

"You can, it's ok – "

"- I want to but I'm frightened."

"It's a frightening thing to do, but you'll feel better. So much better."

"Will you be there for me?"

Hugo sounded like a child now.

"Yes, of course I will."

"Always?"

"Always, Hugo. I'll be with you until the end of days."

"Truly?"

"Truly."

"Where will I go, if I let go?"

"You know where."

"With you, I'll be with you?"

"Yes, we'll be together."

"Until the end of days?"

"Until the end of days."

I reached out and Iago jumped onto my lap. I stroked his head and under his chin, letting him rub the sides of his face against my hand. He soon settled down and curled up tightly as I continued to stroke him from the top of his head to his shoulders. He began to purr. I noticed our breathing was beginning to synchronise. As I slowed my breathing down, so did Iago's. I let my breathing get slower and more shallow. Slower and slower and more and more shallow.

Iago's purring stopped.

I looked down at my old cat. He was still and peaceful. And Hugo had left him.

Chapter 36

0618

I'm lying on my back when I open my eyes. I hear the slightest suggestion of snoring coming from my left. I try and slide out of the bed, as gently as possible so as not wake her, and silently open the bedroom door. I make my way down the landing towards the toilet.

0620

The kitchen is how I left it the night before, and I scurry around putting plates and glasses in the dishwasher while the kettle boils. It's a new game, every morning, Try and get the tidying up done before the kettle clicks off. Today, I win the game.

0623

As I'm pouring in water to warm the teapot, I still half-expect to see Iago, or to feel him curling himself around my ankles. Instead I feel the brush of long hair and a nuzzling kiss on my neck. I close my eyes in the bliss of the moment, an unwise thing to do at that precise moment.

"Simon, the water!"

I came to, reluctantly, and stopped pouring the hot water all over the worktop. I shrugged and went to re-fill the kettle as Pascale mopped up the water.

"I love you," she said.

"I know," I replied.

Ooph!

Still there, I thought.

*

1056

I opened the stable door of the barn conversion in the development in which we have all taken refuge. The late summer sun is creeping higher in the sky but is notably lower than a few months back when we first came here. The air was still warm enough for us all to meet outside, around the millstone the developers had left to mark the centre of the former farmyard, and around which we all took a seat. Me, Pascale, Isobel, Patrick, Janice and my mother, Marine. We chitchatted and drank whatever drinks we'd brought out from our separate quarters, enjoying the company and conspiring in avoiding talking about the increasingly urgent challenges ahead.

1103

"My dear friends, and family. I think it's time for us to make our move."

The assembled group looked serious as they nodded or grunted their assent.

"It's time we struck back and dealt with FoDE and their followers decisively. Marine, Mum, are the First Nation travellers prepared to listen to our requests?"

"They are, Simon."

"And Isobel, do you have the box with the inscription?"

"I do, Simon."

"Then I suggest we begin."

Coming in 2026 – the second book in The Ancient Society of Hypnotists.

Printed in Dunstable, United Kingdom